Dhul wheeled to see Bo aiming center-mass at his chest, and he screamed, "Allah Akbar!" as he lunged forward at her.

Bang! Bang! went the Glock as Bo did a military double tap, placing two shots into his chest that could be covered by a quarter, but the nine-millimeter pistol was not large enough to stop the behemoth. He swung and open hand knocked the gun from Bo's hand.

Grinning evilly, he went after the woman, who barely reached his mid-chest. Women in the aircraft, seeing the charge, screamed loudly. Bo stood her ground, concentrating, and waited until he was right on top of her. His plate-sized hands grabbed her upper arms, and she stomped down on his foot, breaking it with the edge of her foot, and he bent over in pain, screaming . . .

CRIMINAL INVESTIGATION DETACHMENT
BROKEN BORDERS

DON BENDELL

BERKLEY BOOKS, NEW YORK

THE BERKLEY PUBLISHING GROUP
Published by the Penguin Group
Penguin Group (USA) Inc.
375 Hudson Street, New York, New York 10014, USA
Penguin Group (Canada), 90 Eglinton Avenue East, Suite 700, Toronto, Ontario M4P 2Y3, Canada
(a division of Pearson Penguin Canada Inc.)
Penguin Books Ltd., 80 Strand, London WC2R 0RL, England
Penguin Group Ireland, 25 St. Stephen's Green, Dublin 2, Ireland (a division of Penguin Books Ltd.)
Penguin Group (Australia), 250 Camberwell Road, Camberwell, Victoria 3124, Australia
(a division of Pearson Australia Group Pty. Ltd.)
Penguin Books India Pvt. Ltd., 11 Community Centre, Panchsheel Park, New Delhi—110 017, India
Penguin Group (NZ), Cnr. Airborne and Rosedale Roads, Albany, Auckland 1310, New Zealand
(a division of Pearson New Zealand Ltd.)
Penguin Books (South Africa) (Pty.) Ltd., 24 Sturdee Avenue, Rosebank, Johannesburg 2196,
South Africa

Penguin Books Ltd., Registered Offices: 80 Strand, London WC2R 0RL England

This is a work of fiction. Names, characters, places, and incidents either are the product of the author's imagination or are used fictitiously, and any resemblance to actual persons, living or dead, business establishments, events, or locales is entirely coincidental.

CRIMINAL INVESTIGATION DETACHMENT: BROKEN BORDERS

A Berkley Book / published by arrangement with the author

PRINTING HISTORY
Berkley edition / December 2006

Copyright © 2006 by Don Bendell Inc.
Cover photo by Ali Jasim/Reuters/Corbis.
Cover design by Steven Ferlauto.
Interior text design by Kristin del Rosario.

ISBN: 0-425-21257-2

BERKLEY®
Berkley Books are published by The Berkley Publishing Group,
a division of Penguin Group (USA) Inc.,
375 Hudson Street, New York, New York 10014.
BERKLEY is a registered trademark of Penguin Group (USA) Inc.
The "B" design is a trademark belonging to Penguin Group (USA) Inc.

PRINTED IN THE UNITED STATES OF AMERICA

10 9 8 7 6 5 4 3 2 1

My apple trees will never get across
And eat the cones under the pines, I tell him.
He only says, "Good fences make good neighbours."

—ROBERT FROST, "MENDING WALL"

This book is dedicated to some special people in the Special Forces (Green Beret) community. All SF personnel have my undying respect and love, but these people have a special place in my heart for a variety of reasons. In no particular order: my wife, Shirley A. Bendell, wife of a Green Beret and mother of two Green Berets, "an incredible breed of woman"; my two youngest sons, SF SSG Brent Bendell and SPC Joshua Bendell; retired SF LTC Dennis Yost, my adopted "little" brother; retired SFer the Honorable Rudi Gresham, presidential appointee and my "Bro"; my friend Robin Moore, author of *The Green Berets* and the "Ballad of the Green Berets," *The French Connection*, and more, and his wife, Helen; my friend and fellow author and SFer Jim Morris; my close friend Roxanne Merritt, for years curator of the Special Forces Museum, but more importantly, official historian of U.S. Army Special Forces; my friends retired COL Roger Donlon, Medal of Honor, and Norma; my friend and SF and CIA legend retired SGM Billy Waugh; my friends SF legend retired SGM Jimmy Dean, the late SGM Joe Seyers, the late SGM Charlie Telfair, and H. Ross Perot; my friends retired GEN Bob Kingston, LTG Jack Singlaub, MG Bob Disney, MG Geoff Lambert; and SF legends the late COL Aaron Banks and the late LTG William Yarborough; my namesake, Clint Eastwood, the late John Wayne, and the late Martha Raye, Bo Derek, fellow Green Beret and friend U.S. Surgeon General VADM Rich Carmona, MD; and last, but not least, every one of my SF "Brothers" who served with me at Dak Pek, ODA-242, Co B, 5thSFGA, 1st SF, Republic of Vietnam: COL Joe Dietrich, COL Jim Selders, CPT Mike Sizemore, 1LT Mel Light, CSM Tom Weeks, CSM Joe Kope, SGM David Smith, MSG Don Williams, MSG James "Doc" Phillips, the late MSG Steve Olson, SFC Joe Howard, the late SFC Harry Boyle, the late SFC Chuck Challela, SGT Larry Crotsley, SGT Larry Vosen, SGT Dennis Afshar, SGT Karl

McKinley, SGT Ray Hill, and interpreters Nhual, Suat, Tieh, Tuan, and finally, the late Plar, a wonderful little Montagnard girl who will never be forgotten.

De Oppresso Liber
Don Bendell

THE FRIENDLY SKIES

Bobby Samuels was so happy he and Bo were able to get the two seats just behind the flight attendant's galley separating first class from the rest of the low-life passengers like him, he humorously thought. He at least had a little more legroom, and only needed to worry about noisy brats behind him. Bobby swallowed the rest of his drink and wondered if they were bringing any more of the little bottles.

Bo guessed he was thinking that and hoped they would not. Bobby was such a good man, but she hated it when he drank, and he had started downing Wild Turkey and Coke in the airport lounge when they laid over at DIA, Denver International Airport. Bobby did not realize he'd already had several drinks. He simply wondered why he'd never gotten into bed with his beautiful coworker Bo Devore. She had high cheekbones, entrancing green eyes, long curly auburn hair, and a body that made men stare with longing and women stare with envy. Even in Class A's, or B's, or even in BDU's, she could not hide her obvious figure.

He then quickly realized why he never did try to pursue

her romantically. She reminded him of Arianna, and it made him very sad. Sometimes the alcohol anesthetized the pain, but usually not. He was also her senior officer, rank-wise, and felt it would be unprofessional and dangerous to have a relationship with his partner. On the other hand, as macho as he was, Bobby Samuels was a romantic, and the job would not have interfered if it were not for the memories of his late wife.

Even though he had started drinking, Bobby was still Bobby and was always aware of his surroundings. He acted as if he was cracking his neck, and glanced around, looking out of the corners of his eyes.

An alarm went off in his senses. One little thing jumped out at him. It was almost imperceptible.

He summoned the flight attendant and asked for coffee, black. He wanted to be alert, and his order of coffee alarmed Bo in return. It had been her experience that he would not just stop when he started to drink. Bo's training, experience, and mindset were also to spot things wrong or out of place, just like Bobby would.

Bobby politely excused himself and walked to the restroom in the rear of the jet, and the women along the way could not help but watch him as he walked. His shoulders seemed wider than the aisle and his head seemed closer to the ceiling of the jet than that of any of the other men on the flight. Bo always felt his looks reminded her of a cross between the younger versions of Harrison Ford and Tom Selleck, if that could be, and the sight of her partner frequently took her breath away.

In the tiny lavatory Bobby had to squat down just to function. He splashed cold water on his face, and looked in the mirror shaking his head in disgust. Why had he started drinking? he wondered. He wiped his face with paper towels that were simply too small. He put his hands on the counter and looked at himself in the mirror. Usually, he would smile and make faces at himself, but never lately when he drank. He slapped his face several times and wondered what passengers would think of the strange noises in the restroom, if they heard him. He splashed more water on his face and dried off. Bobby headed back to the front of the jet.

Four seats back from his seat on the port side of the jet, Bobby's left, there was a man in the aisle seat who wore a brand-new suit and looked to be Mexican. He wore a Mexican flag lapel pin. He had a laptop opened and looked to be typing, but Bobby noticed the words "Allah Akbar" in the text in several places as he walked by. Now he was even more concerned, very concerned. He was trained to avoid denial in such a circumstance.

Thankfully, the coffee had arrived, and he asked the flight attendant to bring more.

When he sat down, Bo whispered, "Fourth seat back on the left? Mexican guy?"

Bobby nodded. He sipped the coffee and smiled when the flight attendant handed him another, which he gulped down.

Bobby whispered, "Go to the restroom. On the way back, check out his shoes and the laptop. See if anything is out of place."

Bo got up saying aloud, "Excuse me, please," and smiled at Bobby as if he was a new friend she had just met on the plane.

Bobby went through another tiny cup of airline coffee before she returned, and was anxious to hear her report when she sat down.

Bo whispered, "HP laptop. New one. Looks normal. Shoes look fine, wingtips, black. Brand-new. No wear on them."

Bobby whispered, "Do you have a compact?"

Bo said, "Yes."

She just waited for his directions, knowing he would tell her what was up when the time was right.

Bobby said, "Take it out and pretend like you have something in your eye. Keep watching his hands. See if he tries to pull anything from the laptop or pockets."

Bo complied while Bobby, holding the folder jacket his ticket came in, walked forward to the flight attendant smiling.

He held it up so the Mexican passenger could see it and said, "Ma'am, I have a question about my baggage."

When he got close to her, he whispered, "This is an emergency, keep smiling, and lead me behind the galley. I'm a cop."

She forced a smile, saying, "Let's get out of the aisle, sir, and let me answer your questions."

As soon as they went around the bulkhead, he pulled his badge out. It was gold and embedded in a leather fold-over wallet. The badge read on the outside, "Department of the Army," and on the inside, "C.I.D. Agent." He pulled out his military ID and showed it, as well.

Bobby whispered, "My name is Major Bobby Samuels, and the woman with me is Captain Bo Devore. We are C.I.D. agents, army plainclothes detectives. Is there an air marshal on this plane?"

She said, "No, sir, what is wrong?"

"The aisle passenger with the laptop in seat five on the port side of the jet, the Hispanic-looking guy in the blue suit, he has done several things which are really troubling me."

The flight attendant stiffened, "Sir, we cannot discriminate because someone looks troubling."

Bobby got closer to her face, "I really don't have time to start arguing with you. He is not Hispanic. He is Middle Eastern, and is in fact a Muslim."

She stiffened. "All the more reason, Major, to not—"

Clenching his teeth, he interrupted, whispering, "You remember all the events on September 11, 2001, don't you?"

Face reddening, she said, "Of course, but I don't—"

Bobby interrupted. "Remember when the World Trade Center was bombed in 1993?"

She nodded and started to speak, but he cut her off again. "Do you remember all the U.S. Marines that were killed in their barracks in Lebanon?"

Meekly now, she nodded.

He said, "The USS *Cole* that was blown up?"

"Yes, sir," she said.

Bobby said, "Know what every one of those terrorists had in common?"

"No, what?" she replied, ready to cry now.

He said, "They all looked very similar to the passenger in the aisle seat in the fifth row on the port side of the jet, and they loved to scream 'Allah Akbar!' before dying, which he was writing on his laptop a minute ago. Now, are you going to cooperate, or take a chance I am wrong and get your throat slit by a box-cutter?"

She nodded and wiped a tear away.

Bobby gently dabbed her eye with a napkin, smiling, and said, "Sorry I had to get forceful, but I need your help. You're from New York City, I'll bet?"

She tried to smile bravely, saying, "Boston."

Bobby smiled.

He said, "I need you to tell the pilot to slowly turn us and get us to the nearest airport and report what I told you. Other than that, act perfectly normal. Jot this down. Tell him to report my name, Major Bobby Samuels, and my partner is Captain Bo Devore. We are U.S. Army C.I.D agents and operate out of the Pentagon. I do not have time to explain, just get him to call it in and turn the plane slowly, and tell them I said 'terrorist incident.' I have to get back to my seat and investigate. Don't you worry. We will be okay."

She smiled bravely, saying "I'll do it, I promise. I'm sorry, it is just they tell us so much . . ."

He smiled, gently shushing her. "I understand. You're doing fine. Don't worry."

Bobby walked away from the galley and looked back at her smiling, saying, "Thank you very much, ma'am."

He wouldn't even glance toward the Middle-Easterner. He knew Bo would, and the man might be looking closely at him for a giveaway.

Bo was still blinking one eye and acting like she was trying to get a pesky eyelash. He sat down and leaned toward her.

"It is getting called in," he whispered, "He reached in his shirt pocket for a pen earlier, and a couple blue-tipped matches started to come out of his shirt pocket. That is what alerted me."

Bo said, "He has pulled a wire from the right side of the laptop, with a small plug. Several times, it has looked like he is trying to reach inside his shirt, but is worried about me seeing him in the mirror, so he moves his hand back. The woman by his window is fast asleep."

Bobby whispered, "How many smokers on a plane carry a bunch of blue-tipped matches loose when they can carry a matchbook? He is dressed like a Mexican and spoke with a Spanish accent at the ticket counter, but he was typing in English type, and I saw the words 'Allah Akbar' several times as I walked by. The suit is brand-new. His pants still have a clear plastic strip he didn't see on the back of his right leg that says Size 34 over and over."

When Bo heard Bobby say "Allah Akbar," she felt a chill run down her spine. She had heard the words, meaning "God is great!" many times while watching Abu Musab al-Zarqawi, the head of al-Qaida in Iraq, sawing off the heads of captured American civilians and taping it. He and his helpers, who would hold the captives down, would yell those words over and over while he sawed with his long knife.

"Bobby," she said using familiarity the two used only when alone together, "we have got to nail this bastard before he can do anything."

Bobby replied, "A headshot would do it, but he has passengers behind him and around him. You using Corbons in your Glock?"

She whispered, "Yes."

He said, "Me, too. We also can't just light him up without knowing definitely he is a terrorist planning something. I don't want to spend the rest of my life in Leavenworth for smoking a Mexican computer salesman, do you?"

She gave him a sarcastic look.

She thought back to June 8th, 2006. It was about four o'clock in the morning and Bo awakened, wide awake, with indigestion. She held her stomach and that did not help. Bo finally got up and like her dad, grabbed the old Arm and Hammer baking soda. She poured a small glass of tap water, then stirred in a half-flat teaspoon of baking soda. She drank it and returned to bed. Bo decided to turn on the TV and catch the current world news. She switched to Fox News and stared at a photograph of a very dead Abu Musab al-Zarqawi. She heard the announcer tell about Zarqawi being killed, and Bo pumped her fist, saying, "Yes!"

She grabbed the phone and dialed Bobby.

His sleepy voice said, "Hello."

Bo started to answer, but burped really loud.

Bobby said, "Who in the hell is this?"

Bo was so embarrassed her ears turned red. "Bobby, it's me. I am sorry. I bumped my lamp, and it scraped the top of the nightstand. Sorry."

"Okay, what's up?"

Bo said, "Turn your TV on to Fox News."

Bobby said, "Okay."

Several seconds elapsed while the two watched their respective TVs.

Finally, Bobby said, "Why, that was my boys that lasered his sorry butt."

Bo said, "Task Force 145?"

Bobby said, "Yep. This is great!"

Now the two had another terrorist to deal with, close up. An obvious Muslim posing as a Mexican businessman, and more obviously a jihadist.

"What do you think he is up to?"

Bobby replied, "My guess would be that he is wearing a suicide belt, made out of C4 molded to conform to his midsection with no metal parts, and the plug from the laptop will have his detonator. The blue-tip matches would be a simple backup. He might even have a firecracker or cherry bomb in his pocket, too."

"When will he try to detonate it, do you suppose?"

"We're flying to LAX, Bo. That answer your question?"

Bobby whispered, "If we pull our weapons on him, he will plug in and detonate. If we try to question him, he might do the same thing. If I knock him out and immobilize both arms before he can detonate the bomb, we will be okay."

Bo said, "What if he is innocent and there is no bomb?"

"The government will have to make a heavy-duty apology to Mexico, and I will get my ass handed to me by some general," he replied. "I'll probably get court-martialed, or at the least get a major reprimand or maybe an Article 15."

He went on. "Because of that, I do not want you involved."

"I am your partner!" she replied.

"That was not a question or suggestion, Captain," he said.

"Yes, sir."

Bobby smiled, adding, "Besides, these AQ guys are trained to always have backups. While I take this one down, you have to watch for a partner to appear."

"What if the partner is wearing a suicide belt?" she asked.

Bobby replied, "We are screwed. If there is one, go for a head shot if this one does have a belt on, but you have to watch about putting a round through the aircraft skin or a window."

Bo asked, "How are you going to take him down?"

Bobby chuckled softly. "Punch the hell out of him."

Bo grinned and slipped the Glock 17 out of her shoulder holster well hidden next to her left breast. She carefully pulled back the slide and jacked a round into the chamber. The Glock has one safety, which is a little button on the trigger, which you press while you fire. She hid the gun under her blanket and waited, watching.

Bobby gave her a wink and walked back, palming handcuffs and his badge in his left hand. He walked down the aisle until he was right in front of seat five and simply said, "Sir?"

The faux-Mexican businessman looked up at Bobby startled, and his hand had started for the side of the laptop when Bobby suddenly lashed out and up with an uppercut that sent shock waves all the way into Bobby's shoulder. The punch lifted the terrorist a few inches up off his seat, and blood spurted from his mouth as several teeth shattered. Two women screamed and then more, and Bobby held up his badge, yelling "Relax, Police!"

He grabbed the right wrist of the unconscious man and slapped a handcuff on it, yanking the man's body onto the floor of the aisle. Stepping on the other limp arm, Bobby yanked the man's shirt open, with two women screaming as flying buttons startled them. Strapped around the man's midsection was a tight suicide vest with Velcro connecters holding six-inch-by-eight-inch blocks of C4 plastic explosive. Bo stood behind Bobby looking back at all the passengers holding up in the air with a two-handed grip her Glock 17 nine-millimeter semiautomatic while carefully screening each passenger's face.

Several passengers started praising God, and several more praised Bobby and Bo, while she maintained a vigil and Bobby carefully searched the terrorist.

The unconscious man on the floor was named Abdul Baari and was indeed a member of al-Qaida, as were his two compatriots working specifically on this flight, which they planned to send to the ground in flames as it passed over the highly populated areas of Los Angeles. And as members of al-Qaida, they always had a contingency plan, something always insisted upon by the Director, Osama bin Laden.

Faarooq Ghasaan was the man who remained on the ground; in fact, he was part of the ground crew at the airport in Washington. Faarooq had cleaned and maintained the inside of the cabin and cockpit before Bo and Bobby and the other passengers boarded. As soon as his helper, a young black female, whose name he never even bothered to learn, walked down the steps to the tarmac carrying two white bags of trash, Faarooq worked quickly and efficiently as he had practiced over and over in the mockup in their shared Georgetown Apartment. At each of the bolt lock points of the newly strengthened door separating the cockpit from the first-class cabin, he molded a liberal chunk of C4, quickly spraying them all with the model paint that blended them into the gray color of the rest of the door. He stuck the spray can back in his cargo pocket on his leg, and inserted the blasting cap and remote processor just inside the cabin door. So far, it had escaped detection.

Now with the operation compromised and Abdul Baari in custody, the third member, Dhul Fiqaar, had to use option two to effect their plans. He would bide his time and watch back into the cabin from his seat in first class, until he saw an opening. He would have to bring the plane down well before Los Angeles, but there still would be a great loss of life of infidels and more terror in the skies for the hapless, stupid Americans. He held his Mexican daily newspaper *Pulso* over his open briefcase. Below it rested the innocent-looking garage door opener, which he'd quickly explained in thick Spanish accent when going through the security checkpoint.

He had been so embarrassed, he'd said as he explained that he was running late when he got out of his car in the large parking lot at Dulles Airport in DC—where, he said, he worked at the Mexican Embassy—and had actually stuck his cell phone in the visor over the driver's seat and grabbed the garage door opener and dropped it in his briefcase. The expensively dressed Mexican businessman was allowed to board with his carry-on.

Dhul Fiqaar was also wearing a Brooks Brother suit, a brown one with a gold and brown checked tie, and he too sported a Mexican flag lapel pin. Like everyone else on the aircraft, he was now standing watching Bobby back in tourist as he expertly searched and cuffed the still-unconscious Abdul Baari.

Bo, simply being a good cop, turned to give a little attention to the passengers in first class. That was when she noticed the man at the very front of the jet, a well-dressed Hispanic-looking man in a brown suit who towered above everybody in first class. Even with the suit, he looked like he could well be an NFL offensive lineman. He was much taller than Bobby and even wider in the shoulders. Then

Bo, eyes scouring and searching for details and anything out of place, noticed on the left lapel the tiny little Mexican flag. Even at that distance, Dhul Fiqaar noticed her immediate recognition of the pin, a too obvious attempt at camouflage suggested by Faarooq Ghasaan when they saw some for sale by the cash register while eating at a Mexican restaurant in Alexandria.

Dhul ducked down into his seat, grabbing the garage door opener, and he rushed behind the next seat ducking.

In the meantime, Bo, aiming her Glock, screamed, "Everybody down!"

She ran forward as fast she could, yelling over her shoulder, "Major Samuels, accomplice in first class!"

Abdul Baari, at the same time, sat straight up looking around him in a daze, and Bobby shoved his shoulders back down. Dhul pushed the garage door opener, and the high-frequency detonator in the cabin blew the door inward, actually cracking Dhul's right kneecap. Nonetheless he jumped up limping and rushed into the cabin, Bo behind him but unable to get a clear shot because of confused screaming passengers still in the way.

Dhul Fiqaar hit the copilot with one sweeping backhand that sent his head against the bulkhead, and he slumped in his seat unconscious. Then Dhul swung to the left, hitting the pilot with a slapping blow that knocked him out of his seat and against the side window. He was not out totally, but very woozy and disoriented. The navigator had been thrown by the blast into one of the observer seats in the cabin.

Suddenly, Dhul wheeled to see Bo aiming center-mass at his chest, and he screamed, "Allah Akbar!" as he lunged forward at her.

Bang! Bang! went the Glock as she did a military double tap, placing two shots into his chest that could be covered by a quarter, but the nine-millimeter pistol was not large enough to stop the behemoth. He swung and his open hand knocked the gun from Bo's hand, sending it flying back into the first-class cabin.

Grinning evilly and starting to feel faint, he went after the woman, who barely reached his mid-chest. Women in the aircraft, seeing the charge from the killer with two streams of blood draining from his chest, screamed loudly. Bo stood her ground, concentrating, and waited until he was right on top of her, ready to grab her. His plate-sized hands grabbed her upper arms, but she stomped down on his foot, breaking it with the edge of her foot, and he bent over in severe pain, screaming.

Remembering all she could from the years of training in tae kwon do she'd had as a girl, she stepped back and then skipped in, pivoting her hips as she kicked as hard as possible and executed a sidekick with her stiletto heel imbedding itself in Dhul's windpipe. He tried to scream, but it was only a gurgle of blood. Bo withdrew her foot and her high-heel shoe stayed in his Adam's apple. He yanked it out, eyes open in sheer rage. He started for Bo, but fell back as the jet started into a steep dive. The pilot, barely conscious, now grabbed the controls and leveled it out somewhat. And the giant, knowing he was near death, started toward Bo again. Her eyes searched all around for a weapon. Her pistol had disappeared under a seat. His left hand clutched his throat, frothy bubbling blood working its way out between and around his fingers.

The man was almost upon her again, blood streaming from several holes now, and she was not sure how she would attack, but she stood her ground and determined she would try attacking with kicks just above and directly on his knee he was limping on. Bo simply knew that she had to get past him. The plane was headed for the ground.

At the last second, Bobby's voice from behind her yelled, "Bo! Down!"

She dropped to the floor immediately and heard Bobby's double tap, as she saw two bullet holes appear in the forehead of Dhul Fiqaar, former giant Taliban fighter from Sar E-Pol, Afghanistan, who now looked up cross-eyed, seemingly at the holes in his forehead. In actuality, he was dead on his feet. He fell backward, as more screams rang throughout the rapidly descending aircraft. Without looking, Bo waved at Bobby over her shoulder as she rushed to the cabin, stepping on and running across Dhur's body to get there.

2

WHITE DEATH

She heard Bobby yell, "Folks, fasten and tighten your seat belts and prepare for a crash landing! Don't you worry, we will all be okay!"

The jet was already turned around and on its way back to Denver. The pilot was semiconscious, and the copilot and navigator were still out cold with concussions. Although it was now May, and most passengers wore summer-type clothing and carried no heavy clothing with them, Bo was now looking down at a ferocious late-spring blizzard hitting the snowcapped peaks of the Colorado San Juan Mountain range in the southwestern part of the state. She slapped the pilot across the face and tried to bring him around, to no avail.

The Pratt & Whitney JT9D turbofan engines were working hard to power the Boeing DC10 Model 40 series through the raging blizzard, but their thrust range had dropped to 40,000 pounds from 54,000 pounds. It was losing altitude fast, and Bo saw the looming mountains below getting closer and closer. Bobby appeared next to her and tossed a glass of water into the face of the pilot, but the man was still half out of it.

Bobby said to the pilot, "We are going to crash in the Rockies. We have to pull out. Wake yourself, man!"

He looked back and saw the nervous flight attendant running around with another attendant getting people buckled in.

As if he were given a silent signal, the pilot sat up and looked around. He pulled himself behind the controls and looked at Bobby.

"What happened?"

Bobby said, "Terrorists! How can I help?"

"Pray, and you two get buckled in. I cannot pull this up," he replied, "I can only try to find us the best place to crash."

There was a little break in the blizzard, and they could see fourteen-thousand-foot peaks looming all around and above them. Below them was a gentler slope coming off one and heading right down to the bank of a frozen glacial lake.

The pilot lowered flaps and his wheels to cause more drag and slow the jet as much as possible. A flashing light and buzzer came on with the word "stall" flashing on the tiny screen.

"I am going to try to skid it across the lake and hope those trees keep us from going over a cliff or into one."

He quickly grabbed the mike and started to key it, then yelled, "Shit!" instead.

Bobby and Bo both looked and saw the radio literally bashed in, apparently from the door being blown earlier and something flying against it. Bobby looked back and saw the flight attendants were now apparently buckled in and people seemed to be bent over in their seats.

The plane bounced off some unseen boulders, which tore a hole in the belly and knocked off one set of wheels. They hit the lake surface and the ice held, as the plane collapsed the second set of wheels and skidded fairly straight toward the evergreen and aspen forest to its front.

Bobby wrapped his large-muscled arms around Bo and

held her tightly against his chest, his eyes staring out the window at the looming trees. The jet went into them with loud crashing and screeching noises. The entire right wing tore free from the plane and exploded into flames. The pilot had wisely shut the engines down before hitting the lake. Trees were being clipped off with great cracks, and Bobby, still holding Bo tightly, was thrown forward, gashing his forehead open on the copilot's headset cradle, which had become draped over the seat. His head started bleeding profusely, and he blinked blood out of his eyes. The jet slowed suddenly and smoke started pouring from the engines on the existing port wing. With a great grinding sound, it stopped and listed to the left.

Bo immediately jumped up and unbuckled the captain and threw his left arm over her shoulder lifting him to his feet. Bobby lifted the copilot and placed him across his shoulders in a fireman's carry.

As they left the cabin, Bobby yelled, "I need somebody with strength to carry the navigator!"

A young man in a whitewall haircut ran up to the cockpit and picked up the navigator.

Bobby, bearing his own load on his shoulders, winked at the young man, who explained, "Marine Corps, sir. Cherry Point."

Bobby said, "Semper fi."

Bo yelled, "Do not go out the exits on the wing side of the plane! When you hit the ground get away from the plane, but stay in a group!"

Bobby carried the copilot to the emergency exit and following the Marine and his charge, dropped the man on the chute. Two men stood at the bottom of the chute grabbing all who slid down.

Bobby then started back toward the fifth seat, where he had knocked out Abdul Baari a second time, so he could take aim and shoot Dhul Fiqaar. The man was still out, and Bobby picked him up like a baby.

He carried the limp man toward the exit and yelled at the Marine, "Jarhead, I need your help."

The Marine ran over and Bobby handed him the terrorist.

Then, Bobby pulled out his Glock and shoved it in the Marine's belt, saying, "I need you to follow him down the slide and take charge of him for me. What is your name?"

"Bobby, Sir," he replied, "Lance Corporal Bobby Kennedy."

Bobby laughed. "You have got to be kidding! No relation, I assume?"

"No way, sir," Bobby said, "My family are hardcore Republicans, Protestants, and most are blue-collar workers and proud of it."

Bobby said, "Since my first name is Bobby, too, I'll refer to you as Corporal or Kennedy."

"I'm used to it, Major," Bobby responded. "I'll take this raghead off your hands, sir. You know, my best friend is from Mexico originally, and it really pisses me off these guys were trying to pass like they were, too."

He walked to the exit door and tossed the unconscious prisoner out onto the bright yellow ramp and followed him out the little door. At the bottom, two men, who immediately took up the responsibility when the plane stopped, caught the terrorist and set him off to the side, then grabbed the arms of Lance Corporal Bobby Kennedy as he hit the bottom.

Bobby and Bo both made sure, along with the flight attendants, that every passenger got out safely. There were assorted injuries, most minor, though, it seemed. Then the one engine burst into flames, and Bobby could tell both attendants were very nervous.

He said, "Ladies, you have been great, but you need to get out now. I will make sure everyone is clear. You, too, Captain Devore."

Bo started to argue but stopped herself, simply saying, "Yes, sir."

The two attendants were going to argue, too but both felt very comfortable with Bobby in charge, so all three headed toward the exit door. The flames started spreading to a fuel line and Bobby worried about a tank blowing.

Smoke started pouring into the cabin and the snow started falling again outside.

Bobby yelled down at Bo, "Get all the passengers to form a group close enough to be warmed by the fires, but far enough to avoid an explosion. I'll be down as soon as I check the plane."

Bobby ran into the forward restroom, and the cockpit. As he started heading back looking under seats just to make sure, the cabin really started filling with smoke. He yanked an oxygen mask from its tether and placed it over his face, sticking the end of the tube inside his shirt. This would filter some of the smoke.

Outside, a woman came running forward crying, and Bo calmed her down.

She screamed, "My baby is in there! My little boy Daniel ran to the restroom after we stopped and the crowd forced me to the exit and out. He has not showed up! Please!"

Bo interrupted, speaking softly, "Please don't worry. Major Samuels will find him and bring him out."

She gently handed the woman off to two other women who escorted her into the crowd. Bo had already removed one high heel, and was only in her nylons in the snow. She ran over to Bobby Kennedy.

"Corporal, I need you and these other two men to stand on each other's shoulders and make me a human ladder on the emergency ramp."

They understood and quickly complied, with Kennedy the top man. Bo climbed up over their backs and onto the Marine's shoulders, but still could not reach the emergency opening in the jet.

The corporal grabbed her feet and yelled, "On three, ma'am, jump! One, two, three!"

She jumped while he shoved, and she went flying upward, and grabbed the edge of the emergency opening, where heavy smoke was now pouring out. Bo pulled and kicked with her feet and, holding her breath, scrambled into the blackness. She could not see.

Bo yelled, "Bobby!"

She heard a faint muffled answer.

"Bobby," she yelled, "there is a little boy on board!"

She now clearly heard him yell, "Go, now!"

Bo knew enough about Bobby to know that she should not argue, question, or hesitate. He was a former Green Beret, a member of Delta Force, and knew what he was doing better than anyone around in any type of emergency. She complied, and slid down with all three men catching her. They backed away, standing with the other passengers. The lance corporal tried to offer her his shoes, but she flatly refused.

One of the fuel tanks on the opposite side of the plane blew, and the mother screamed, "My baby!"

It was a bloodcurdling scream and unnerved many there, some now with tears in their eyes, and all eyes were glued on the tiny emergency exit in the side of the big jet.

Smoke billowed out; then suddenly the suicide belt of C4 came flying out and hit the bottom of the inflatable ramp. Bo, wanting to give her feet some activity anyway, ran forward and grabbed it. Bobby suddenly came flying out of the smoke, feet-first, his shirt removed and wrapped around his head leaving only a crack for his eyes. In his arms was a little boy wearing an oxygen mask with the tube going into a water pitcher from the galley with Bobby's tie shoved into it making an airtight seal. Bobby had something wrapped around his neck, and slid all the way down quickly, hitting the ground with a thump on his back, but still holding the boy protectively in his arms. Bo and the three men rushed forward, as well as the mother and two women.

His butt and back covered in mud now, Bobby stood and removed the mask from the boy's mouth. He removed his own shirt and replaced it on his body.

The mother, in tears, wrapped her arms around her son and smiled broadly at Bobby, crying out, "Thank you! Thank you! You saved my son!"

"We were fine, Mom," the boy said nonplussed. "Bobby said we are perfectly safe. He's cool!"

Bo felt a shiver go down her spine. Then Bobby turned, and she got tears in her eyes, easily camouflaged by the now hard-falling snow. He walked over to her, pulling off Bo's Nike running shoes that were hanging by the laces around his neck. They had been in her carry-on bag.

Bobby handed them to her, saying, "Thought you might need these. There is a pair of your socks inside."

She could not help herself. She stood on her frozen tiptoes and kissed him on the cheek.

Bobby called for all the people to come forward. Behind him the smoke was trailing off, but flames still shot up on the other side of the jet, steam was rising everywhere, and one lone dead tree was aflame. All the people on the jet gathered around in a big semicircle, and suddenly one old man started clapping for Bobby and Bo. Others joined in, and soon all were clapping for them in the midst of a blizzard. Bobby, embarrassed, raised his hand and the clapping died down.

He yelled, "Folks, just because things go better with just one chief, does anybody object to me being in charge?"

The old man yelled, "Sonny, if they do, I'll club 'em with one of these logs."

People chuckled.

Bobby said, "I know it looks bleak, but we'll be okay, but I'll need help right away. The fire from the fuel will help keep us warm a little bit longer, and I don't think we'll have any more explosions, but I do think the blizzard will put it out soon. Now, I need the C4 plastic explosive in those vests torn into small strips. If we light it with matches, it makes a great fire itself or fire-starter."

The Marine raised his hand.

"Kennedy," Bobby acknowledged.

"Sir, that is C4. It won't blow up?"

Bobby smiled. "Well, if you stick a firecracker in it, but if you simply light it, it will make a nice little cooking fire that burns a long time. Speaking of that, I need several groups of volunteers. The first group will get water off the plane when the fire and smoke clear, then food. Another group will help me start tearing the padding out of the seats. Another will unload as much carry-on and especially regular luggage if we can get to it."

Kennedy said, "I have one question, Major. I thought army C.I.D. agents were only warrant officers or enlisted swine, like me. How did you both become C.I.D. agents?"

Bobby said, "Well, we still have to wait on the fire anyway. Because of 9/11 they created a special C.I.D. unit headquartered in the Pentagon that is generally kept pretty quiet. Captain Devore and I are the senior officers of the unit. To become an FBI agent, Treasury agent, Secret Service, or whatever, you have to have at least a college degree. Not so with C.I.D., and a lot of investigation requires a lot of records and file searches, so they created this unit to work alongside other Homeland Security-type officers with education and experience equal to FBI and other federal agents."

A young man raised his hand, and Bobby pointed at him.

"Major—I think they said," he asked, "why are you going to tear up the seats? Can't they be used for beds?"

Bobby said, "Good question, sir. We would have trouble removing the seats, but more importantly, we will have comfortable beds out of pine boughs. We are all dressed for summer, but we are right at timberline somewhere in the Colorado Rockies in a blizzard. We will use the luggage to insure everyone is wearing a long-sleeve shirt or jacket and long pants. Then we will stuff the seat padding down the sleeves, body, and legs of everybody's clothing. We will tie off the cuffs and ends of sleeves, and the padding will act as very good insulation, so it will be like you are all wearing a snowmobile suit. If we run out of padding, we will use dry leaves or pine needles. They work, too."

A big murmur ran through the whole crowd.

The wife of the old man said, "Young man, are you a professional hero or what? I swanee!"

Bobby got embarrassed as people cheered again, and even more so when Bo held up her hand and said, "Yes, ma'am, he is. Major Samuels is an MP detective, but he was a Green Beret in the Gulf War and earned two Silver Stars, and General Perry, army chief of staff, nominated him for the Distinguished Service Cross for his actions in Iraq."

"Captain Devore!" Bobby yelled. "More than enough about me. We have to survive this blizzard. Are there any doctors or nurses or EMTs here?"

Several people raised their hands.

Bobby said, "Please find out about injuries and treat them. I need you two large men in the back there to go into that thicket of evergreens and find a place where you can pull the tops of trees down in a long line and tie them down. Have the airline personnel tell you where there are ropes, electrical wire, whatever."

One of the two said, "Major, I am a scoutmaster and Order of the Arrow advisor. We'll get it done! One giant lean-to coming up!"

Bobby was pleased. The man's background in scouting should make him quite capable of making an effective shelter for the entire group paying attention to wind direction, thickness of cover, and so on.

Everybody divided themselves up and started rushing to accomplish the various tasks Bobby gave them.

Kennedy ran up, saying, "Major, if we can cut away the emergency ramp, wouldn't that make an excellent tarp for us?"

Bobby said, "Great, Corporal. You're in charge of that. Maybe we can get the other emergency ramps, too. One could be set up as a giant reflector."

The passengers were very motivated and excited. Bobby had not let them even consider the possibility of perishing in a high mountain blizzard. They all worked diligently. Bo had checked for a sat phone, but not a single passenger had one, and no cell phones were working.

Network news was already reporting that it was believed that the flight was taken over by terrorists and blown up over the Rocky Mountains somewhere. This had the President in a very angry state of mind. The original Mayday had been monitored or leaked by air traffic controllers and was now very much in the public domain. Network news teams were racing to try to secure passenger lists, bios on the flight crews, find out if celebrities were on the plane, and of course, do a complete breakdown of everything they could learn about Major Bobby Samuels and Captain Bo Devore. If possible, some of those TV and print news personnel were going to try to find out how many freckles Bobby and Bo had on their bodies, and see if there were any Peyton Place episodes lived out in their respective families.

General Perry, now chief of staff of the U.S. army, would not have any of the gossip, passing it, or listening to it. He had dealt with the news too often. He would make his own decisions based on the most current intelligence from U.S. and military satellites, humintel, and USAF overflights and other electronics. He was also going to "personally kick the shit out of any sumbitch that gives information out about two army plainclothes detectives and endangers their lives, especially our two best ones."

The snow was still falling at two A.M. but the passengers who were hurt had been treated. A giant lean-to had been built with numerous small pines side by side, bent over, and tied to boulders on the ground with heavy-gauge electrical wire. All the passengers were fed by three who had worked as cooks, and one who was a gourmet chef on vacation from an upscale restaurant in Crystal City, a Washington suburb. Skin from the wings had been used to cover the bent-over trees and to set up a giant reflector. All the emergency chutes had been converted to giant ground cloths, and numerous small fires reflected plenty of heat throughout the giant shelter.

Three people were having problems with altitude, and

two of them were cardiac patients. So the doctor and EMTs were now trying to get them oxygen from the jet's supply.

Bobby and Bo were wearing rucksacks formed by tying the bottom of the pant legs on two pairs of jeans from the luggage, and then attaching them to the butt area. With the waistline of each pair as the top of each pack, rope was strung through the belt loops and pulled tight to close the packs. The packs contained ammunition for their nine-millimeters, bottles of water, a pair of binoculars and hunting knives from someone's luggage, and extra clothes.

The prisoner was left in Bobby Kennedy's charge.

Bo said to Major Samuels, "Bobby, why are we wearing packs? Are we going to try to make it to civilization?"

Bobby said, "No, we would get killed. We're going to try to hunt down some meat for all these people."

"Oh," Bo said, but she suddenly felt a need to vomit.

She must have eaten something that was really hitting her system. Her legs started shaking almost uncontrollably. Then diarrhea cramps hit her.

Bo said, "Ooh, I have to go to the restroom. I'll be back!"

Bo ran into the darkness of the trees on the other side of the aircraft and vomited. She rubbed snow on her face and started calming herself down.

She spoke to herself. "You are an army officer. Straighten up, Devore!"

She pulled her shoulders back, knowing passengers might be counting on her and Bobby. She masked, something familiar to Bo for years, and walked back. The cramps had already subsided, but her heart was still pounding, and she simply decided to hold it together.

Bobby was going to attempt to find any small herds of deer or harems of elk, holed up in the dark evergreens during the storm. He did not want to take a chance on how long the storm might last, and he wanted to insure there was fresh meat.

He was concerned about Bo, but she returned smiling bravely.

Bobby said, "You okay, partner?"

Bo smiled broadly. "Yep, I'm fine."

Major Bobby Samuels was a detective and noticed everything. Bo's glance went down and to her left, which he knew is what suspects do when they are lying, look down to their left. Bo was a very honest person, so it was even more obvious with her. He knew she was not fine. He would deal with it when he felt the time was right.

"Have you ever hunted before?" he asked.

Her eyes shifted down to her left as she replied, "No, never."

He said, "Do you have a problem with killing animals?"

"Oh, no!" she replied eagerly, "Not at all. The Bible says that animals are here to serve us. I am fine, really."

He smiled softly and turned, walking into the blizzard.

They had made it less than a mile, and Bo wondered how Bobby could ever find the plane again the snowfall was so blinding. Suddenly, he stopped, hand up, and she froze. She had no idea why he stopped, but she knew to trust him. Bobby turned slowly, and grabbed her gently by the arm, kneeling down. She looked where he pointed on the ground. There in the falling snow, now already barely discernible, were several large sets of prints that were like giant upside-down V's and the size of a pony's hoofprint. Snow had them almost covered already.

Bobby put his mouth right up to her ear, pulled back the makeshift hat and muffs he had fashioned from somebody's sweater, and whispered softly, "Elk right in front of us. Probably were stirred by the crash and are settling down now. They are walking and the wind is in our favor. It's blowing towards us, and they travel with the wind blowing into their faces so they can smell danger first, so we are behind them. They have very large ears, eyes, and noses, so be very slow and careful. Hopefully, we will catch them bedded down. If we shoot at two, when I wave, count one thousand, two thousand, three thousand, and fire from the time my hand goes down. Aim low behind the left shoulder. If you miss the heart, you will hit the lung, and

again, do double taps. I will point out which one to fire at if
we see two at once. Okay?"

She smiled at him and gave him the thumbs-up, and felt
a chill down her back from his lips being so close to her
ear. They moved on slowly, very slowly, Bobby directly in
front. Bo just had no clue what was going on other than
blinding, blowing snow.

She saw everything get darker, and realized they were
dropping into a deep bowl surrounded by tall trees, evergreens. The snow was somewhat shielded here. Bobby suddenly stopped and dropped silently into the snow. Bo
followed suit. He turned and put his fingers to his lips. Inch
by inch, they crawled forward, and suddenly she noticed
the dark boulders in front of them were moving a little.
There were about twenty elk, bedded down in the bowl,
most under low-hanging tree branches. Bo's heart started
pounding in her neck and temples. They were now moving
forward at the pace of wounded caterpillars.

After ten minutes, Bobby crawled up behind a small
snow-buried boulder with Bo directly behind him. He
slowly moved and held his index finger up to his lips in a
shushing gesture. With his hands, he indicated that there
were two elk lying down close to them. She was to shoot
the one on the right, and he, the left.

Slowly, carefully, gun in hand, Bo crawled up next to
Bobby, feeling her heart pounding hard in her temples
and her ears. He nodded, and they both slowly rose, and Bo
lost her breath. Lying directly in front of them, less than
ten feet away, was a giant bull elk and a large cow. They
looked to be as large as horses to Bo. She realized she was
almost gasping, as she watched the giant breaths of warm
steam coming from their noses, and both animals, apparently frozen in shock, stared intently at Bobby and Bo.
Bobby's finger went down, and she silently counted to herself, one thousand, two thousand, three thousand, as she
centered her front sight just behind the cow's left shoulder
and down low. Boom! Boom! Both guns fired twice as one,
and the bull jumped to his feet and fell back on his rump.

Bo's cow fell over sideways, her four mighty legs kicking out toward Bo as if running. She choked back a tear, feeling sorry for the animal, and put two more shots into the elk's under-chest, aiming where she figured the heart must be. It lay still, one leg slowly twitching even after death.

Bobby stood and walked forward and pumped four rounds into the struggling bull, and he lay still. Blood was everywhere on the new-fallen snow, and steam poured off the animals' bodies. Bo's knees almost gave way, and she wondered why she was rubbery-legged. She had faced death from a man shooting at her before, but this was different. Being a good cop, Bo masked well, but maybe Bobby just knew her well.

He set his gun on the bull's body and wrapped his arms protectively around Bo in a tender hug. She put her face on his massive chest and sobbed.

Bobby said, "You okay, partner?"

She wiped her tears, saying, "Sorry. I don't understand. I've never hunted before."

Bobby wiped a tear, saying, "Bo, people who live in big cities and lobby against hunting have no clue about the beauty and majesty of wild animals like this. Most hunters do, but the antihunting lobby portrays them all as bloodthirsty, mindless killers. The fees from hunting licenses is what provides for most of the wilderness for them to live in, and most hunters hate to actually bring death to the animal, but it is a necessary part of the whole ordeal."

She said, "Bobby, I'm not against hunting. It just . . ."

Bobby smiled. "You don't need to explain. I understand. It will help to remind yourself we have a planeload of people in a mountain blizzard who may need this food to survive before we are rescued."

"I know," she replied. "I don't feel guilty, just feel bad for these two elk."

Bobby smiled and said, "I have to get busy. Why don't you gather us some firewood from the low-hanging dead branches in these pines around this grove." She did, and was surprised at how many elk had been bedded down. All had fled when the shooting started. Their bed marks were all around the grove.

Bobby had the knife out and was cutting away the testicles and penis from the bull and cutting around the anus. Gathering wood, she glanced over and saw him tying a string from his pack around the colonic tract going to the anus. Then he slit the hide and flesh halfway up the elk's body. He made a slit higher up across the throat and reached inside, apparently cutting the esophagus.

He called Bo over and quickly took her wood and made a blazing fire.

He then returned to the bull and asked for her help. They swung the hind legs over to the downhill side, and he started removing the elk's intestines and lungs.

While she got more firewood, he started working on the cow, and was soon cleaning the knife. Bobby handed her his water bottles, as he stood and looked off into the flurries. She had no clue which way they'd come from.

Bo almost panicked. "Where are you going?"

He replied, "Kid, we can't carry these monsters ourselves. I am getting help."

Bo jumped up, proclaiming, "I'm going with you."

Bobby said, "You can't. You have to stay here and protect this meat from predators."

"What if a bear or mountain lion comes?" she asked, "You already told me we probably couldn't bring down any elk with our Glocks, but we did."

Bobby said, "Bears are all hibernating and are shy about humans anyway. Mountain lions are the same. Besides, they like to kill their own prey, usually deer, almost always deer. They are scared of grown humans normally."

Bo said, "Well what kind of predators are you talking about?"

Bobby smiled and responded, "Rocky Mountain tigers and Sasquatches."

"What?" she said, knees secretly shaking.

Bobby started laughing. He picked up his pack and slung it on his back.

"I'll be back shortly. Just keep wood on the fire and watch for coyotes, foxes, things like that," he said.

Bo said, "No problem."

She did not really mean that. Bo had no idea what was wrong with her. She was really frightened now, and even more so when she looked at the large trees surrounding her and felt almost claustrophobic.

Bo felt so all alone. The wind was blowing more softly now, but she was more frightened. Bo patted the grip of her Glock 17 for relief, but it wasn't that. She could not understand what was going on with her.

"Bobby" she whispered into the breeze, "Please come back. I'm scared."

She whispered it in the manner of a little girl with monsters in the closet. She looked at the bloody field-dressed bodies of the two elk, and suddenly had to relieve her bladder. Bo ran a few steps and squatted down.

She tried to avoid looking again, but could not help herself. She looked at the animal carcasses again, and immediately began sobbing. Bo curled up next to the fire and reached out, placing more branches on it.

"This is bullshit!" she exclaimed, sitting bolt upright, and said, "You are a captain in the U.S. Army! You are a cop! Why are you crying?"

It was as if the question had to be asked for the answer to pop into her conscious mind.

Bo fell forward, really bawling now. Racking sobs came out. She'd never dealt with it before. Every single time it popped into her mind, it was pushed back down again. Bo cried for several minutes, then sat up, and wiped away the tears. She stared into the fire. Every time anybody ever asked if she had ever hunted, she always said, "No," but never understood why she lied.

Her mind went back to that day. Her Uncle Ken was her father's older brother, and she always felt uncomfortable with the way he looked at her. One time, when she was very young, she saw her mother slap Uncle Ken across the face, right after he came to visit and simply hugged her.

Her mommy was very angry, but was keeping her remarks from young Bo's ears.

As Bo entered her teenaged years, she started developing her breasts, which were larger and better-shaped than all the other girls'. When Uncle Ken came to visit, his hands always lingered too long as he removed them from his too-tight hugs. She then understood what happened with her mother years earlier.

It was with the normal denial of family dysfunction and avoiding parental disapproval that Bo agreed to go deer hunting with Uncle Ken, as she was "his favorite niece."

Bo was a fifteen-year-old-virgin with a figure that would have made any grown woman jealous. She had dreamed romantic dreams about the man she would love someday, fully and totally. In fact, most of her free time just thinking involved letting her imagination go wild while formulating that man. Her father, a well-respected general in the air force, was the outline for that man to fit into. Bo became an overachiever as a young girl, because she always wanted "Daddy to be proud," even now, years after his death.

By admitting the incident, she would have to actually get angry at her father, even in death, for insisting she go with his big brother. Bo was uncomfortable the whole trip, but she did get her deer, a two-year-old eight-point whitetail buck.

To celebrate, Uncle Ken told her he could not help himself because she was such a great niece and he loved her so much. He pinned her to the ground, panting like a worn-out coonhound, right next to the deer's still-warm body, and groped and bit and pinched and squeezed.

He forced himself on her totally, forcing himself into the innocent recesses of her body that she was saving for that special man.

Afterward, he cried and apologized profusely, until Bo told him she would tell her dad.

Then, he turned into the scariest person she had ever

seen. That look on his face was one of murder, and he told
her if she ever told anybody, it would cause a big family
rift and nobody would believe her. He would deny everything and his kid brother would believe him over a teenager.
He never threatened to kill her if she told, but his body language and his looks told her.

Until that day, Bo had wanted to become an art professor, but the following day, she made up her mind to become
a cop. Sometime later, she decided to join the army and become an MP after getting her degree first. She got her degree in police science with a minor in psychology.

"Oh, my God," Bo said aloud into the wind. "Oh, my
God!"

She stared at the outlines of the giant evergreens with
tears now dripping slowly off her cheeks. All these years
the memory had remained suppressed, but now was flood-
ing into her stream of consciousness. Bo was a rape victim.
Bo was an incest victim. The thoughts were rushing in now.
She started understanding some of her silly peccadilloes,
like losing her breath whenever people would even mention hunting trips, chills she would get whenever she saw a
deer, even along a highway, the diarrhea cramps, and vomiting. Now, she felt like two tons had just been lifted off her
shoulders.

Bo's head was spinning. The beautiful captain was a
survivor, for certain, and she now made up her mind that
she would have to deal with this later, after they were safe.
Bo, however, missed Bobby right now probably more than
anytime ever. She caught herself picturing having him
wrapping his massive arms around her protectively and letting her rest her head on his bulging chest. She knew she
would feel totally safe in those arms.

Bo shook off the thoughts and added wood to the fire,
and decided to break more branches, and she kept herself
busy adding more wood to the pile until Bobby arrived with
six men from the jet. They were all excited to see the elk.

A very large man stepped forward, saying, "Major, ah
was born and raised in my pop's huntin' camp in Montana.

My ole man was a big-game guide and outfitter. You let me take charge, and we'll have these puppies dressed, quartered, and ready to pack in no time."

Bobby said, "Absolutely. What is your name, by the way?"

"Rainbow Flowers," he said, "but folks call me Rain."

"Rainbow?" Bo said.

"Mah mom and dad were also kinda hippies," he said with a chuckle.

Bobby said, "Are you a guide?"

Rain said, "No, sir. Computer software company out of Chicago."

Bo asked, "What do you do there?"

"President and COO," he drawled. "But I hunt and fish a lot when I can get away."

Bobby glanced toward Bo, and she diverted her eyes briefly, but he was a cop. Something was wrong, and he knew it.

He grinned at Rain, saying, "Great, Rain. You're in charge. That will help because Captain Devore thought she saw the outline of a cabin over that way, so she and I will check for it, if you men don't mind."

Rain said, "Get outta heah. We got it handled."

Bo was clueless why Bobby said that, but she knew to play along without changing expression.

One of the men said, "Thanks for all the firewood. It's going to help staying warm."

Bobby grabbed a large stick from the fire, one end burning like a torch, and led Bo away from the grove and past the big trees. Little hiss sounds emanated from the burning end of the stick as they walked along, as snowflakes hit the flames.

They only went a quarter of a mile, when Bobby found a grove of large rocks up against a large cliff overhang. He immediately broke some low-hanging branches off nearby trees and built a log cabin fire by fashioning the larger sticks in the shape of a box, with smaller ones on top. He then filled the center of the box with pine cones and dried pine needles. He then stuck his torch in and the flames shot up, with tongues of flames soon licking out at the falling flakes on all sides. Bobby cleared the snow away back up under the cliff, and prepared seating spots for them side by side.

He pulled a small coffeepot from the plane out of his pack and scooped if full of snow and balanced it on the fire. After adding more snow, he soon had water boiling and added coffee to it. He produced two cups from his pack with cream for Bo.

They started to drink, and she put on her best smile.

Bo said, "Okay, why the mystery, Boss?"

Bobby smiled.

"You and I are partners," Bobby said, "and I could tell something happened with you while we were gone."

Don't look down and to the left, Bo instantly thought to herself, or he will know I am lying, and smiling, she stared into his eyes, saying, "Bobby, you are loopy. Nothing happened. Nothing is wrong other than being stranded high in the mountains in a blizzard."

It was only a split second, he sensed, before she answered, but that was too long. Part of her wanted to tell him.

Bobby said, "Did I do something to make you angry?"

"Oh no! Absolutely not!"

Bobby felt guilty himself now, saying, "Did you get upset when I had a couple drinks?"

Why did he ask that? he wondered. And again there was a split-second hesitation before her answer. "No, that is none of my business if you want to drink a bit."

"Hey, it's not like I'm an alcoholic," Bobby said, "So what if I enjoy a drink or two now and then?"

Damn, why I am I talking about that? he thought to himself.

Bo got irritated, saying, "Bobby, can we go back? Your drinking is your own business and none of mine. I personally won't let myself get where I can be out of control, but what you do is your business. I don't care how much you drink."

"Out of control?" he shot back angrily. "I am never out of control just because I have one or two drinks."

"Whatever," she replied, staring into her coffee cup.

Bobby said, "Bo, what is wrong?"

"Nothing, dammit!" she snarled glaring at him.

He felt really guilty now, saying, "You felt like I was letting you down as your partner on the plane before the crash, because I had downed a few drinks, didn't you?"

"You! You! You!" she raged. "Why do you have to insist that it has anything to do with you? Can't I just have my own problems?"

Bobby got calm and smiled softly, saying, "I thought you said that nothing happened, that nothing was wrong."

Bo started to reply, but realized in her anger, she had let him know something was wrong. She fought the feeling, but felt the tears bubbling toward the surface like molten lava gurgling up the esophagus of a mountain waiting to spew out. Then, just as suddenly, the tears erupted from her eyes, and she threw herself against his chest. He was taken aback, but gently stroked her long beautiful auburn hair. Now that the floodgates had burst, Bo could not help herself. She sobbed, and Bobby leaned back against the cliff side and just let her lay her head on his chest and cry.

"Whatever it is, partner, I am here," he said almost in a whisper, "You cry all you want to. It's going to be all right."

Bo cried for a good five minutes, and felt so much better having Bobby's protective embrace around her. Bobby gently lifted her chin up to within inches of his face, and he smiled. He stared into her hazel eyes, now showing green, and something in him wanted to kiss her so badly. He thought of Arianna and felt guilty, as if he was thinking about cheating.

A soft smile appeared on Bo's lips and her breathing deepened. Oh, how she wanted him to be with her, right there in the snow and the cold, by the fire. She did not care. If she could look into his intelligent eyes while he was joined with her, it would be heavenly. If she could give herself totally to him, nothing else would matter.

Bobby was so tempted, especially after her lips parted

ever so slightly. He started to move his lips forward, and paused inches from her face.

An impish smile appeared on his face, and Bobby said softly, "You know, Bo. If you were a male partner, I would not be holding you like this."

She sat up laughing, wiping away her tears, saying, "I sure hope not."

Bobby breathed a deep sigh of both relief and regret. Bo was his partner, he reasoned, and he knew he could not, should not, have any romantic thoughts about her. She reminded him too much of Arianna and that much love hurt, deeply.

He remembered the day he was flown into Germany and told of Arianna's death on Highway 401 in Fayetteville, North Carolina, and the death of his unborn son. He remembered his feelings when he heard it was a head-on collision with a drunken driver who went left-of-center. It was odd how he turned his grief into rage and hate, and he left the army to seek a job in the LAPD as a cop, with one goal: Bust as many drunken drivers as possible. He was so experienced and overqualified that his goal did not work out, as he quickly worked his way into the role of homicide detective. He could not help himself. It was odd that while all that went on, he tried coping by drinking himself, many times, way too much. Bobby just could not imagine life without her. She was his lover, best friend, wife, mistress, confidante, and the only person in his life he had ever really opened himself up to. An obvious adrenaline-junkie, he loved the serenity of simply lying in bed with her and stroking her hair, while he stared into her beautiful eyes and could not believe he was so blessed to have such a woman as his life-partner.

Bobby stood and kicked the flaming embers into the snow, seeing chimneys of steam and smoke trailing upward into the black, snowflake-littered sky. Then, smiling warmly, he reached down for his partner and lifted her to her feet with no noticeable effort. They headed back toward the harvest of wild game.

It was much closer to dawn than it was to the previous sunset when the meat packers and army cops arrived back at the campsite. Bobby nudged Bo with his elbow, as they looked at the camp. Those with injuries had been all treated, ladders had been constructed of logs and sticks lashed together, and two crude ladders went up into the emergency doors of the jet. Three crude restrooms had been made using pieces of metal from the jet, and were set up behind the tail of the plane. Luggage had been removed from the jet's belly, and fires were burning all around. Two men were busy working on continually improving the water and wind-proofing of the giant shelter. A cheer went up when they saw the meat being brought in.

Bo said, "When people like to say Americans have grown weak, I wish they could see things like this."

3

CALL TO ACTION

General Jonathan Perry, chief of staff of the U.S. Army, had not slept. He had just left the White House and a late-night briefing of the President, and was now headed back to the Pentagon. The front of his limo sported a flag with four stars. Bobby Samuels and Bo Devore were his pet projects, and he would do all he could before his retirement to see that their careers were always proceeding on the right track.

Right now, however, he had a much greater concern. He wanted to know if Bobby and Bo were alive or dead. Just since he'd known them, Bo had survived a shootout with a jihadist in a hotel room in Canton, Ohio, Bobby had survived captivity by al Qaeda terrorists in Baghdad and escaped before being beheaded, and eliminated a major al Qaeda assassin in Iraq who had infiltrated the U.S. Army and was a sergeant who killed from within. Now, they had gone down in the Colorado Rockies in a late-spring blizzard in an obvious terrorist incident, and all indications had been that they were probably dead.

When the general got seated behind his desk, there was a buzz from the little box on his desk.

"Yes, Top," he said to Sergeant Major Will Rossberg in the outer office.

The general's aide, a colonel, was good, but was home asleep this night. But Sergeant Major Rossberg never seemed to sleep, or eat, or leave his post near the "Old Man." He made everything function properly around the general. Louisa, the general's civilian secretary, the colonel, the limo drivers, the valet, even the gardener, all came to the sergeant major when they needed problems solved or if the general needed something immediately.

"Sir, I got Major Niger on line three, from the air force. Says he has important information for you."

"Thanks, Top, and go home and get some sleep," the general said, pouring a cup of coffee and sitting behind his big walnut desk.

He grinned when the voice came back, "Yes, sir. Wilco, right after you leave."

The general picked up the phone. "General Perry here."

"General," the voice said, "this is Major Robert Niger, sir. I am at Peterson Air Force Base in Colorado Springs. We got orders from up the chain to get some fast-movers out to try to locate that downed commercial craft. We did some high altitude flyovers, sir, as the storm towers with that blizzard go up to higher than fifty grand. We have been looking with IFR instrumentation, COMINT (communications intelligence), which didn't pick up anything, SAR (you know, sir, synthetic aperture data), and MTI (moving target indicators). I have some good news, sir."

"Affirmative!" the general said enthusiastically. "What have you got?"

"We have a large group apparently in one area, maybe a campsite, sir. But the good news is people are moving around," the major replied, "MTI picked up a small group moving out a couple clicks from the main group and then returning a few hours later. Lot of activity, General, but they are staying put. Our analysts figure it is the crash site."

"Outstanding!" he replied. "You have any SAT lock-on?"

"Affirmative, sir, NORAD has a spy in the sky watching and will keep us updated."

The four-star responded, "You are supposed to be asleep, Major. Why are you up in the middle of the night?"

"Air Force never sleeps, General," the major said with a chuckle into the phone, not revealing he was officer of the day for Pete Field.

Perry laughed. "The air force, huh? Why do you suppose the army has a four-button here working when it is starting to get light outside?"

Niger said, "We never question, sir, but are here to serve at your pleasure. In fact, none of us ever sleeps."

Jonathan grabbed his pen, saying, "Well, you have done a good job, and I appreciate you keeping me informed. How is your name spelled?"

"N-I-G-E-R, Robert A., General."

"Well, Robert A.," General Perry countered, "pass on our thanks, and I will be meeting with the air force chief of staff in a few hours and am passing on your name to him."

"Thank you, sir!" Niger said. "Niger, out."

"Good morning, Major."

General Perry called the 10th Special Forces Group at Fort Carson, Colorado, just eight or nine miles from where Major Niger was. He was soon on the phone with Lieutenant Colonel Phil Rickerson, deputy commanding officer of the 10th Group.

"Sir," the DCO said, "we have been alerted of the commercial jet crash and I have got two ODAs (operational detachments-alpha, or twelve-man A-Teams) deployed at Peterson waiting to board a C130. As you know, sir, most of our men are currently deployed to Iraq. My boss is there now. The two teams have parachutes and are packed with winter gear. One detachment specializes in mountain ops. They are ready to insert as soon as we have some clear weather."

"What about Blackhawks or Chinooks, Colonel?" Perry inquired.

"Negative, sir," Rickerson replied. "Too much worry about icing up rotors and lift problems at altitude. Until we have a major break in that storm, we don't want to risk choppers. That may happen tomorrow, but if we can get a small window, we can drop both teams in."

"Drop them?" General Perry said. "By parachute? In a blizzard at maybe twelve thousand feet elevation?"

"Sir," the Green Beret commander said, "we are SF. People are at risk. That is what we do."

"Okay, Phil," the general gave in. "Just hope you've been reading all your FMs (field manuals) and TMs (technical manuals) and not watching too many Rambo movies."

"Sir," the SF leader said, chuckling, "Rambo was a pussy. If you'll have a talk with God about clearing this storm a little, we'll safely get our men on the ground with commo and medical supplies. I've been interfacing with 4th ID (Infantry Division) command, and they have food, blankets, and med supplies ready for air-dropping. Whatever is needed. First we have to get eyes on the ground with direct comm, so we can apprise and address the situation."

Perry said, "Colonel, sounds to me like you have your stuff in order. I'll go have that talk with God. Thank you."

"Yes," Phil replied, "And General, a favor?"

"Yes?"

The DCO said, "When you're having that talk with God, sir, could you ask him to strike my ex-wife down with some horrible disease?"

Perry laughed, relieved by the brief levity. "Wilco! You let me know if you need anything at all. Perry, out."

He took a sip of coffee and rubbed his eyes, still chuckling and thinking about the lieutenant colonel's sense of humor. He really reminded Jonathan of Bobby Samuels. The general figured that most snake-eaters must be that way. At least the ones he had worked with were.

Lieutenant Colonel Rickerson called the staff duty NCO into his office, saying, "Sergeant Telfair, I need you to stay

on top of things until the command sergeant major gets in.
I am heading to Pete Field. If anybody needs me, I am going out with the team on that SAR mission."

"Got it covered, sir," the E-8 replied.

Abdul Baari was glad he was sheltered with a piece of fuselage over his head and behind him, as he had worked loose
a small strip of metal and a screw to use as a rake and pick
to try to pick the handcuff lock. He had learned how to pick
locks in his al-Qaida training camp near Tall-Afar in north-
ern Iraq, and these handcuffs seemed to be finally cooper-
ating. He had been warm with a fire near his feet and pants
and jacket stuffed with Bobby Samuel's expedient insulation. His eyes had been taking everything in, so he could
grab items quickly once he got loose. Finally, the left cuff
was free. The Marine was busy with others working on the
survival camp, giving him occasional cursory glances. Abdul wrapped his airplane blanket higher around his shoulders, and moved his hands to his front, so he could work on
the second cuff.

After five more minutes, he was ready. His second hand
was free, and he held the cuff at the ready under the blanket. Lance Corporal Bobby Kennedy was walking toward
him carrying a knife loosely in his right hand. The knife
was a fishing knife taken from a suitcase. Bobby had been
helping cut strips of blanket cloth to be used for braiding
into ropes by two women.

Abdul gave Bobby a nod, as if he needed something, and
the young Marine approached. As he bent over, the terrorist's right foot shot out from under the blanket and caught
Bobby on the shin. He fell facedown, and Abudl Baari's
hands came out from under the blanket, slapping the cuffs
on one hand and then the other wrist, while Bobby was trying to catch and brace himself.

Abdul, before Bobby could yell, snatched the knife up
and held it against the Marine's throat, holding his other
hand up with a shushing gesture with his index finger.

Bobby's mind immediately flashed back to high school.
Delbert Cornwall was the school bully, maybe because of
his name. He was a big bumbling guy who was just naturally very strong with thick bones, and he almost always
looked down at people where he could see the top of almost everybody's head.

From seventh grade to tenth grade, Delbert had one
single comment for Bobby every time he saw him. He nee-
dled him constantly, but would not try to hit him because
he knew Bobby would fight back and fight hard.

Every time he saw Bobby, making fun of the future jarhead's name, Delbert would say, "You know, Kennedy,
you're gonna get assassinated when you're still young."

It got so tiring, one time in the tenth grade, Cornwall
said it while they sat in the bleachers in the gym watching
a film on hygiene during health class. Delbert was sitting
next to Bobby and they were on the end of the fifth row up
in the bleachers. Bobby swung his right hand and punched
Delbert right in the corner of his left eye, and shoved as
the big bully leaned toward the end of the bleacher. Delbert fell and landed on his side, bruising the side of his
knee, which kept him out of school for three days. He
never said another word to Bobby, but the bully's words always haunted young Kennedy.

Lance Corporal Bobby Kennedy laughed to himself,
because he thought only of Delbert's prophetic words now,
and because he decided right then that he was a U.S. Marine and this man was a jihadist terrorist, and he would be
damned if he would keep quiet, even if he had to die. He
started to yell, and felt the knife pass through his windpipe,
and it also cut so deeply into his neck, the point sliced
through the carotid artery running up the right side of his
neck. Delbert was correct! That is what Bobby thought, as
he fought panic, starting to choke and drown on his own
blood.

He tried to raise his cuffed hands to his throat, deciding
to hold his throat and yell with his last breath, but Abdul
held the cuffed hands down easily. So Bobby head-butted

the terrorist as hard as he could. Abdul fell back with blood spurting from his broken nose. He plunged the knife into Bobby's chest and belly over and over until the body stopped twitching.

Covered with blood from the gruesome murder and his broken nose, Abdul grabbed the items he wanted, crawled under the fuselage, and disappeared into the white-floored blackness. Seconds later, he heard a woman's scream and then other screams.

Abdul ran. He wanted to live. He would gladly die for jihad, taking the lives of infidels, but not being chased in the snow in the land of the infidels. It never dawned on him that not a single one of the mullahs who told him about dying a martyr ever did it themselves. They all seemed to be older, most with gray or white hair and beards, and had been around a while, but like most ignorant suicide bombers, he never wondered why, if they could achieve Paradise and have seventy-two virgins, they didn't kill themselves.

Abdul Baari spent plenty of time in the high mountains in the Afghanistan-Pakistan border. In fact, at one point he was all over the North West Frontier Province in Pakistan, the NWFP, as one of the many bodyguards of the Sheik, the Director himself, Osama bin Laden. He had been removed as one of dozens of bodyguards for two reasons. Things had been heating up with the U.S. bent on capturing or killing bin Laden, so his security force was cut down significantly so as not to call attention to him. More importantly, Abdul had walked into a private room in the giant cave that could sleep six hundred, and caught Osama bin Laden in a compromising position performing fellatio on one of his bodyguards. Abdul was shipped out the next day to another front on the orders of bin Laden himself.

He ran around trees and into every thicket he could find, heading downhill the whole time. The blizzard had stopped, and all was covered with a deep thick blanket of white, and in some places, Abdul found himself stepping into depressions filled with snow. His sides were heaving with exertion, and he was limping. Osama bin Laden was

six feet five and a half inches tall and almost skin and bone,
plus he walked with a cane. Abdul always wondered how
he could move around as well as he could well above ten
thousand feet in the Peshawar Mountains of Pakistan. Being away from altitude for a while was having an affect.

His plan may well have worked except for one important fact: Bo Devore competed in Olympic-style triathlons,
just to keep in shape and as a hobby. She would have to
swim one mile, ride a bike twenty-five miles, and run six
miles. Bo was not acclimatized, but she was an American
soldier in pursuit of an al Qaeda killer, on American soil no
less. So, Abdul was shocked to see the woman approaching
when he had to finally stop and try to breathe. She pointed
a 9mm Glock at him, he could tell, but he was not fazed.
She was a woman, he figured he would easily outwit her
and kill her. He stood at the edge of a high steep cliff, and
had planned to run along its edge for a while hoping pur-
suers would slip and fall. Bo had a serious menacing look
on her face and kept advancing, careful to keep her double-
hand grip on her weapon steady. That bothered him. His
mind raced through options, as she stopped at ten feet. The
bloody knife was still in his hand. She looked down at the
knife and never smiled as she looked in his eyes.

He started to make a demeaning remark about women
to goad her into coming closer, but she cut him off, saying,
"Never bring a knife to a gunfight, asshole."

He heard the five bangs and his upper body went numb
as he looked down at the growing red stain on his chest.

He looked up at her, and Bo said with an evil grin, "You
guys think pigs are filthy animals, Guess what, we are going to feed you to a bear. They are in the pig family."

He could not move, and was seeing flashing lights all
over now, and felt her foot as it shoved him backward off
the cliff, and the last words he heard were Bo saying softly,
"Let's roll!" as she kicked him into open space.

He panicked, and then clearly saw solid rock before he
slammed into it at 120 miles per hour after falling for six
hundred hundred feet.

Bo heard clapping behind her, and turned to see Bobby applauding.

Her knees gave way, and she sat down cross-legged in place, her whole body shaking.

Bobby came up and looked out into space, saying, "It never gets easy taking a human life, even an enemy's."

Bo said, "I hope it never does. I'll handle it, and I'm sorry, I know everybody would have wanted to interrogate that guy."

Bobby said, "That Kennedy was a very brave young Marine."

Bo got tears in her eyes and wiped her cheeks.

When they walked back into the fire circle, Rainbow said, "Did he get away?"

Bobby shook his head, saying, "No. When Captain Devore approached him to place cuffs on him and arrest him, he attacked her with that knife, and she was forced to kill him. He fell over a cliff, but was already dead."

A man in the crowd yelled, "Hooah!"

Everyone started applauding very enthusiastically, and kept applauding.

When the applause and cheers died down, a loud yell of "Airborne!" emanated from the back of the large crowd, and out of the shadows stepped Lieutenant Colonel Phil Rickerson followed by his A Detachment carrying several boxes of supplies. All the men had been wearing night-vision devices on the front of their K-Pots, or Kevlar helmets, and heavy rucksacks. Now the crowd really cheered as they stepped forward. Bobby and Bo walked forward saluting Rickerson, who returned it. Then the team members saluted Bo and Bobby, and they returned their salutes and shook hands with everybody. Cheers went up through the crowd. Team members immediately went to work, and were all noticing how comfortable the cold-weather survival camp actually was.

Rickerson identified himself, as did Bo and Bobby, then Bobby asked, "HALO, sir?"

"Roger that," the field-grade officer replied, "We landed

on the frozen lake. And have plenty of supplies cached there. How'd you go down, Major?"

Bobby said, "Arab terrorists posing as Mexicans. Two are dead and there is a third working as a ground crew member somewhere. The pilot's cabin door was rigged with explosives. We found the name of an accomplice. It is Farooq Ghasaan. Probably him. Do you have a sat phone?"

The commo sergeant of the ODA overheard the conversation, and handed the sat phone to the senior officer, saying, "Sir, I got the Pentagon for you. General Perry is online."

Rickerson took the phone and reported the news about the terrorists and then handed the phone to Bobby. "He wants to speak with you, Major Samuels."

Bobby took the phone, saying, "Thank you, sir." Then, into the phone, he said, "Bobby Samuels, sir. Sorry to cause you to be up in the middle of the night."

Perry said, "You and Bo okay?"

Bobby said, "Affirmative, sir."

"What happened?"

Bobby said, "We stopped an apparent al Qaeda jihadist, General. He was going to blow the plane with a suicide belt of C4. He had a partner who blew the cockpit door with explosives already planted. We killed him, too, but the jet was already on its way to crashing at that time. Later, the first one was being guarded by a Marine on leave, and apparently picked the locks on his handcuffs, killed the Marine with a knife, and got away. Captain Devore had to light him up when he attacked her."

General Perry replied, "Wish we could have interrogated them, but glad you two smoked the bastards."

"General?" Bobby said.

"They were posing as Mexicans and one at least spoke Spanish, but they are definitely Alpha Quebec of Middle Eastern descent. Also they have to have an accomplice on the ground who rigged the cabin door to explode with a detonator. Probably at Dulles. The colonel gave the name of that one that we found in their carry-on," Bobby said,

"They did have a lot of documentation, but Bo and I do not read Spanish."

The general said, "I have given orders for you two to be transported back here ASAP for a debriefing for the CINC (commander in chief), SECDEF (secretary of defense), and me. Bring all the material with you and do not surrender it to anybody. Good job, son. Put Rickerson back on."

"Thank you, sir," Bobby replied, humbled. "Wilco, Samuels, Out." And he handed the phone to the lieutenant colonel.

"Captain Devore," Bobby said, "We're on our way to DC to get debriefed, and brief the President, secretary of defense, and General Perry. We're supposed to carry all evidentiary material with us and hang onto it."

"Yes, sir," she replied since others were within earshot. "I'll make sure we have everything as well as the digital pictures we took afterward."

4

BACK HOME

The following morning, four U.S. Army CH-47E Chinook Special Operations helicopters flew in to extract the passengers. Each Chinook was capable of carrying forty-four passengers, as well as the gear and supplies, with no effort. But before the first Chinook came in, an MH53J Pave Low III special ops helicopter came in to lift out Bobby, Bo, the body of the remaining terrorist, and the evidence they had gathered. Used extensively in Afganistan and Iraq, the big helicopter, capable of flying day or night in rugged terrain and adverse weather up to sixteen thousand feet elevation, was ideally suited for this mission. In fact, this mission was chump change for the rugged state-of-the-art helicopter, which brought in more 10th Special Forces Group operators as well as an investigation team from the NTSB, the National Transportation Safety Board. Two FBI forensic specialists came in, too. One of the Chinooks carried supplies in to set up a secure camp around the aircraft, and several Homeland Security personnel flew in with that.

Bo and Bobby were extracted off the frozen lake along

with the evidence, the luggage, and the terrorist's body within ten minutes time from touchdown. The two General Electric T64-GE-100 engines cranked up to over four thousand horsepower each and the bird lifted off. Its forward-looking infrared (IFR), inertial global positioning system (IGPS), Doppler navigation systems, terrain-following and terrain-avoidance radar, onboard computer, and integrated avionics enabled the Specops big bird to precisely navigate the steep ridges, canyons, and gulches of the San Juan Mountains of western Colorado as it made its way eastward toward Peterson Air Force Base in Colorado Springs on the Front Range, where they would transfer to a fast-mover for the trip to Washington. The eighty-eight-foot-long, forty-million-dollar bird made it to Pete Field in less than an hour and a half.

At Peterson Field AFB in northeastern Colorado Springs, the Pave Low brought Bobby and Bo in on the tarmac landing next to an Air Force C-21, a military version of a twin-turbofan eight-passenger Lear Jet. Dispatched from Illinois, it was waiting to take them to Washington, DC. While the two SF troopers who accompanied them were quickly offloading the body, evidence, and luggage from the Pave Low to the Air Force Lear, two FBI agents drove up and identified themselves to everyone present.

One, who was white, stopped the troopers, and the other, Garrett Wilburn, who was black, spoke with Bobby. "Major, I understand you are headed to DC, but we were ordered to take charge of the evidence and body and transport them immediately to the national FBI labs so this case can be expedited."

Bobby said, "Sorry, Agent. I have been given orders by the chief of staff of the U.S. Army to transport all matériel to Washington and not to let it out of my sight."

Wilburn's lips tightened. "I understand your predicament, Major, but we have been commanded by the national FBI directorate to immediately take charge of that evidence. I can have a court order in less than a half hour.

Your general understands due process. You won't be in trouble."

Bobby said, "I know I won't, because I am following my orders, Agent Wilburn."

Garrett said, "Look, pal, I am chief resident FBI agent of—"

Bo interrupted. "Who gives a rat's ass? You are the FBI. That's nice. We are the U.S. Army, and we have more guns and bigger ones, too. The major explained our position, and we have an urgent mission to achieve. The only way you will get this evidence is to shoot us first, and we are loading it now. I am willing to die to follow my superior's orders. Are you willing to die trying to stop me?"

Wilburn looked at his partner, who was suppressing a grin. He spun on his heel and stormed to their black sedan. It drove off. One of the SF troopers chuckled, picking up his end of the body bag.

"She should be SF, sir," he said.

Bobby smiled. "Roger that, Sergeant."

Bo blushed and suppressed her own grin, but felt very complimented. She went into the military Lear and sat down feeling elated. The jet had to stop to refuel at Wright-Patterson Air Force Base in Dayton, Ohio, but still made the 1,400-mile flight in much less than four hours.

Three days later, Bo and Bobby sat in General Perry's office in the Pentagon, their heads spinning from the constant interrogations and opinions from staff officers, two senators who got wind of it, general officers, Homeland Security personnel, an obnoxious INS investigator, and a complaint about Bobby and Bo from a high-level FBI manager. The latter brought the man a stern rebuke from General Perry, and the FBI honcho left the building with a great deal more respect for both officers. In the meantime, Bobby and Bo simply tried to keep their sense of humor.

Bobby stood up and said, "Let's get out of here and go get supper somewhere."

"Sounds good to me," she said.

They hopped on the metro and headed to Capitol Hill, and went to the Banana Café on 8th Street, where they talked about their adventure, as Bobby ate Cuban Picadillo, which was ground beef and pork loin cooked in a creole sauce with capers, olives, and raisins. Bo had the Ropa Vieja, which was shredded flank steak cooked with tomatoes, onions, peppers, and spices.

Then Bo made the error of agreeing to them both drinking mango margaritas while they listened to music from the piano and enjoyed the Latin artwork adorning the walls. She should have known that with Bobby, one drink would beget another.

Bobby awakened with a start and looked at the blazing sun streaming in the window. He kept blinking his eyes and rubbed the pounding headache throbbing in his temples. His tongue felt like a used lint remover had been rolled over it a dozen times. His bladder ached. He got up fully clothed in Class As and strolled into the bathroom. It was really hot, he thought as he sat down on the toilet seat to urinate. He was in no mood to stand up. The room was full of steam, and he looked up as a fully naked Bo Devore stepped out of the shower. She stared at him, but did not cover herself. Then, she calmly wrapped a large towel around her voluptuous body and shook her head in disgust walking from the bathroom. Bobby was astounded. Number one, he had been here before. This was Bo's bathroom in her townhouse. How did he get here? he wondered. Had they slept together? What had happened? Bobby remembered leaving the Pentagon on the metro.

The image of her in her full nudity haunted him. He had no idea she was even more beautiful unclothed than he had ever imagined. Bobby shook off the thought, thinking he could not go there. She was his subordinate.

He washed his hands, splashed water on his face, found some toothpaste and rubbed it on his teeth with his index finger, sloshed the residue and water around in his mouth, and walked out of the bathroom.

Bobby remembered the kitchen and walked in there, where Bo was in a long terry-cloth robe making eggs, bacon, and toast. The smell made him sick to his stomach, but he thought he might be hungry. Bo was very cold toward him, and then he noticed a single tear in the corner of one eye.

"Good morning," he said cheerfully, almost hopefully.

She said coolly, "Coffee is on the counter. Do you want any eggs?"

"Over easy, please? Can I help?"

"No."

Brrrrrrrr!

"Bo," Bobby said, "I am sorry. I cannot remember a thing about last night. How did I get here? What happened? Are you mad at me?"

"Mad at you?" she said staring at him, her face reddening, "Here's your eggs, you son of a bitch!"

She dumped the plate of eggs, bacon, and toast on his lap, and he jumped up, brushing it away and screaming in surprise, as Bo, sobbing, ran from the kitchen.

Bobby cleaned up the mess as he heard the bathroom door slam, and then he carefully made two plates of breakfast. He poured two cups of coffee and carried it all into her small dining room and set everything down on the table, returning for silverware and napkins.

He walked up to the bathroom door and tapped, "Bo, please come out. I made us breakfast. Let's talk? Please?"

Bo opened the door and sat down at the table, while invisible curtains of ice hung all about her as a protective shield.

Bobby said, "Bo, I don't remember a thing about last night. If I did anything wrong I am sorry, really, very sorry, but I have no clue."

"No clue?" she fumed.

Captain Devore was still smarting very much emotionally from her revelation up in the mountains of southwestern Colorado.

Bobby said, "Look, we are partners. Sometimes we'll get mad at each other, but we have to depend on each other. We can't have this much anger between us."

"No, Major Samuels," she said coolly. "We are not partners! You are my immediate supervisor."

Bobby said, "Bo, please?"

Bo got up and walked over to her window, looking out at the distant Potomac. She stared at the sky and then returned to her chair.

"Bobby, how could you? First, as usual, you had too much to drink and became loud and embarrassing in that restaurant," she raged. "Then you said that I have beautiful tits and grabbed one of them in front of everybody. I was so humiliated."

Bobby's head spun. He literally thought he was going to faint. Without speaking, Bobby got up and rushed to the bathroom. His eyes welled up with tears, and he stared at himself in the mirror. He poured cold water into the sink and filled his hands with it, splashing it all over his face. It did not help. Bobby spun and dropped to his knees vomiting into the toilet. He finished and drank water from the sink to clean his mouth. Then he spun and vomited again.

Ten minutes later, Bobby Samuels emerged from the bathroom. Bo wondered what was going through his mind. Bobby walked over to the table and pulled his chair up so it was directly in front of hers. He took both her hands in his and looked into her eyes.

"Bo," he said humbly, "I just don't know what to say. Of all the people in this world, you are the very last person I would ever want to hurt."

His eyes filled with tears, and he tried to blink them back.

Bobby went on. "Bo, I could never hurt you. I lo . . . I like to think about us as the closest of friends besides being partners. I don't know what to say. I am just so overwhelmed."

Bo started to cry again, and ran into her bedroom and threw herself down on her bed sobbing.

Bobby drank his coffee, hearing her sobbing in the other room. He didn't know what to do. Finally, he went in there. He sat down on the bed and put his hand gently on her back.

After several minutes, he turned her and simply lay down next to her, placed her head on his chest, and stroked her hair while she cried.

Bobby said, "I deeply apologize. I will watch my drinking from now on, and I will never ever do anything to hurt you."

He meant it, too.

Bo sat up, angry again. "You will watch your drinking from now on? Do you know how many similar comments you have made since I have known you, Bobby?"

Again, Bobby did not know what to say. He sat up, too. He looked around and realized he had been lying on Bo's bed with her. He got up and paced around her bedroom.

"Bo, what do you want me to do?"

"Get some help, Bobby!" she said. "AA, counseling, something."

Bobby lifted his hand and pulled out his cell phone. He held up an index finger.

"Hello Colonel, Major Samuels," Bobby said, "Can I talk to the Old Man? Thank you, sir.

"Hello, General Perry. Fine, but kind of worn out. How are you, sir?"

Bobby paused and listened, then went on. "Sir, Captain Devore and I have not had a minute to recuperate from the ordeal on the mountain. I know we have a War on Terrorism to fight, but can we just take twenty-four hours for R and R, sir?

"Yes, sir. Thank you very much," Bobby said, smiling and winking at Bo, "We'll see you day after tomorrow, sir, ready to lock and load. Thank you, General."

Bobby hit the end button, and put the cell away.

Bo said, "Thank you."

Bobby said, "They translated all the material and are creating an emergency task force. We are being assigned to it. I guess al Qaeda discovered just how porous our southern border is. But first he ordered us both to rest."

Bobby did not want to think about not drinking. He had done it so many years. It was simply part of his life.

He stuck out his hand and helped Bo off the bed, saying, "More coffee?"

They walked to the kitchen, and he poured two cups from the coffeemaker. They sat at the table.

"Bo," he asked, "do you think I'm an alcoholic?"

Bo said, "It doesn't matter what I think. What do you think?"

"I just don't know. I don't want to be. For one thing, I can't take the time to go to those stupid meetings."

Bo took a sip of coffee, smiled sweetly, and said, "Yeah, you're right. Instead you can arrest guys for rape at work, and then drink at night and feel women up without their permission."

Bobby got tears in his eyes again, and Bo now panicked. "I'm sorry. You apologized. That was a little resentment coming out, but I didn't mean it."

He replied, "It's okay. I deserve it."

"Yes, you do, but it was not classy of me to do that."

Bobby said, "Bo, all I know is we have al Qaeda posing as Mexicans infiltrating our country. We cannot have another 9/11, and you and I can, must, help prevent one from happening. I am just worried about what I would have to do if I am an alcoholic."

Bo said, "Bobby, all I can tell you is that you are definitely not a social drinker."

His face reddened and his ears burned. He felt so much shame, he was really searching for what to say.

Bobby headed toward the door, saying, "Bo, I need to go and search things out. I'll get a handle on this. Number one, as a military officer and your superior, I should never ever put you in a position where you feel uncomfortable or where you can be adversely affected in your OER (Officer Efficiency Report) by how you respond to anything I say or do. More important than anything is that I despise sexual assault. There is no excuse for what I did, and to be so drunk it happened to my partner, my best friend, well, I just cannot apologize deeply enough. I will never get over this."

Bo stepped forward and stood on her tiptoes. She leaned forward and kissed Bobby softly on his lips, and stepped back. He touched his lips.

She stepped back again, saying, "I forgive you, but I do insist you finally do something about this, and follow through on it. If something like that ever happened again, I would not be able to forgive you."

Bobby held her upper arms, saying, "Partner, I give you my word. I will take care of this somehow."

She hugged Bobby, and he could fell her nakedness under the robe and wanted to run away quickly, the image of her stepping from the shower still in his mind.

Bobby left.

At his apartment, he literally tossed himself on his bed and sobbed. No, he opened the floodgates.

The next morning, Bobby called Boom Kittinger, who told him he most certainly could talk. Boom and Bobby's father had both been recovering alcoholics, but Bobby never knew his father was until years after his death. Boom was more open about his long-term sobriety and was easy to talk to.

Like Bobby's old man, a retired command sergeant major, Boom was a legend in Special Forces, a demolition/engineer specialist extraordinaire.

Bobby told him what happened and asked what he should do.

Boom said, "Don't do a thing until I get there."

Bobby said, "Get here? Boom, you can't do that."

Boom replied, "What are you, my nursemaid now? I can do what I want. Remember. I am retired."

That was a joke. Boom had journeyed to Iraq under a large retainer by the Department of Defense to help Bobby out, traveling there in the personal jet transport of General Perry, who had at that time been commander of coalition forces in Iraq. Boom had helped Bobby get rid of an al Qaeda mole who had grown up in the U.S. and infiltrated the U.S. Army as a sergeant and killed U.S. soldiers from within. Thanks to Boom's hard-core imagination and extensive experience, the mole had died a grisly agonizing death.

Prior to that, working for the CIA as an independent contractor, who was doing a joint exercise with the DEA, Boom had assassinated a hard-to-get-to Colombian drug lord the U.S. government wanted out of the way badly.

Boom was one of those typical Special Forces types, but he fit in just as well as a close friend of Bobby's late father and Bobby, too. There were quite a few like him who seemed ageless but could go anywhere in the world and hold their own with anybody.

Bobby thought back to the excitement of his teenaged years the first time he and his father visited Boom at his Colorado ranch. Boom lived on the side of a mountain with a large wooded ranch and joked that his main bumper crop was rocks.

In actuality, in the early 1990s, Boom had a psychologist tell him that he was often the victim of the "gunfighter syndrome" and always would be, and Boom asked for an explanation. She said that, because he was a retired Green Beret, plus some knew he was a black belt in the martial arts, he was a target for those with great insecurities. She did not just mean they would challenge him to physical confrontations, but they would challenge him in business deals, as well. In either case, they would feel like they had stood up to, or even backed down, the fastest gunfighter in town, so to speak. She added that because of his background, most of these people would know that he would not fight them over just words, but only if actually attacked. In this way, they would sometimes really "push the envelope." This all made sense to Boom.

Boom had a neighbor who had three very large sons in their late teens and early twenties, and all three were always in trouble for one thing or another, but usually fighting. The neighbor was a fourth-generation cattle rancher with no business sense or ability to hold his liquor. He had gone through his family's cattle fortune, ending up selling off the whole herd and eventually the whole ranch. He caught his wife one day reading Cosmopolitan magazine, and it just sent him into a rage. She argued back and got beaten up for her trouble. She filed for divorce the next day, and Tom Smith, the man, was issued a restraining order. That did not stop him. He broke in with a mask on and beat her badly, blackening both eyes and pulping her lips. Having no relatives, besides the police, she called Boom.

Boom ran into the man at the local Safeway store, and gave him a straightforward lecture in front of the bread racks. Tom Smith was not a learned or even intelligent man. That was proven when he decided to argue with Boom. It got heated, until Boom got angry enough to whisper.

He reached out and grabbed Tom's index fingers in a viselike grip and bent them backward, then pulled the man close.

Boom said, "Smith, it is simple. This conversation is over. I have no use for men who beat women. If you stalk your wife anymore, or if she even falls getting out of the bathtub, you are going to die. Nod your head if you understand me clearly."

Grimacing in pain, the bully nodded, and Boom let go and simply walked away, but Tom Smith remembered.

Boom's sister was visiting, and was on the way home from the feed store with a load of horse hay cubes, dog food, and chicken scratch loaded in the back of Boom's one-ton pickup. She was followed by two of Tom Smith's sons, even into their long ranch driveway. When she had to get out and open and close a gate, they pulled up behind her and one jumped out of their car.

In a deep commanding voice, she yelled, "Stop!"

He did.

She said, "What are you doing here? This is private property! There are signs everywhere. Get the hell out of here, now!"

The hoodlum complied, but the other one, who was the shirtless one, covered with prison tattoos, walked toward her rapidly. Leaving the gate open, she wisely jumped in her car and roared up Boom's driveway another third of a mile to the house.

Running in to the house, she approached Boom, eyes wide open in excitement. He thought she had been attacked by a bear or something.

"What's wrong, Sally? What happened?" he tried to say calmly, so she would stay that way.

Sally said, "There are two guys at our front gate in an old white car. They came at me, and I—"

He interrupted. "Did they hurt you?"

"No, no," she said rapidly. "I put my hand up and ordered them to get out of here. This was private property. The one guy headed back toward the car, but the other came at me. I jumped in the car and left the gate open. I'm afraid your horses will get out . . ."

He jumped up and ran to his gun cabinet, saying, "Screw the horses. We'll catch 'em later. You did the right thing. Dial 911."

He grabbed a .22 rifle, a .45 revolver, and shoved a bowie knife down the front of his pants and grabbed the phone. They answered on the first ring.

"Nine-one-one. What is your emergency?" the woman's voice answered.

Boom's adrenaline was pumping at full volume, but he tried to stay as calm as possible. This was hard to do, because his right foot kept wanting to start his body out that front door, while his left foot wanted to stay firmly planted and give full details about the situation.

As calmly but quickly as he could, he said, "This is Boom Kittinger," and he gave his address, adding, "My sister was just confronted by two sleeze-bags at our front gate, and they have a beat-up old white car. I am heading down there now to hold them until a deputy arrives."

The operator said, "Mr. Kittinger, please stay on the line with me. There are numerous deputies in the area and someone will be there right away. They could be very dangerous, please just stay—"

Boom interrupted. "Yeah, right. Gotta go."

He ran to the door, yelling over his shoulder, "Lock the doors, Sis, and grab a pistol out of my gun cabinet. Stay close to the phone."

Jumping in his car, he quickly roared back down the driveway, arriving at his front gate at the same time as a cruiser with two deputies pulled up to the gate. They happened to be within a quarter mile of his driveway when Boom called 911. More cruisers started appearing down the drive, too. The white car was deserted, with both doors standing open. He ran to it and looked at the ground at their tracks. One man had run to the left toward a nearby fertilizer company that was closed for the weekend. The other had very clearly walked backward along a deer trail running up a bushy gulch that ran all the way to the side of Boom's house. The tracks went right into some thick brush where deer frequently bedded down.

Pointing, Boom told the deputies, "One went that way. The other walked backward to throw us off and is hiding in that brush." Pointing again.

One of the deputies, a young one who Boom did not know, said, "No, look at his tracks. He came to the car."

Inside, Boom was very frustrated, but used to such stupidity from his many years in SF. Again, he was being discounted, and this was a simple trail to read. He did not even want to explain that it was easy to tell that the guy walked backward by the way the dirt piled in the tracks, or by just asking, where did the person walk from and how did he get there? Or why wasn't he still there if the tracks led *to* the car? Boom just bit his tongue, which he first learned to do quite often in Special Forces.

The deputies held, waiting for backup. Colorado Department of Corrections bloodhounds were then dispatched, with their handlers on the trail of the guy who ran toward the fertilizer company. They did not strike on the other trail. This deputy, who apparently was in some supervisory capacity, had sent them toward the fertilizer plant to the left, but ignored the other Boom warned about to the right.

Boom even heard him say to others that both men took off toward the fertilizer plant.

Then the sheriff showed up with more deputies and knowing him, Boom ran up and explained the situation to him.

He said, "I don't want to interrupt, Boom. I have a sergeant in charge and really don't want to tell him what to do."

Boom said, "Sheriff, your sergeant is an idiot. That trail goes into that thick brush and deer bed down there all the time. The guy's tracks go backwards into the brush and do not come out. He is hiding in there. Right now."

The sheriff smiled condescendingly.

Boom knew he could never serve as a deputy or a police officer anywhere, because he would end up shooting a boss.

Frustrated, Boom resorted to his old SF sanity-sustainer, humor.

Smiling, he said, "Sheriff, that thicket is on my property, so I can say or do whatever I want? Can't I?"

The sheriff nodded.

Moving away with his .22 rifle at port arms in front of him, Boom walked down from his driveway to a spot about twenty feet above the brushy thicket. He had already learned from the deputies that the two were Smith's sons, or at least the car would make it seem so.

The first punk, Andrew Smith, who ran toward the fertilizer company, was picked up by the bloodhounds and then tackled by a gung-ho sheriff's deputy who chased him into a semitrailer full of white powdered fertilizer. The man was cuffed, and the two came back up the hill to the cruisers by Boom's front gate, looking like cousins of Casper. The Department of Corrections officers and deputies howled with laughter and teased the deputy who was covered with the white powder.

Boom knew the two younger brothers were frequently together, so he reasoned the one in the thicket had to be Derek. He yelled out, "Derek Smith, I know you are in the thick brush right below me here! You have a bunch of cops here who care about your Constitutional rights, but I sure as hell don't! I care about my family and property, and you have threatened our safety! Here's the deal! I will give you exactly one minute to surrender to them, or I will begin shooting bullets through my thicket here, and you will be deader than shit!"

He heard chuckles from two deputies, who headed toward the heavy bushes finally, as a pair of arms came out of the brush! A minute later, Derek was in cuffs.

Boom was angry because the sanctity of his home had been threatened, but more importantly, they had scared his sister and his adrenaline was still going full tilt with battle lust. As they had both men lying handcuffed across the hood of a cruiser, Boom's anger kept building, and he walked up and dropped his baseball hat down in front of their faces. It was white and had a green beret on it and dagger behind the beret. It read: "Special Forces Association."

Boom said, "You two are real geniuses. Of all the places you pick in this county to attack, you pick my place. Spread it around in the jail, and with your daddy, if anybody else comes here again, I'll call the coroner, not the sheriff."

He knew the law didn't intimidate them at all, so Boom decided that maybe they could be intimidated by him instead. So he added, "Now, when you punks get out, if you want to get revenge on me, you know where I live, and my name is Boom Kittinger. Hell, bring your buddies. I'll kill them, too."

While deputies chuckled again, the sheriff, grinning, gently grabbed Boom's upper arm and led him away from the two hoodlums.

Two weeks later, Bobby and his family showed up for a visit. Bobby was a young teenager. Sally and Boom were leading young Bobby, now in middle school, for a horseback ride through the trees and up and down ridges. Bobby had come to Colorado just one day before and had no experience riding horses. Boom had him riding good old dependable Prince, the three-decades-old sorrel gelding that Boom always put guests on who had not ridden much, if ever. Boom called him his "dude horse." In fact, Prince was going on thirty-seven years of age (which is like Dick Clark's age, in horse years) and still loved to have children on his back. Boom was in the front on his big paint, and Sally followed about fifty feet behind him on her Appaloosa, with Bobby close behind her on old Prince.

Where Boom lived was at the boundary between the fringes of civilization at the outskirts of town and the wilderness of the San Isabel National Forest. People would sometimes come into the area to fire weapons, ride dirt bikes, or just hike, because of the proximity to town. Riding around the rugged mountain ranch, mainly in the trees, most of the time they were blocked from view from Boom's house.

Bobby's mom, Bonnie, was having fun working in the flower garden behind Boom's house. Bonnie was in the terraced lower garden about twenty feet below the house, and bending over to pick some mums, when she heard what she thought was a hummingbird, or large bee dive-bombing her, but dirt kicked up from the ground a few feet to her left. She looked around puzzled, and bent over again, when the same thing happened. She also heard a gunshot afterward coming from a long finger of a ridgeline, which paralleled the one Boom's house was on. The ridgeline was wooded and about seven hundred feet away. It dawned on Bonnie that someone was shooting at her.

She scrambled up to the house and ran up to Bobby's dad, who was on crutches from ACL surgery, saying, "Honey, somebody just shot at me twice from that hill!"

Honey was the actual nickname that everybody called Ted Samuels by.

Honey hobbled to the gun cabinet, grabbed Boom's 7-by-50 binoculars and a Winchester Model 94 rifle, and ran out onto the back deck to spot and warn Boom. He told Bonnie to call 911.

At that time, out of sight of the house, Boom, Bobby,

and Sally emerged from trees in the small valley the sniper had fired across and headed across, to one of the natural springs on the property where deer, elk, bears, and lions often watered. The spring was a couple hundred feet or so up the side of the small mountain, with a small creek running down the ridge and across the valley.

As Boom led the way, they approached the spring, and suddenly Eagle, his horse, stopped instantly, stuck his forelegs out, locking them tight, ears forward and nostrils flaring in panic. He stopped so fast, Boom actually moaned in pain as his groin struck the saddle horn.

Alerted, he patted the horse's neck and softly said, "Easy, boy. What's wrong, Eagle?"

Boom strained to spot a lion or bear at the spring above him, which was his initial thought.

Totally shook up, Eagle bounced around a little stiff-legged, and flinched to the right just a little, and just then, a loud crack went by Boom's left ear, within an inch or so, and then he immediately heard the whoomp sound of the rifle's muzzle report. He even felt the power of the bullet passing so close to his ear, and he saw the muzzle flash next to a large oak tree just above the spring. Then movement. The bullet just missed Sally, scaring her to death, and the next thing Boom knew, docile old Prince was dancing wildly in total panic, with Bobby grabbing a hold of the saddle horn and hanging on for dear life. A second shot made a loud bang, and Boom knew automatically from experience that the sniper was shooting away from them, probably over his shoulder, as he ran. Boom had been shot at enough times to know that bang-whump double sound you hear when you are being shot at, and he never enjoyed the noise.

Quickly turning his head, Boom yelled, "Get out of here now and call 911!"

Sally stared at him with a wild-eyed, shocked, and colorless expression on her face and yelled, "What's happening?"

He knew she knew what had just happened but was in

shock, as he hollered back, "We're being shot at! Go! Now!"

Turning his head to the sniper's position, which was just above the spring, maybe seventy feet above him and to his front, he scoured the vegetation for the sniper, who was none other than his illustrious neighbor Tom Smith himself. Boom saw movement as the sniper bolted away through the trees, but Tom was wearing camouflage. His mind automatically catalogued the second rifle report as an approximate thirty-caliber. He was furious. The shooter was on Boom's property, and he felt violated, totally violated. Whenever Boom helped teach women sexual assault prevention at the various martial arts school he trained at over the years, one technique he would teach them was to use very foul language to upset and unbalance a potential attacker, plus using the loud foul language would bolster the woman's self-confidence. This is what he immediately thought of, because Boom had not carried a gun with him, like he normally did in the mountains. He yanked his sheath knife from its holster on his right hip and put the spurs to Eagle, heading him at the sniper's position. Maybe it was because he was still on active duty then as a master sergeant (and would become a sergeant major before retirement) and was always carrying guns on MTTs (Mobile Training Teams) and various deployments around the world, and he just wanted to relax.

Boom screamed at the top of his lungs, "Come on, motherfucker, shoot me! Shoot me, you fucking pussy! I'm going to cut your fucking balls off!"

There was no courage involved in this, as far as he was concerned. After years in Special Forces and teaching the martial arts, his immediate instincts took over and he felt the only solution was to attack and try to unnerve his opponent. To him then, running would be making him a sitting duck, and he would easily get shot in the back. While Eagle lunged up the steep mountainside, Boom yanked his other knife from its sheath attached to the back girth strap on his saddle. Scared, Eagle balked, and Boom, very much in shape from his constant training, finally jumped down and led him by the reins, running up the ridge toward the sniper's position. But Smith was gone, running through the trees along the mountain.

Now, it was the time to go easy. First, Boom mounted up and galloped back along the six-inch-wide trail across the face of the mountain, not a recommended exercise for Eastern horses that are used to green pastures. He ran out on a piñon-covered ridge directly across from his back deck. Honey spotted him from inside the house and dashed out. Sally was directly across the valley leading Bobby and his horse up through the trees.

Honey yelled at Boom at the same time that Boom yelled at Sally.

Pointing at the ridgeline beyond Boom, Honey yelled, "Somebody shot at Bonnie, twice!"

Simultaneously, Boom screamed at Sally, his voice echoing across the mountain valley, "Don't walk! Run!"

Boom looked over at Honey, yelling, "We were shot at, too! Call 911! Take care of them!"

The old Green Beret, leaning on a crutch, raised the rifle in agreement and hobbled inside, as Boom wheeled Eagle and tore back across the suicide path along the mountain. He knew all would be totally safe with Honey Samuels until the sheriff got there.

In some places, the deer trail was only wide enough for his horse's hooves, and to his left, it went straight down a hundred feet or more, with dozens of trees along the way waiting to knock him out of the saddle.

The tree the sniper hid behind was a large oak and was along the trail fifty feet from the spring. Arriving, Boom jumped out of the saddle and led his horse, looking for sign. He found where the man had knelt behind the tree and fired at him, but Smith was at least smart enough to grab his brass, the spent shell casings. Boom felt very blessed and protected by God, because if the man was smart enough to police his shells, he should have been more careful to nail Boom with his second shot. Boom could tell he was right-handed, because he had knelt on his left knee on the left side of the tree, apparently bracing the rifle against the side of the oak. Boom had already figured he was one of the Smiths and remembered the oldest son was a lefty.

He followed the man's trail across the face of the mountain. He wore size-nine-and-a-half-or-ten boots, with hardly any tread, and Boom guessed that they might have been old-style army combat boots. He knew Smith had been in the army years earlier. As usual, in this type of tracking, he watched the ground, and his gaze would sweep left and right in front of him, moving out in ten-meter arcs, so he would not run into an ambush. Up close, he would also watch each branch overhanging the trail for threads, strands of hair, or any other useful evidence. Being on the side of a steep mountainside, Boom also had to keep looking up above him, which most animals and people did not do. Now he didn't want to gallop, or he could easily end up being bushwhacked. If he were the sniper, Boom figured, he would have run a short distance and would have set up a hasty ambush for himself, and would have simply shot Boom point-blank out of the saddle. Apparently, Boom must have given the shooter too much credit, for the man's tracks showed him that his mind was telling him, "Feet, don't fail me now!"

It didn't take Boom very long to reach the ridgeline where the bushwhacker had knelt down to shoot at Bonnie. He tracked the guy for some time, and finally saw what he was looking for. Tom Smith had been running directly away from his own home, but now started a slow circle back toward his house. That told Boom what he wanted to know for sure. Now he could carry out his plan of action, certain it had been Tom Smith. The sniper had run through and fallen in an area of wet gray clay. Boom slipped in it, too and was covered with gray clay. He was wearing a white T-shirt, and white cowboy hat, so he decided to cover his face, T-shirt, and the white parts of his horse's legs and chest in dark gray clay, and tied his cowboy hat behind the saddle. Being a target was one thing, a bull's-eye something else, though.

He mounted up, and went on another fifteen or twenty minutes in thich trees switchbacking back and forth up a steep ridge, then down the other side, and back up another; then he smoked his horse's heels along another narrow deer and elk trail for two miles. He knew the trail where Tom Smith would surely come hotfooting through.

Boom jumped down and tied his horse, climbed over a small ridge and down to the trail. He had to work quickly. He had his lasso from his saddle, and the clear monofilament line from the telescoping fishing rod he carried in his saddlebags. Boom made it out to Colorado to this ranch he inherited every chance he got, and loved to take his horse up to high mountain lakes above timberline and go fishing for rainbows and cutthroat trout, the best eating around.

He found a large sapling and tied the lasso around the top, bending it back so it was parallel to the trail. He quickly tied the fishing line across the trail to one tree and set it down on the other side. He grabbed some small pine sticks and whittled them into sharp points and lashed them onto the end of the sapling with pieces of fishing line. He then cut a notch into one small tree and stuck the sharpened end of one of the sticks into it, which was tied off to the lasso. He cut another stick, sharpening both ends, and made a Figure Four out of it, the notched tree, and the stick with the rope attached. He carefully tied the fishing line across the trail onto it and inserted it between the two stick to complete the Figure Four.

Boom brushed out his tracks and hid uphill behind some scrub oaks. No sooner was he there than he heard a noise down the trail. Sure enough, along came Tom Smith, wearing sweaty camouflaged coveralls and a deer-in-the-headlights look. Boom drew his knife and waited. Right at the line Tom stopped, sides heaving. Boom thought he had spotted the line, but the man set the rifle against a tree and pulled out a canteen, drinking deeply, and pouring some over his head. He looked behind him nervously, as he put the canteen away and picked up the rifle, slinging it over his shoulder.

He took two steps when his thigh hit the trip wire. Feeling it across his thighs, he looked down and got a look of sheer horror on his face; then he saw the big sapling whipping at him from alongside the trail. It was too late. Tom Smith screamed in pain, as Boom's expedient Malayan Gate swept across the path at high speed and one pine punji stake tore into the flesh of his upper thigh and the other went into his hip, breaking as it stuck into his hipbone. Tom dropped the rifle, and Boom sprang forward from the trees before Tom could react.

Tom Smith felt the knife at his windpipe and his life flashed before his eyes.

He sobbed in pain and abject fear. "I'm sorry, Sergeant Kittinger. Please don't kill me?"

To his relief, and the total relief of his bladder and bowels, Boom responded, "I'm not going to, idiot. I am a warrior, not a murderer. I am making a citizen's arrest. Yer going to jail, not passing go, and sure as hell won't collect two hundred dollars. Now, ya son of a bitch, I have to make a travois so I can haul your sorry carcass to the cops. Wish they'd invent small radios people could carry, like the army has, so people could call each other from anywhere."

Months later, Tom Smith pled guilty to felonious assault in exchange for a dropping charge of attempted first-degree murder, criminal trespass, and aggravated menacing, and ended up losing what money and property he had left and spending six and half years in the Colorado State Penitentiary, where he was told daily how lucky he was he'd attacked a Green Beret and was still alive.

Bobby remembered going into town a couple days later

with his dad and Boom, and men tried to buy both men drinks, but both refused and settled for handshakes. Now Bobby understood why.

One good thing that came out of it was that Tom Smith's oldest son became very close with his mother and entered the priesthood, vowing to only do good the rest of his life.

5

VILLAINS

Bahiy Udeen's name meant Magnificent of the Faith, and he often impressed young members of al Qaeda, because it was known he was personally trained by Ayman al-Zawahiri, the AQ's number-two man, but more importantly, he held one singular honor that he never spoke about. For a period of two years, Bahiy Udeen was a primary bodyguard of the "Sheik," "the Director," Osama bin Laden himself, but during that time he also had a homosexual relationship with bin Laden. In fact, he was the man who Abdul Baari had seen in the cave with bin Laden when he and the "Sheik" were fellating each other. Abdul was also the terrorist Bo Devore shot and sent flying into space in Colorado.

Bahiy Udeen was also the man responsible for starting the al Qaeda program in Mexico. He was a graduate of Universidad Nacional Autonoma Mexico, the National Autonomous University of Mexico. Founded in 1551, the second oldest university in North America, it has over 269,000 students, but more important to Bahiy Udeen was that after receiving his bachelor's in Mexico City, he did graduate work on his master's at the big branch of UNAM located within the U.S. border at San Antonio, Texas. A university that produced four Nobel Laureates would not seem to house a major al Qaeda operative, especially on American soil, and that was exactly their plan.

During his time in Mexico and Texas, Bahiy Udeen extensively studied the problems along the U.S. border. Like most other members of al Qaeda, he felt the infidels were extremely stupid, and even further, he felt our arms-open attitude could be exploited to become our downfall.

The way he saw it, the Republican and Democratic Parties in the United States did everything they could to destroy each other, and he could not understand why they did not work together to protect the country as a whole. Divide and conquer: That would be easy enough.

He also saw that many Americans were spoiled and lazy in his view. They could hire Mexicans to work for them as maids, housekeepers, nannies, gardeners, and cheap laborers for their businesses. Because of this, nobody seemed to care about the constant stream of illegal immigrants coming from and going back into Mexico. This could be exploited.

As time went on, and he studied the situation further, he figured that many al Qaeda could be smuggled across the border, if they simply learned to speak a little Spanish and posed as illegal Mexican workers, migrants and domestics mainly, so even if caught, they still might not be detained.

After presenting all of this in meetings in Pakistan, he was praised, and it was discussed much further. The infidels were fools, they figured. He explained that in his view, the Democrats in America constantly told minorities how oppressed they were, and the minorities always believed them, so most of them would vote for Democrats. This Hispanic voting block seemed very important to the Democrats, so they courted it. The Republicans seemed in his view to be in favor of big business, and their lobbyists and corporate donors wanted the cheap labor the illegals provided, so the Republicans, too, did not want to upset the apple cart and encouraged looking the other way when people crossed into the U.S. In the mind of al Qaeda it was ridiculous anyway and the U.S., they felt, would be much better off with a theocracy.

The main thing that came out of the meetings was a plan to carry out the long-term goal of Osama bin Laden. For years he stated he wanted to create an American Hiroshima. Specifically, Osama bin Laden wanted to detonate two nuclear devices simultaneously in two major American cities with large Jewish populations, and even more specifically, during daylight hours to multiply the terror factor.

The al Qaeda leadership frequently laughed about how the American news media and Democrats attacked Bush for not finding weapons of mass destruction in Iraq, and everybody knew they had been moved to Syria by plane and convoy, very easily in fact. On top of that, meeting with black-market arms dealers in one of Saddam Hussein's palaces, representatives of al Qaeda purchased a truck containing several suitcase nuclear bombs, a backpack nuclear bomb, and two nuclear artillery warheads, all left behind when the *muhajideen* defeated the Soviets in Afghanistan.

The Soviets, before their country crumbled, confessed to losing twenty nuclear devices left behind in Afghanistan, but U.S., British, and Israeli intelligence forces secretly estimated that the number was actually well in excess of fifty devices, with most being backpack and suitcase nuclear bombs with blast capabilities ranging from one all the way to five kilotons. Then in 1997, Retired General Alexander Lebed, Russia's former security chief, admitted publicly that eighty-four nuclear devices were missing from Russia's arsenal and could not be found or accounted for.

Specifically, a "suitcase" bomb is an extremely portable nuclear weapon, and some have the dimensions of only twenty-four by sixteen by eight inches. The smallest possible bomblike object would be a single critical mass of plutonium (or U-233) at maximum density under normal conditions. Most of the suitcase nukes from the Soviet arsenal were one to two kilotons and weighed just over fifty-seven pounds each. It doesn't take much more than a single critical mass to cause significant explosions ranging from ten to twenty tons. The warhead consists of a tube with two pieces of uranium, which, when rammed together, would cause a blast. Some sort of firing unit and a device that would need to be decoded to cause detonation could be included in the "suitcase."

The "backpack" nuclear bomb is even smaller. The Soviet nuclear backpack system was made in the 1960s for use against NATO targets in time of war and consisted of three "coffee-can-sized" aluminum canisters in a bag. All three must be connected to make a single unit in order to explode. The detonator is about six inches long and had a three-to-five-kiloton yield, depending on the efficiency of the explosion.

Further research by Bahiy Udeen revealed that the very vicious MS-13, an El Salvadoran-based street gang, had pretty much taken over the drug-smuggling trade between Mexico and the U.S. It was decided, for lots of money, that al Qaeda might get them to smuggle the nuclear devices into the U.S. and take the fall if caught. The idea was nixed, however, because there had even been television news stories about the MS-13 gang, so they figured the FBI or DEA had probably already infiltrated undercover agents into the gang.

Udeen reported, however, that a little known but equally vicious Rio de Janiero-spawned street gang had had no press at all so far, and would be better to utilize. O Grupo Grande was ruled with an iron bloody fist by a dark-skinned seven-foot-tall muscle-bound giant named Ramiro Maureo. All intelligence reports indicated he was psychotic and very much a sadist.

One American DEA agent grew up in Sao Paulo and Buenos Aires, the son of a U.S. tire executive, so he spoke fluent Portuguese and was olive-skinned and black-haired, as he was the offspring of a Sicilian-born mother and father whose family came from Naples.

The Portuguese-speaking Italian-American cop did not last a week undercover, maybe because he was simply a newcomer. Ramiro broke most of the bones in the cop's body with a two-by-four, then personally sliced the man's entire groin off with his pocketknife, and packed a bag of ice on the wound, so the man would stay awake and the bleeding would subside. He then crammed the genitalia into the officer's mouth and pinned the officer's upper and lower lips together with ten large safety pins. He left the man sitting in his office in the corner for two days until he finally died of shock, and the whole time Ramiro conducted business as if the American was just a piece of furniture. At one point, with the dying man moaning just a few feet away, the cold-blooded killer even shared a romantic interlude with his main woman, Paola Mirari, a beautiful seductive murderer herself.

With the blessings of the al Qaeda leadership, after separate meetings with Osama bin Laden in his most frequent hideout in the NWFP tribal area in Pakistan, and al-Zawahiri, who was at that time very near the Khyber Pass almost right on the border, Bahiy Udeen was officially put in charge of what al Qaeda secretly referred to as *Iid Min Mawt,* the Festival of Death, the simultaneous daytime nuclear attacks on New York City and Miami, Florida. Funding came from an initial outlay of American money, and more would be delivered to him by courier, mainly already implanted cells in the host country he was in at the time. Funding for this aggressive but highly secret program was unlimited, with most coming from very wealthy private backers in both Riyadh and the Ash Sharqiyah province of Saudi Arabia, as well as one in Kuwait.

He initially met with Ramiro Maureo and Paola Mirari in San Antonio at The Longhorn Café, as all three wanted a really good American hamburger and were told that was where they would get one. Bahiy lusted after the beautiful seductress, and secretly lusted even more so for the dark, muscular seven-footer, but notwithstanding, they did not like each other. If not buddies, they were all three very mercenary. O Grupo Grande would indeed smuggle any of the al Qaeda personnel across the border, as they wanted at $20,000 a pop, and arrangements were made to take the backpacks and nuclear suitcase bombs across the border using horses at $50,000 for each device. They would go in a rocky area along the Arizona-Mexican border not too far from Willcox, which was rough enough that they could get through with surefooted horses but not four-wheelers or dirt bikes, so the Border Patrol would only be able to apprehend them with helicopters, a rare commodity.

Ramiro even asked for reassurances from Bahiy Udeen that, whatever the AQ was planning, he wanted to know his grandmother in Miami would be totally safe. Bahiy gave his word, not caring about doing so, because in his mind, Ramiro and his bitch were also infidels just as much as the Americans. Infidels were "unbelievers," and it was perfectly all right to lie to them.

The stage was set and arrangements were being made to smuggle the "nukes" into Mexico for transport into the U.S.

Ramiro Maureo was very well suited to the task. He became the leader of O Grupo Grande in a rapid fashion. In fact, his ascension to power in the gang was immediate. The founder of O Group Grande was Duarte Liberio, who could best be described as one mean son of a bitch. Duarte's father trained and fought alongside Che Guevara in the rain forests of Bolivia and high mountains of Chile. He was a revolutionary and the cause was usually not important to him. He was simply fascinated with killing, and this fascination was passed on to his son Duarte. Duarte killed his first man when he was twelve in the streets of Rio. He grew up as a murderer, robber, rapist, extortionist, and all-around bad guy. Then one day, he saw he could expand or actually multiply his criminal prowess by forming O Grupo Grande. In a psychological sense, it was like getting a penis extension.

Then along came Maureo. O Grupo Grande really

started developing a rep around Rio and money was flowing for protection alone, besides all their other criminal activities. Ramiro Maureo saw the potential and power base and was very used to taking whatever he wanted, whenever he wanted. The gang was meeting at a large abandoned warehouse on the outskirts of Rio. Ramiro invited himself into the group meeting, and there was a total hush when he entered the building. One reason was because he was an outsider, but more pronounced was the fact that he stood seven feet tall but was built like an NFL defensive end who enters bodybuilding competitions in the off-season. Adding to that, he removed his shirt and entered the building holding an American-made bowie knife in his big right hand. The fact that Uzis, MAC 11s, and other guns were leveled at him as he approached Duarte did not seem to faze him. In actuality, he decided in order to carry out his plan, he would have to be totally fearless and merciless.

The leaders of the gang were seated at a table that was fashioned by connecting four old doors together and placing them on legs. Duarte sat in the largest chair at the head of the table. Ramiro never broke stride, just walked rapidly right up to Duarte, who, shocked at the intrusion and boldness of the newcomer, was not sure how to react.

Ramiro Maureo looked him in the eye and in Portuguese said, "You are sitting in my chair."

Duarte did not like this.

Boldly, he challenged, "Who are you? You pup! I am the leader of O Grupo Grande. The only way you could ever sit in that chair would be to kill me first, and you would find that a very difficult job."

Ramiro smiled, saying, "No, it would be easy. Watch."

He grabbed Duarte by the throat with his left hand and lifted him off the floor, then viciously thrust the bowie knife into Duarte's abdomen and twisted it over and over while Duarte screamed and twitched in pain, eyes wide open in horror.

Before Duarte died, Ramiro smiled at him, saying, "See, I told you it would be easy."

When the body went limp, Ramiro dropped him on the concrete floor. He bent over and wiped his blade off on the dead gang leader's pants, then stood erect and looked at all the shocked leaders.

The first words out of his mouth were: "I am your new leader. Now, you will all start making very much money. If any of you wants to be the leader, just kill me, like I have done. Who wants to fight me to the death?"

One by one, after looking at each other, the leaders sat down in their chairs.

6

12 STEPS

Retired Sergeant Major Brand "Boom" Kittinger called Bobby as soon as he arrived in Washington.

Bobby answered and Boom said, "I'm in town. You still park your car in that same lot?"

Bobby said, "Yes, but I—"

Boom interrupted, "Hop on the metro and meet me there ASAP. I'm in a white rental SUV. I'll wait."

Bobby showed up twenty minutes later. He hopped in Boom's car, and they shook hands.

Bobby said, "Boom, I can't believe you hopped a jet and flew across the country."

"Look, kid, yer SF and yer Honey Samuels' son, period," Boom said.

Bobby said, "Yeah, but you dropped everything and flew all the way across the country—"

Again, Boom interrupted. "Look, this doesn't mean you and I are going to share a sleeping bag and play reach-around or share meaningful moments of midnight magic together. I will help get you headed in the right direction, and you will listen and learn, or I'll hop on the next jet back. Fair enough?"

Bobby said, "Affirmative, Top.

"Where we going, Boom?"

"You'll see," Boom said,

A short while later, Boom pulled into a church parking lot. He pulled a note out of his pocket, and glanced at it.

"This is it," he said, "We need to find the basement."

Bobby said, "Boom, I don't have time to go to AA meetings."

Boom opened the car and got back inside.

Bobby jerked his door open, saying, "What are you doing?"

"Bobby," Boom said firmly, "I don't have time to fly across the country and waste my time on losers who won't help themselves. Let's go. I have a plane to catch."

Bobby's temper flared, and he hopped in the car, slamming the door, and peered straight ahead.

He said, "Fine, let's go!"

Boom started the vehicle and put it in gear, but Bobby suddenly stepped on top of Boom's foot on the brake.

Softly, he said, "I'm sorry, man. I'll go, and I won't whine. Please, let's go in?"

Boom again turned off the car, and the two men got out and found the way to the church basement. They heard laughter coming from a room off the hall, and Bobby asked a man where the restroom was. He went in there and splashed water in his face while looking in the mirror.

He said to himself, "How did you get yourself in a predicament like this?"

Just then a toilet flushed, and a tall man with red hair walked out chuckling, and walked to the sink, nodding at Bobby.

"Probably drank too damned much. That's how." He laughed.

He walked out the door chuckling at his joke.

Bobby looked in the mirror again, and noticed his face

was red with embarrassment. He laughed at himself and went out the door.

Bobby was glad this was a smokeless AA meeting. He looked around at faces, people drinking coffee and all smiling, it seemed. He did not want to be there. He always figured AA was where losers went. Some guy who seemed to be in charge identified himself as "Tom, a grateful recovering alcoholic, thanks to this program and my higher power." He seemed to be telling the rules or how the meeting would be conducted. Bobby wasn't sure, because he really wasn't listening closely. His mind was racing too much. Then, Bobby noticed men and women around the room were telling their first names and each one said they were an alcoholic, and some were saying how many days, months, or years they had been sober. Before he had time to figure out what to do or say, it came to him.

Bobby did not know what to say. He looked down at his feet.

Tom said, "Friend, this meeting is voluntary and you do not have to share if you don't want to. We were just hoping to learn your first name so guys would know what to call you."

He looked up and said, "It's okay. My name is Bobby. I guess I'm an alcoholic. I haven't had a drink for two days, I guess."

Everybody clapped. The man next to him shook hands with him.

Inside Bobby's head was where the real turmoil was going on. Had he copped out? He had called himself an alcoholic. How could he? he wondered. He'd earned not one but two Silver Stars and a Purple Heart in the Gulf War. He was currently waiting to be awarded the Distinguished Service Cross, or a third Silver Star if the DSC got downgraded. He had earned his Green Beret. He had been with Delta, and was a cadre member of the HALO Committee. He had been captured by al Qaeda in Iraq and was going to be beheaded, and he'd escaped. How could he be an alcoholic, one of those guys in a trench coat and a paper bag that sleeps under bridges?

Bobby looked up as people clapped. General Roget was in civvies standing at the podium. He was a lieutenant general, a three-button, who worked in the Pentagon. Bobby had been in meetings with him, had lunch with him along with General Perry one time, and had attended several parties with him. A West Point graduate, he was known as an outstanding officer, who'd been an airborne infantry officer and commanded a Ranger Company, a battalion of the 101st Airborne Division, and was the commanding general of the 82nd Airborne Division. He was at the Pentagon serving at the pleasure of General Perry and waiting for a fourth star. How could he be there? Bobby wondered.

The general spoke. "Hi, my name is Carl and I am an alcoholic. In fact, through the grace of my Higher Power, who I choose to call Jesus Christ, and the men and women and twelve steps in this great program, I have been a recovering alcoholic for exactly eleven years today."

Everybody applauded, and the three-star general smiled and winked at Bobby. He winked. Bobby became glued to the man's story. During the talk, Bobby noticed people were getting up all the time getting cups of coffee. He did, too.

The general talked about how he first got sober, and Bobby was fascinated.

Carl said, "By profession, I am in the military, and my job is fairly important, I think."

Bobby laughed out loud and subconsciously looked around, embarrassed.

Carl went on. "I hosted a large formal party at my home in Falls Church, and there were some real bigwigs in attendance. I was nervous about the party, because I had been hoping to get promoted to a higher rank, and this get-together had people way out of my league as far as rank is concerned. I was so nervous, I decided I needed a martini to fortify myself."

People in the room laughed, and Bobby could not figure out why.

Then Carl continued. "I have been the same rank in the

military for over a decade. Do you know why, boys and girls?"

Somebody chuckled and yelled out, "Booze!"

Carl laughed and said, "Partially, but the real reason is because I am an alcoholic, and I cannot sip on a martini all night long like others. I don't eat one chip. I eat the whole damned bag! It is my personality. I am a creature of excess, a perfectionist, I am highly sensitive, I am prone to depression.

"I have been the same rank for eleven years, because a normal social drinker would never have told the wife of the secretary of defense that she had great tits and legs and she should be ridden like Secretariat."

The room roared and howled. Tears flowed down the cheeks of everyone, but Bobby's were not from laughter, although he masked it that way. All he thought about was how he'd betrayed Bo.

It took five full minutes before Roget could speak again. People were laughing and murmuring with each other.

"You see," Carl continued, "I don't even know what the woman looks like. I don't remember saying anything. All I remember is the first martini to calm down, but there must have been a bunch of them. I was told later what I said, and that was not the only thing I did that night. I have the sweetest, most loving wife in the world, and I embarrassed and disrespected her publicly by calling her a nasty bitch in front of others, because she tried to get me to stop drinking!"

This time he winked at the other side of the back of the room, and Bobby saw Carl's wife, a beautiful classy woman, Bobby had met before. She smiled at Carl and blew a kiss.

"The next day, my wife got into Al-Anon, because, you see, our family members and loved ones are the ones with the real scars. For years, they become our victims and our enablers, and they end up as sick as we are. Because of the selfishness of this damned disease," Carl added, and Bobby heard a sniffle behind him.

Carl continued. "You know what is weird? The army encouraged my alcoholism but never meant to. If you are an officer in the army, you will be toasting, you will drink to everything, and after work, you will head to the O-Club to schmooze and try to deal with the fact that you control to a great extent the lives and sometimes deaths of young men and women."

When the speech ended, Bobby jumped to his feet with the others applauding, and he realized tears were running down his cheeks. They all sat, and then different members would stand and thank Carl and each seemed to try to drop a pearl of wisdom. Bobby felt like the whole meeting and all the comments had been set up specifically for him.

When Boom stood up, he said, "Hi, Carl," and Carl answered back, "Hi ya, Boom. Glad you could make it. He lives in Colorado, folks."

Then Bobby spotted a woman he knew from the Pentagon. She was a major who was a JAG (Judge Advocate General) officer, an attorney, but today she wore her hair down and was in a sweatshirt and culottes. She actually was quite pretty, Bobby noted.

Looking around the room, he also recognized a sergeant first class he knew who was an MP at the Pentagon.

Boom said, "My name is Boom, and I'm a drunk."

People chuckled.

Boom went on. "Carl, thanks for your lead, your story. It is an inspiration to me and others. We always have to keep a little crack open in the door to our past, so we never forget where we come from, and always remember we cannot take that first drink, 'cause it's not the caboose that kills us when the train runs over us. It is the engine."

After the comments, people stood and held hands and said the Lord's Prayer together, then kept holding hands and raised everybody's hand up, all saying, "Keep coming back. It works, if you work it."

Then people mingled and hugged each other. There were a few handshakes, but mainly hugs, and Bobby could tell these people genuinely cared for each other. Many came over to him and hugged him and greeted him.

Finally, Bobby saw Boom coming toward him carrying two cups of coffee. He handed one to Bobby, and they drank. They gave each other knowing looks, and Boom never said a word.

Bobby walked over to Carl and shook hands.

Sheepishly, he said, "General, this is my first meeting."

Carl interrupted. "Not here. Call me Carl."

Bobby said, "Yes, sir," and then they both laughed.

"So what do you think?" the general asked.

Bobby said, "I'm overwhelmed. It's not what I thought it would be. Eleven years. I have two days. I feel like a private E-1."

Carl smiled, "Yeah, but when you were out there drinking, you were a draft-dodger."

Bobby laughed.

Carl added, "Bobby, the reason I have been sober eleven years is because I did it one day at time, not a year at a time. You get a big book and learn the twelve steps and start working them. Here is my card with my home number. If it is three A.M. and you are having an anxiety attack, you feel like you're going to have a drink, anything like that, just give me a call."

Bobby was overwhelmed.

"Thank you," was all he could mutter.

The ride away from the meeting was very quiet. Bobby was deep in his thoughts, and Boom turned Rush Limbaugh on and listened to his broadcast.

Bobby suddenly said, "Can I buy you a cup of coffee somewhere?"

"Sure," Boom replied.

They pulled into an IHOP and got coffee and talked about the meeting.

Bobby finally said, "I really started drinking after Arianna died. Most of it was alone."

Boom said, "Many of us get started that way, trying to drink away a hurt or pain."

"I have a big problem, Boom," Bobby said, leaning forward in a whisper. "The AQ are smuggling terrorists into the

U.S. as Mexican illegals, and they want to sneak backpack nukes in and blow up New York and Miami with 'em."

Boom didn't change expression, "Gee, don't I look shocked, just like any other Specops guy that would hear that."

Bobby said, "We are just now forming a task force to deal with it."

"Task force?" Boom said. "Isn't that politispeak for a cluster fuck?"

Bobby laughed and replied, "Probably, but I will SF around the obstacles. I may be calling on you for help."

Boom took a sip of coffee and kind of toasted Bobby with his cup, saying, "When it positively, absolutely has to be blown up overnight, call me."

Bobby said, "What about my brand-new sobriety?"

"Well, old son," Boom responded, "did you manage before to get drunk even though you were swamped with trying to save the planet?"

Bobby thought for a second and started laughing. Then he got serious. "This is scary, Boom."

Boom said, "Nukes are just bombs that are real grown up."

Bobby explained, "No, I mean getting hit with sobriety right now."

"Well, it always is. The real question is how are you gonna handle it?"

Bobby said, "I'll try the best I can."

Boom replied, "Your sobriety must come before everything. It must. Only way the program works. No matter what, you cannot ever take that first drink."

"I got that point clearly today," Bobby said.

"Yeah, but hearing it is one thing," Boom came back. "Living it is another."

Bobby pondered this a moment and responded, "Well, Boom, I guess I'll just have to do it one day at a time."

Boom took a healthy swallow of coffee and nodded for more.

"That-a-boy," he said, "I'm going to stay a couple days, and we'll get as many meetings in as possible."

"Thanks," Bobby said, "I know I'll be in meetings all day tomorrow."

Boom said, "There are midnight meetings. We'll catch up on sleep after we're dead. Don't worry."

Bobby and Bo were told to meet in the SECDEF's briefing room the next morning at 0800 hours (eight A.M.) in Class A's. They met ahead of time outside the Pentagon and talked, both in uniform, which was unusual. Bo saluted and Bobby returned it.

Bo smiled. "You are looking strac today, except your shaggy civilian haircut."

Bobby grinned. "You are standing tall yourself, Captain, but I think you should get yours cut high and tight."

She chuckled.

Getting serious, Bobby said, "Bo, it is going to take me a long time making it up to you. I just can't put into words how sorry I am for what I did. You are my partner, and I want you to know beyond a shadow of a doubt that you can always count on me."

Bo smiled. "Bobby, I have always known you were there and that has not changed. It is just that, when you drink—"

"I know," Bobby interrupted. "That is why I do not drink anymore. I am an alcoholic, and I can never take the first drink."

Bo could not help herself. She got tears in her eyes and leapt into his arms, almost, and gave him a big hug and a kiss on his cheek. She stepped back smiling, feeling as if a two-ton anvil had just fallen off her shoulders.

They went inside and headed to a big conference room. When he saw all the brass around, all Bobby could think about was Carl's party and how he'd messed it up by simply having a martini. Now Bobby understood why everyone laughed when Carl said that. Once Carl had a martini, a second, third, and so on were inevitable.

Before he and Bo sat down, introductions were made

around the giant shiny mahogany table. General Perry was there along with the other chiefs of staff and the chairman of the joint chiefs, the deputy director of the FBI, secretary of defense, the secretary of homeland security, the deputy director of the CIA, several National Security Council officials, Secret Service agents, two agents from the DIA, a DEA executive, the surgeon general, three officials from the Immigration and Naturalization Service, and of course a plethora of staffers. Bobby and Bo were going to sit at the table, but a homeland security official and senior FBI agent who had been talking crowded ahead of them and sat down in the last two seats.

General Perry spoke. "Mr. Defense Secretary, Mr. Homeland Security Secretary, ladies and gentlemen, we are gathered here today for an emergency meeting requiring tremendous cooperation and a real urgency to mission accomplishment on our part. The very security and safety of our citizens depends on our ability to operate together. By the way, his hair does not look like a soldier's because he operates undercover frequently. I would like to introduce to you two of the finest members of our military, Major Bobby M. Samuels and Captain Bo Marguerite Devore."

Everybody applauded while Bobby and Bo stood at attention and smiled.

General Perry spoke again. "As you all know. Major Samuels and Captain Devore identified and combated two al Qaeda terrorists, homicide bombers aboard a domestic flight, took them out, and it was later learned they were planning to explode the plane with a bomb as it flew over the streets of Los Angeles. The plane crash-landed in the very rugged Rocky Mountains during a blizzard, and the two of them took charge and successfully evacuated passengers, set up triage, and significantly reduced potential loss of life. They, in essence, were solely responsible for the safe and healthy escape of a couple hundred passengers, and their immediate survival in high-altitude blizzard conditions, and at the risk of their own lives."

Everyone applauded again.

General Perry went on. "Come here, you two."

Bobby and Bo walked forward and stood at attention before the general.

He continued. "Did I just sound like I was reading an award citation? Well, I wasn't. I was expanding on the actual citations."

He held up two framed certificates, then set them down and then lifted up two blue and red striped medals.

He continued. "Major Bobby Samuels and Captain Bo Devore are being awarded the Soldiers Medal for the action named, the U.S. Army's highest award for heroism outside a hostile combat operation or environment."

He pinned the medal on each of them, and they saluted; then he shook hands with them, handing them their framed citations. All the others stood applauding, and came up and shook hands with them.

A man came into the room and whispered to the secretary of defense, who called Perry over.

General Perry said, "You two stay right here."

Bobby and Bo gave each other a quizzical look.

Two men, both in dark blue suits, came into the room. The surgeon general and both secretaries came forward and stood by Jonathan Perry.

The secretary of defense said, "Ladies and gentlemen, the President of the United States."

General Perry hollered, "Atten-tion!"

Heels clicked and locked simultaneously throughout the room. The President entered the room with an entourage, including many members of the press corps.

He yelled, "Carry on, please!"

Everyone stayed on their feet. The President went around the room shaking hands.

The President was introduced to Bobby and Bo, and just grinned and shook his head. Then, he got a serious look.

The President stood by Perry and summoned Bobby forward two steps.

The President said, "Mr. Secretary of Defense."

The secretary of defense pulled a framed citation out of his briefcase and handed it to General Perry and nodded.

While the President pinned the Distinguished Service Cross, only the fourth one awarded in the Iraq War, on Bobby's uniform, Jonathan Perry read the official citation.

The general put on reading glasses and began. "The Distinguished Service Cross is awarded to Major Bobby M. Samuels, U.S. Provost Marshal's Office, Criminal Investigation Detachment-Special Operations Unit (Airborne), Headquarters, Department of the Army, for extraordinary heroism in action during the period of 20 to 30 September, 2005, while engaged in combat operations during *Operation Enduring Freedom.* As an undercover military police officer, Major Samuels was kidnapped by a squad of al Qaeda terrorist insurgents who ambushed and killed Major Samuels's companions with automatic weapons in a Baghdad restaurant. Major Samuels was handcuffed, beaten, tortured, and held in an al Qaeda safehouse in Baghdad proper. Preparations were being made to videotape and behead Major Samuels, when he, using his extreme initiative, training, and experience, escaped his bonds and set out an expedient signal for allied rescue forces and fought and dispatched, using hand-to-hand combat, an estimated reinforced squad of heavily armed insurgents and successfully escaped, thus demoralizing the enemy and single-handedly destroying a powerful enemy cell. His unparalleled courage under fire, decisive leadership, and personal sacrifice were directly responsible for the success of the rescue operation and were further instrumental in ensuring preventive measures against further kidnappings of American personnel. Further, during this same classified operation, Major Samuels successfully operated undercover, exposing himself to tremendous danger, and eliminated a dangerous al Qaeda infiltrator and saboteur. His personal example has added yet another laurel to the proud military history of this Nation and serves as the standard for all others to emulate. Major Samuels's gallant deeds were truly above and beyond the call of duty and are in keeping with the finest traditions of the military service and reflect great credit upon himself, the military police branch, the United States Army, and the United States of America."

There was a thunderous round of applause and a long, cheering standing ovation in the room.

Then the President called Bo forward and pulled out a Silver Star as Perry read her citation, too. He pinned it on her, as Perry read, "The Silver Star is awarded to Captain Bo M. Devore, U.S. Provost Marshal's Office, Criminal Investigation Detachment-Special Operations Unit (Airborne), Headquarters, Department of the Army, for extraordinary heroism in action during the period of September 25, 2005 and extraordinary valor in a shoot-out with an armed and vicious al Qaeda terrorist and jihadist. Working as an undercover plainclothes military police officer, Captain Devore, while investigating the activities of an armed terrorist on American soil, was set upon and attacked by the spy and avowed terrorist by cowardly ambush, while she was showering. Using her training and experience, Captain Devore quickly slipped on her body armor and when attacked, took deadly bullets in the heart plate of her protective vest, and stood her ground returning fire with her nine-millimeter handgun, dispatching the al Qaeda combatant and potentially saving the lives of countless Americans. Her valorous actions were in keeping with the finest traditions of the military service and reflect great credit upon herself, the military police branch, the United States Army, and the United States of America."

Again, there was much applause, and Bo and Bobby shook hands professionally with each other; however, he gave her a smile and a wink.

Bobby was then awarded a Purple Heart for the wounds he sustained in Iraq, second Oak Leaf Cluster, from the secretary of defense. He had received his other two Purple Hearts during the first Gulf War, as well as two Silver Stars, and a Bronze Star for meritorious service when he served as an A-Detachment commander with the 3rd Battalion of the 5th Special Forces Group and, shortly after, went to Delta Force.

Everyone sat and the staffers got out of their seats to let Bobby and Bo sit at the table. The press was escorted from the briefing room.

The President said, "Ladies and gentlemen. We are facing a dangerous time right now. I am counting on all of you to pull together as a cohesive force to eliminate and counteract this grievous threat to our nation. You are all part of a top secret task force, ordered by me, and it will be overseen by the secretary of homeland security. Major Samuels and Captain Devore will spearhead the investigative process of this operation and are to be given wide latitude in how they handle the problems and challenges they will be confronted with. They are to be given whatever support they need, immediately. I am counting on all of you, on each of you. Your country is counting on you. Now, on a personal note, these arrogant jihadist bastards think they are going to blow up our citizens on our soil with nuclear devices. We will not let that happen. Anybody who leaks anything to the press, or tries to politicize anything about his operation, will have my size-ten Presidential-sealed cowboy boot right up their ass. Do we all understand the import of this task before us?"

"Yes, sir," came numerous simultaneous shouts around the table.

He started for the door, saying, "You will all be briefed by General Perry and his staff, and he will give you the security warnings about the classification of the briefing. Those same tenets apply to what I just said. Thank you all. I have to go visit with the president of Afghanistan in the Oval Office, and by the way, he once again sends his sincere 'Thank you,' to all of our military, especially Special Forces."

Everyone stood as he left the room.

General Perry warned everyone of the Top Secret classification of the briefing and materials they would read. Each document passed out had a cover that was yellow and white with the large letters "TOP SECRET" on it. General Perry and his J2 gave an intelligence briefing based on what happened on the flight and on all the information they were able to get from the information the terrorists had. Plus, it was reported that Faarooq Ghasaan, the accomplice who was in the ground crew at Dulles, was apprehended by FBI and federal air marshals at work, and was immediately taken to Guantanamo Bay for interrogation. He had been, according to Jonathan Perry, "singing like an Elvis impersonator at a convention of recently divorced women." They were able to assign a higher probability to his testimony, as much of what he confessed was verified by paperwork of the other two.

After the intelligence briefing was concluded, a fancy catered lunch was brought in for everyone in the meeting. Bo and Bobby finally had a chance to talk privately and congratulate each other as friends. The whole time Bobby was talking, he kept picturing Bo coming out of the shower that morning. He could tell she had a great body just by seeing her clothed every day, but he was haunted now by visions of just how great her shape was. Then, he would get upset with himself.

They went off to a corner of the room to eat, and she excitedly said, "Can you believe we were just awarded medals by the commander in chief!"

Bobby said, "I know, It was awesome!"

Bo giggled and said, "The President of the United States of America!"

Bobby said, "I know. It's cool."

Bo said, "The single most powerful man in the world!"

Bobby replied, "Come on, Bo, cheer up."

Bo grinned mischievously and said, "Bobby, you received the nation's second-highest award for heroism, the DSC. Only the fourth soldier in the Iraq War to receive it so far."

Bobby said, "Yeah, that's neat."

Then, as if she had read his mind about the bathroom incident, Bo said, "What if when all the national press was in here, I told everyone you sit down to pee?"

Bobby had his iced tea come out his nose, he laughed so hard. Seeing what happened, General Perry walked over and shook hands with both, congratulating them again.

"Something must have been awful funny, Major?" he said.

Bobby still laughing, looked over at Bo, and back at the general, saying, "Captain Devore is acting like a total asshole, sir."

The general looked at Bo grinning, saying, "I find that very hard to believe, Major Samuels."

Bo said, "Believe it, sir. I have a mean streak sometimes."

He laughed and said, "I am not pursuing this conversation any further, especially since you both carry handcuffs."

After lunch, Perry turned the meeting over to the secretary of homeland security to discuss the Concept of the Operation and the actual Execution. In short, a lot of electronic surveillance was going to go on along the Mexican-American border, humintel would be increased well over five hundred percent, Bobby and Bo would be the investigative and operational spearhead of the entire operation.

After the briefing, the FBI deputy director said, "Mr. Secretary, this is unprecedented, sir. The FBI is responsible for domestic investigative operations in regards to national security. These two are soldiers. We have agents—"

An INS official stood and interrupted. "Hear, hear. We are talking about an operation involving the investigation of illegal foreign nationals, and that is our bailiwick, Mr. Secretary."

The secretary of homeland security said, "Gentlemen, if you listened to the President, he asked that we all cooperate for the sake of our country."

The deputy director of the Border Patrol stood and raised his hand, smiling politely. "Mr. Secretary, if I may."

The secretary nodded.

"Everybody in the U.S. Border Patrol is very aware of the dangers following 9/11, and we all want to cooperate, but this is a question of jurisdiction. We are the agency with the jurisdiction here, sir. We are more familiar with Mexican border jumpers than any other agency."

The FBI agent said, "Yeah, you guys have done a great job! We only have had eleven or twelve million slip through your grasp."

Several in the room chuckled. Bobby and Bo were both getting exasperated.

The secretary of homeland security said, "We do not need this squabbling starting. Homeland Security has overall jurisdiction."

The FBI senior agent raised his hand again, and the secretary almost made a face, but forced a smile and pointed at him.

The fed said, "Mr. Secretary, This has nothing to do with our patriotism. We are all patriots. As I said, you are putting two soldiers at the head of this investigation—"

The INS deputy said, "Wait a minute. If you are going to argue who will provide the best investigators, this is our forte."

The Border Patrol official said, "And it is dealing with the Mexican-American border. That is clearly our specific jurisdiction, and soldiers should not be involved in domestic, civilian law enforcement."

Bobby raised his hand.

The secretary said, "Major Samuels."

"Sir, Captain Devore and I will be able to work with any of these individuals from any of the respective agencies, but I cannot believe what I am hearing right now, and with all due respect, she and I are tired of being dismissed as a couple of soldiers. Gentlemen, I am sorry but the commander in chief, our President, was just here and asked us all to cooperate for the sake of our nation. He has only been gone from the room a few hours, and some of you sound like a bunch of Crips and Bloods wearing badges, and you're each protecting your hoods."

General Perry could not help himself.

He said, "Hooah!"

The chairman of the joint chiefs and the secretary of defense both chuckled.

Bobby went on. "Sir, we are not just soldiers. We are both law enforcement officers. Good ones, in fact, and we both are very familiar, on a personal basis, with al Qaeda. In fact, we have both had several different shootouts with al Qaeda, and we are both still here, and they are not. We are sworn to protect the citizens of this country, and we are going to. We sure would appreciate all of your help, but we do not have time to argue about it anymore. There are several million Americans whose lives are going to be lost if we sit in a conference room arguing about who gets to shoot the pigeons out of the belfry. Thank you for the time, Mr. Secretary."

The secretary of homeland security stood again, saying, "Major Samuels just summed it all up better than I could have. Maybe when he retires, he would like to become a speechwriter for the President."

Bobby smiled and shook his head negatively.

"You all have heard the Defense Department's J2 briefing," he continued. "And you have heard our operations order. Now, if you have specific questions about either, please ask them, but you all heard what the President said, and the bitching is over, ladies and gentlemen. Your various departments will be here to support Major Samuels and Captain Devore with assets, personnel, matériel, or equipment, as they spearhead the investigative part of this operation. If anybody has a problem with it, you can always get a book deal to talk about how nasty this administration is and go on the speech circuit. I hear both pay very well."

There were several chuckles in the room, and the Border Patrol deputy stood, saying, "Mr. Secretary, Major Samuels, you will indeed have the full support and cooperation of the U.S. Border Patrol."

The FBI official stood grinning and said, "No whining here. We have your backs Major, Captain. In fact, if I get a choice, I would prefer covering the captain's."

Bo said, "The captain's what, sir?"

Challenged now, he grinned and flirtingly said, "Whatever the good captain would like to have covered."

Bo smiled, saying, "You're all witnesses. I would like to have my gas bill for the month covered. Thank you very much, sir."

Everybody laughed.

Bobby gave Bo a private wink and approving nod.

Other officials then spoke, one by one, pledging the full support and cooperation of their respective agencies.

The meetings went on for two more full days. Boom, whose real name was Brand, flew back to Colorado after escorting Bobby to several more AA meetings. It was decided that the task force would set up its command center, under guard, in the basement of the Pentagon.

7

GO WEST

The next day, they all assembled around a large table and listened to a report from the senior FBI official. The chief resident agent of Salt Lake City, like FBI officers all over the country, had been watching for any large purchases of fireworks or chemicals that could be used in the construction of bombs. According to him, several suspicious-acting Mexican immigrants bought five fifty-five-gallon drums each of aluminum metal powder and ferric oxide powder, which is granulated iron. They also bought a five-gallon bucket of potassium permanganate. The materials were bought with a credit card belonging to a Jessan Antonio Tapia.

Everyone agreed that there was definitely a sufficient, actually an abundant, amount of suspicious activity to warrant further investigation. The FBI learned that the same credit card had been used to reserve four rooms in Page, Arizona. This engendered much discussion in the room. It was agreed Bobby and Bo would immediately leave for Page, Arizona, on the first available flight, and try to get a room in the same hotel. The suspects were not checking in until the following day. The secretary of defense was present at the meeting, and insisted that they use his limo and driver. Bo called on her cell phone from the car, and the closest immediate connection she could find was a flight into Albuquerque and a connecting flight into Durango, Colorado, and they would have to get to Ronald Reagan International right away, rent a car in Durango, which hosted commercial jets, then buy clothes and toiletries in Page or on the way.

They were greeted at the airport by two U.S. air marshals, who escorted them through processing and security. Bobby used his sat phone to call the 1st Battalion of the 19th Special Forces Group headquartered just south of Salt Lake City in Riverton, Utah. He gave the commanding officer a list of items he needed delivered to him at Page with an equipment truck standing by.

On the plane, Bobby called Boom Kittinger, who was one of the most legendary Special Forces engineer/demolition specialists in history, quickly briefed him, and then said, "We had suspects buy five fifty-five-gallon drums of aluminum metal powder, five fifty-five-gallon drums of ferric oxide powder, and one five-gallon barrel of potassium permanganate. I have to know what they are planning."

Boom answered immediately, "The biggest damned thermite grenade you ever saw in your life."

Bobby briefed Bo, then said, "Keep talking."

"They will mix the drums together and then probably pour glycerine into the barrel of potassium permanganate. The two together will ignite and get the thermite going. Once it is going, well, you have used thermite grenades in combat, buddy boy. Imagine one that size," Boom said, "Whatever they put it on, it will burn all the way through it, steel, concrete, you name it. You saw demos in the army where the instructor sets a thermite grenade on a safe or an old tank and it just sits there and burns through the steel, making it melt and help it burn."

Bobby said, "What kind of target?"

"Where you headed?"

Bobby said, "Page. Arizona."

Boom immediately answered, "The Glen Canyon Dam, man. That much thermite would burn right through the concrete in the dam and nothing, not even all that water from Lake Powell, could put it out. It would cripple the entire Southwest, and if the dam went quickly enough, there is no telling how much damage you would have downstream."

"It is that powerful?" Bobby said amazed.

Boom responded, "Thermite burns at over thirty thousand degrees Fahrenheit, hotter than any welding torch."

"Whew! Thanks, Boom."

Boom said, "Keep your powder dry. Holler if you need me."

"Wilco, out, " Bobby said, and immediately called it into DC while Bo overheard the details.

"Oh, man," Bo said. "Why can't we just get cases like some colonel's wife gets drunk and kicks him in the balls?"

This really tickled Bobby, and he started laughing in earnest.

They landed in Durango and picked up their SUV, which was waiting for them. As Bo signed for the rental, a man and woman approached.

As the army cops stepped away from the counter, the two people pulled out badges and the woman said, "Major Samuels? Captain Devore?"

Bobby nodded and stuck out his hand, "Yes."

She said, "Hi, I am Sally Mayweather, senior resident agent for the FBI from the Durango office, and this is Donald Kingston, senior resident agent from our Grand Junction office. We are here to expedite your journey to Page. Well, actually, we will accompany you to the Utah state line, and a Utah special agent will meet us there and accompany you to the Arizona line."

They walked toward the rental pickup area, and Bo said, "You have to be kidding. You guys are feds. Why do you stop at the state line?"

Donald replied, "That's how the agency is set up. We cross the line, the agent in charge of the Blanding, Utah, area might get upset. That is his territory, and honestly, we do not get along very well with him."

Bobby gave Bo one of those private looks.

"Oh," Bo said politely.

A few minutes later, they were in their SUV following a black SUV with darkened windows and flashing blue and red lights blinking all over. Ten minutes from the airport south of town, they turned west on U.S. Highway 160 and were soon through the tourist town of Durango, in less than an hour passed Mesa Verde National Monument, and were soon in the Four Corners city of Cortez. On the western edge of Cortez, Bobby thought they would take a southern turn on 491 and go by the popular Ute Indian Casino of Towoac, then 160 would branch off to the west again, passing through the Four Corners, where the states of Colorado, Arizona, Utah, and New Mexico all converge and touch corners, the only place in the USA where four states do so.

Instead, the FBI agents led them on a small two-lane paved road with a sign indicating it was heading toward Hovenweep National Monument, and the tiny Navajo town of Aneth directly west of Cortez.

Bobby and Bo were amazed on the drive toward Aneth. There were beautiful homes along this road and green pastures with small ranches. Then, suddenly, they passed a road going off to the right, with signage indicating Hovenweep as well as Cross Canyon, and immediately they were passing through the lands of the giant Navajo Indian Reservation, and the green disappeared to be replaced by brown. The lush green alfalfa fields gave way to pastures of heat-baked rocks and sand. To their left, a stream, McElmo Creek, snaked its way toward the San Juan River, and it was green along the waterway, which made the varying shades of brown seem even drier.

Soon, they started seeing occasional flocks of sheep or goats and ramshackle homes. Bo was shocked when she saw the poverty on the reservation and told Bobby so. She looked at the numerous little frame houses, many with windows with no glass in them, outhouses behind some. She spotted, by several homes, small dome-shaped buildings.

"I have seen several of those buildings," she said, "What are they?"

Bobby said, "Hogans."

"Hogans?" she asked, pronouncing it the way it is spelled.

Accenting the second syllable, he replied, "No, Hoe-gahns. It is the Navajo family lodge and holds tremendous spiritual significance to the family, the clan. The smaller ones you have been seeing are sweat lodges. Great place to go if you wanna get stoned on peyote."

"Peyote, really?" she queried.

Bobby laughed, "The shamans don't ever call it that. It is called medicine, period. Some just smoke tobacco."

"Medicine, huh?" She smiled. "I think that's what we called drugs in college. I don't remember."

Bobby laughed. "You never smoked a joint in your life, Captain."

Bo raised an eyebrow, saying, "Oh, yeah? What makes you think so?"

"Didn't want to break Mommy and Daddy's heart, especially Daddy." He grinned. "That's why you had straight A's all through school, sang in the church choir, and were head majorette, probably."

Bo started laughing, and finally said, "Well, you, sir, are totally wrong. I was in the school choir, and was head cheerleader, not majorette."

The FBI agents in front of them pulled over. So they pulled over behind them. The four got out of their vehicles.

Donald said, "We can't go into Utah, and the Utah ASAC was supposed to meet us back a ways, but he was not there."

He went to his trunk and came back. He had a black plastic rectangular box with three suction cups and a wire and cigarette lighter plug on it. He handed it to Bobby.

"Here you go," he said, "It's a Gladiator. Portable LED light deal. Just plug it in, turn it on, and rock and roll. You can ship it back to me or drop it off at Sally's office in Durango on your way back."

"Thanks," Bobby and Bo said simultaneously. Then Bo added, "It just amazes me that you are FBI and cannot cross the border."

Sally said, "Well, we are federal agents. We can. It is just that we are supposed to respect each other's jurisdiction and stay out unless we are in pursuit or similar."

Bo just shook her head, and then she and Bobby shook hands with the two agents and exchanged business cards. All four got in their respective vehicles, waved, and drove off.

Five minutes later, the road Bobby and Bo was on came to an end. To their left front was a bridge over McElmo Creek, and on the other side of the short concrete bridge was the small Navajo settlement of Aneth. They turned right and headed down the two-lane highway toward Montezuma Creek just five or six miles away. To their left was the San Juan River coursing its way toward the nearly two-hundred-mile-long Lake Powell. You would not know the river was there, though, as it was barely visible in spots. The river basin here was a mile wide, but next to the fast-flowing river was very thick vegetation, almost all Russian olive and manzanita. To their right were rock cliffs. The entire valley was devoid of vegetation, except right along the river, and there it was so thick it made up for the barren land further out.

Bobby and Bo both seemed to realize how long it had been since they had eaten, and she said, "Bobby, I know we have to hurry, but I need to relax a few minutes and eat."

"I am so glad you said that," he said, "My stomach feels like my throat has been slit. We'll stop at the first place we see."

Five minutes later, he stopped, and at first, she thought they were going into a modern convenience store, but he pulled up to a diner next door to it that looked like it came out of the fifties. He held her door open for her, and they went inside. The inside didn't change the impression gained from looking at the exterior.

They sat down at a Formica-top table and ended up ordering burgers, fries, and colas. All the residents were Navajo and everyone was friendly.

After they ate, Bobby said, "Now, I have been on this reservation before with Boom. Have you ever tasted Navajo fry bread?"

Bo made a face and shook her head, saying, "Fry bread? Never even heard of it."

He said, "You have been missing out on life, girl. It is horrible for your heart, but you have to try some."

He ordered two fry breads.

Bo got hooked, too. In the back, a large deep-frying pan sat on the stove. The cook made a tortilla-type shell out of Bluebird flour and fried it in lard. Powdered sugar was added at the end, and Bobby and Bo added cinnamon and honey to the shells.

"Oh, mmm," she cooed, "this is so wonderful. I want to eat twenty in a row. It is so fattening and unhealthy it is sinful, but they taste soo good."

Bobby chuckled, "Hey, don't hold back. Tell me if you like it or not."

They finished lunch and went into the convenience store next door to buy some bottled water. In the store, Bo was drawn to a little girl who came in with her mother and was dressed in traditional Navajo dress.

Bo knelt down and said, "You sure are beautiful. Where did you get your dress?"

The little girl's big brown eyes twinkled as she smiled, and acted very bashful, occasionally looking up at her proud grinning mother, a nice-looking lady with no shape to her calf muscles and a protruding gut from the very high-fat diet. This was a common sight among some women on the reservation.

The little girl folded her hands behind her back and twisted from side to side, embarrassed by Bo's praise and attention. Bobby just grinned while watching Bo interact.

Her mother said, "Tell her where you got your dress."

In a whisper of a voice, the little girl said, "My mommy made it."

"Well," Bo said, "it certainly is very beautiful and so are you. May I have a hug?"

The little girl threw her arms around Bo's neck and squeezed her tightly. The mother then took her hand and smiling, nodded at Bo and Bobby, and the two walked out the door. Bo wiped both eyes, and turned toward the door. Bobby held it for her.

As she walked by, he whispered, "Ya big softie."

Bo was strangely silent as they drove west toward Bluff, Utah. The land around them was varying shades of brown with a bright glaze to it from the unforgiving sunshine. The few steps between the convenience store and the SUV had been like a walk through a blast furnace being overworked. To their left, though, in sharp contrast, was the San Juan River and the Vietnam-like ultra-thick green foliage. It was like a wet green serpent winding its way through a vast dry sandbox, filled with rocks, as it wound its way toward that man-created giant Lake Powell.

Finally, Bo said, "Did you see the beautiful and expensive silver and turquoise jewelry the little girl was wearing?"

Bobby said, "Did you see what kind of car they drove after they left?"

Bo said, "No, I didn't see them."

Samuels replied, "You could see them behind us in the rearview mirrors. They didn't have a car. They were walking along the side of the road, probably heading back toward Aneth."

"Aneth?" she said.

Bobby said, "Next town a few miles east along the river. It was on the other side of that small bridge when we turned onto this road."

Bo said, "Bobby, turn around, please. We have to go back and pick them up. They can't be out walking in this heat. This is like when you were in Iraq."

He whipped the car around and flew back toward Aneth.

A mile past Montezuma Creek, they spotted the little girl

and her mother. They climbed into the backseat of the ex-
tended car, both wearing big happy smiles, and both grate-
fully accepted cold bottles of mountain spring water.

"Where are you going?" the woman asked.

"Page," he said.

"You are going the wrong way," she said matter-of-factly.

"Yes, ma'am," he responded.

Bobby took them to a house that was just off the highway
that ran through Aneth and Montezuma Creek. Bo could not
believe it when she saw the little box-shaped shack with no
glass in any window. Two dogs barked in the yard.

The little girl looked up at Bo saying, "Please wait?"

Bo nodded.

The little girl entered the house, emerging seconds later
and running up to Bo. She put a little beaded strip in her
hand, three inches long.

"Did you make this?" Bo asked.

"Yes," she said, embarrassed again.

The Washingtonian asked, "What does it mean?"

In a very soft voice, almost a whisper, the little girl,
pointing at the strip, said, "When you go you take a little of
my heart with you."

Bo Devore grabbed her and hugged her. When she let
go, the little girl ran inside.

Bo was visibly shaken, tears streaming down her face.

She said, "Damn you, Bobby Samuels, you son of a
bitch! Get out of here now!"

Chuckling, he pulled away while she wiped her eyes
over and over.

"Is this going to happen to me the whole time we are
down here?" she asked.

"Probably," he replied, and started chuckling.

They drove west again along the San Juan River, with
the highway finally moving a little away from the river.
The treeless mesas all around were completely flat on top.
When they got close to Bluff, there was a small ridge off
to their right about fifty yards off the road. There was a
small Anasazi cliff dwelling there with only two rooms.

The dirt road going to it showed that many tourists spotted it and looked within. Shortly beyond the little ruins, the relatively straight road dipped and curved to the left and a dirt road went left on the curve, which Bobby took.

He slowed suddenly, and it seemed like it was an unplanned stop.

Bo said, "We have got to tell the President about the horrible poverty here."

Bobby laughed. "Here? You might mention the horrible poverty on all the reservations while you're at it."

"You stopped pretty fast."

He said, "This road goes to a swinging foot bridge over the river, and there is a big cliff dwelling on the other side. You'll be able to see it in that red cliff face in a minute. It will only take a couple minutes,"

She watched for a minute and soon saw a naturally hollowed-out bowl-shaped area in the bottom of the cliff, and constructed in the middle of it was the sixteen-room Anasazi ruins. The road dipped down to the river, and they parked by the graffiti-painted rock walls to their left. Bo looked across the river, and started to comment on the ruins. She got concerned looking at Bobby's face.

"What's up?" she asked, getting a chill down her spine.

Bobby shook his head and grabbed a toothpick, sticking it between his lips.

"I can just sense the enemy is getting close to the target," he said, "I had a chill run up and down my spine, and I never feel that anymore. Been through too much. We need to get going."

He turned the flashers back on and peeled out of there.

"Are you sure?" she asked, very nervously looking around at all the thick foliage by the river.

"No," he replied, "I'm a human, subject to being overdramatic, suggestible, and overly enthusiastic, but I am pretty damned certain nonetheless."

Now, she was no longer riding with a man she had secretly fallen in love with. Now she was seeing Major Bobby Samuels, the warrior again, close up. It frightened her in a way. On the other hand, though, it excited her and did make her feel very protected, as if Bo Devore needed protection.

"How do you feel something like that?" she asked as a cop, genuinely curious.

"Deer and other animals that you would consider prey have this sixth sense. I call it a sense of knowing," he replied, "Warriors have it, too. You ever have someone look at your back through a window, and you felt it and a chill ran down your spine?"

"Yes," she said, "when I was a young teenager. Our neighbor snuck around our house and watched me in the shower. I felt it and looked out the window real quickly and saw his face. He fell off our trash can, and my father caught him before I could tell him. Dad beat him up something awful."

Bo got another chill just recalling the incident, thinking about her real horror story with the uncle.

Bobby said, "Well, that is the sixth sense I am speaking about. When I bow-hunt, I always look behind the animal I am getting ready to shoot. The early American Indians believed that looking directly at an animal or enemy was a way to spook the quarry. They felt that the animal would sense that it was being watched. I have a very strong feeling that our al Qaeda perps are at Page or close. I have learned to listen to that inner voice of mine. It has saved my bacon before."

Bobby said, "I was studying all the possible targets in the area on my laptop on the plane, and have come up with only two that would really make a major impact."

"What are they?" she asked.

"The Grand Canyon and Glen Canyon Dam, of course."

"The Grand Canyon?"

He replied, "Those are the two most notable targets in the area, but they could also affect the Grand Canyon, if they took out the Glen Canyon Dam, so I think Boom has to be totally correct. They would not only wipe out Lake Powell, but knock out the electricity in most of the Four Corners area, kill thousands, and disrupt the economy big-time. It would take decades to recover."

It would be that bad?" she asked.

"Probably worse," he said, "Plus, if they take out the dam, there would be a wall of water roaring downstream that could probably knock out the Hoover Dam by the time it got there."

"Like a tidal wave?" she asked.

"Like a tidal wave on anabolic steroids," he added. "The effects would be devastating for years, I believe."

"The wall of water would be that large?" Bo asked.

Just the thought gave her chills again.

"Lake Powell is one hundred and eighty-six miles long, has over two thousand miles of shoreline. That is like driving from here to Illinois maybe."

"Two thousand miles of shoreline!" she said, truly amazed, "That is incredible!"

"There are ninety-six canyons feeding into Lake Powell!" Bobby said enthusiastically.

"Boy, have you been doing your homework," she replied.

"I always do."

They drove for miles, got stopped by a Barney Fife-like deputy west of Bluff, Utah, and both had to educate him in no uncertain terms, and kept flying toward Page driving north of Lake Powell.

Several hours later, they checked into their motel in Page, Arizona, and Bo pointed out a large electrical facility with big transformers just outside town. She asked if that could be a target also.

Bobby said, "Just watch."

A short time later, they drove over a bridge that crossed the narrow, steep, and deep Glen Canyon just below the dam. Then, before taking the Wahweap Marina road, they pulled into the large parking lot and tourist center directly above the dam. Bobby pulled up to a cyclone fence, and they got out. The dam was massive and went down hundreds of feet. To their left the massive Lake Powell stretched out.

Bo said, "Look how large the dam is! And they have

barriers out there in the water, so you cannot get close to it with a boat. That was smart."

Bobby rattled the cyclone fence, saying, "This isn't."

She said, "What do you mean? Look how big and thick the dam is, and how far down. Guards would spot saboteurs as soon as they climbed over this fence. And how could anybody carry enough explosives to even make a small hole in this dam?"

Bobby laughed. "That is why what Boom said makes total sense. They can't blow it, but are going to burn the dam away." He walked back and forth along the fence, looking down, and was strangely silent. She knew he was calculating something, but to her the dam seemed very secure, and she could not understand how anyone could destroy it without getting caught in the process.

The ex-Green Beret went to the truck and opened her door. "Come on a minute, okay?"

She hopped in, and they drove back across the bridge, and on the other side, he switched seats with her, and she drove them back to the visitors center parking lot.

They got out again and looked at the dam and reservoir.

Answering her question from earlier in the day, he said, "Why destroy one little transformer facility like that, when you can take this puppy out more easily? Captain, you need to call DC on our sat phone and send out the cavalry. Have them call us, and we'll meet somewhere. Also, find out if the AQ's are here yet."

The Mexican-looking members of al Qaeda showed up at the empty warehouse outside Page. The large overhead door opened, and they pulled inside with a small U-Haul moving truck. Ramiro Maureo got out of the passenger side of one of the two black Dodge Ramcharger pickup trucks, and greeted the young men. They showed him the rental papers for the truck. The other jihadists got out of the two trucks and gathered around the steely-eyed leader.

Around them were ten blue plastic fifty-five-gallon drums already mixed together. In each drum was a fifty-fifty mixture of granulated aluminum metal powder and ferric oxide powder, granulated iron. There was also a five-gallon plastic bucket of potassium permanganate. One of the members held a jar of glycerine and a package of Fourth of July sparklers. The buckets were quickly loaded onto the truck and two wooden ramps were loaded into the back of one of the pickups. One man tied a strap through a support in the truck roof and suspended the five-gallon bucket of potassium permanganate, with the lid on, over one of the center barrels. When the time was right, the glycerine would be poured into the center of the bucket and the mixture would eventually ignite, serving as a backup igniter for the giant expedient thermite grenade they were creating. When they pulled into the parking lot of the visitors center, two would place the ramps in front of the cyclone fencing at the edge of the parking lot and overlooking the top of the dam, while two more would light the sparklers and drop them into the center of each barrel. This would ignite the thermite, so it would be burning hot already when the truck jumped off the ramps, crashed through the fence, and spilled its deadly fiery contents onto and down through the mighty dam. Just in case, the potassium permanganate and glycerine would be mixed before getting there and would already be starting to burn and ready to drop into the center barrel.

Imaad Udeen, leader of this cell, handed a large packet of money to Ramiro, and the Brazilian-born outlaw smiled, waved at everyone, and left. He'd gotten them across the border, helped them buy materials, and gotten them here. What they did now was not his concern. He was headed back to San Antonio.

Imaad looked at the assembled followers and said, "*Linatruk hunaa. Anaa jaa'I. Aturiid an ta'kula shay-an?*"

Everyone nodded enthusiastically. They all wanted to get out of there and go eat. They were all hungry, too, but more importantly, they wanted to eat, then return to the hotel, place their prayer mats facing Mecca, and deal with their potential individual journeys to Paradise that night.

Because the terrorists had purchased the powder from the chemical company in Salt Lake City, they were now followed by two cars at a distance.

Ramsey Keats was the FBI ASAC for this area, and three other agents were with him. Instead of reporting in, they wanted to follow and see where these men were going.

They kept their distance and switched trails according to FBI SOP (standard operating procedure).

The phony illegals could have created the iron oxide by burning steel wool in tubes, but that would have been too much work. They also could have ground aluminum bars, but again it was way too much work. Ramiro Maureo had told them not to buy all the chemicals from the same place, but they were impatient and did not listen. He did not really care, because he knew they would get caught. He just wanted to make money, lots of it, and gain power.

He knew they wanted to destroy the Glen Canyon Dam and create a major incident. But by the time it happened, he would be in San Antonio reporting about his latest success.

Ramsey Keats got a call from Washington wanting to know if they had the terrorists in town and under surveillance. Reluctantly, he explained that they were all sitting in a Denny's eating, while he and another car with two agents were parked in sight of the Denny's. At this point, he got his rear end chewed up one side and back down the other and was given Bobby's sat phone number, as well as his cell number and Bo's, and told to contact him immediately and cooperate fully.

Ramsey called Bobby on the sat phone, introduced himself, and briefed him on the situation.

Bobby said, "I need you to stay on top of them, but do you have any locals you can trust?"

Ramsey said, "There are three Navajo Tribal Police I have worked with and respect. One is white, married to a Navajo and totally gung ho. The other two are Navajo and just solid cops. There is a very outstanding Arizona Department of Public Safety trooper."

Bobby said, "Huh?"

And the agent laughed, explaining, "Sorry. That is what Arizona says. They don't say Highway Patrol. Anyway, he is a great cop that should not just be writing tickets and measuring skid marks. I like two of the locals here, too."

Bobby said, "I'm in the Wal-Mart parking lot right now, meeting some people, and then we will be in the rocks up above and directly across from Glen Canyon Dam Visitors Center parking lot. I need your other guys to come out there to meet me and set up a stakeout. They will hit tonight."

"How do you know that?"

Bobby said, "Hot intel."

He went on. "You know the area. I'll let you take charge of setting up blocking forces on the road outside the parking lot, and staging the other men where they will not be spotted but can move in ASAP. These guys will move fast, and we need to move faster. You need to have a full fire crew and trucks standing by and ready."

"Fire trucks?" Ramsey asked.

Bobby said, "No time to explain. When you can, call me and all the others with vehicle descriptions and license numbers. Ramsey, one last thing."

"What's that?" the fed asked.

"Tell everybody that these guys are dressed like Mexicans, but are of the same mindset as those who attacked us on 9/11," Bobby said, "They will let themselves be killed to take out any of us. And if you are cuffing them, any of them can be wearing suicide belts. They are jihadists."

Ramsey felt a chill and said, "Thanks, I lost a first cousin in Tower One. All they have to do is blink."

After they hung up, Bobby jumped out of his car and joined Bo at the back of a blue van at the edge of the

Wal-Mart parking lot on South Lake Powell Boulevard. Between Target and Wal-Mart, Bobby and Bo had bought themselves clothing, toiletries, and even small suitcases. Now, they were meeting with two senior NCOs and one officer from the 19th Special Forces Group National Guard unit. They picked out weapons and loaded them and ammunition into their rental car. The National Guard personnel had received orders from DA (Department of the Army) to give Bobby and Bo any weapons or assistance they wanted.

The master sergeant set two boxes of ammo in the back of the SUV and said, "Damn, sir. You starting a war?"

Before Bobby could answer, Bo did. "We sure hope so, Top."

He chuckled and looked at Bobby, saying, "Didn't know they started lettin' women into SF, Major."

Bo felt complimented again.

Bobby said, "If they did, Captain Devore would be the first one in line."

Now Bo was beaming.

When the van was loaded, all shook hands, and Bo signed for all the weapons, ammo, and equipment they got. Two customers driving into Wal-Mart's parking lot gave each other funny looks when they saw three guys in civilian clothes salute a man and woman in civvies, and the two return the salutes, then all get in their cars.

The husband said, "Probably VFW guys or somethin'."

Bobby and Bo immediately drove to their hotel, and both took quick showers and put on the black T-shirts and black jeans they'd bought at Wal-Mart. The army cops got adjoining rooms and opened the door between them. Bobby loaded weapons and set up their tactical vests, while Bo made them sandwiches from the groceries they bought. She also tossed him snack bars and small Gatorades to put in pockets of the vests.

Bobby called Ramsey, and was told the terrorists had left the restaurant and all gone to their hotel.

Bobby got off the phone and gave Bo a report. Then he called Washington and told them.

General Perry had come into the CP, and spoke to Bobby. "Bobby, you were SF. Whatever you do, they cannot destroy that dam."

Bobby said, "Roger that, sir. We have it covered."

"Why did they go back to their hotel?" Bo wondered aloud.

"Same thing we are doing," Bobby offered. "Getting prepared."

Bobby and Bo took off for the dam.

The other cops were there at the parking lot of the visitors center, and Bobby and Bo got out and introduced themselves.

Bobby said, "We will be up on those rocks right across from the visitors center. If I can get help from a couple of you, I need to move our equipment up there and then have one of you take our car with you and hide it."

The highway patrol trooper started chuckling when he unloaded a really, really big gun.

He said, "Barrett .50-caliber rifle?"

Bobby said, "Yes, sir. You guys and the FBI are going to try arresting and cuffing these guys, but I am making sure they do not run their truck through that fence and onto the dam, in case they try, which they will."

They all grabbed gear and climbed up into the rocks, with Bobby selecting a spot a little to the left, so he could get an angle on a driver trying to crash through the fence.

The terrorists had all prayed and checked out of the hotel, Ramsey reported, and were loading their vehicles.

Bobby said, "The bad guys are getting ready to make their move. Listen, we have to obey the laws as far as first attempting arrest, but I am telling you, these guys will fight to the death, and we have to watch for suicide vests."

One of the Navajo Tribal Police officers said, "If it's okay, I am going to stay and hide behind the visitors center, so I can get here quicker."

Bobby said, "It would be better if you had a partner to cover your back."

The white Navajo tribal cop said, "I'll stay with you, Bro."

The third said he would man a cruiser for them and would pull in when they were ready for the bust.

Everyone shook hands, they all wished each other luck, and dispersed. One of the cops drove Bobby and Bo's rental. The two C.I.D. officers went up into the rocks, and they equipped themselves. Bobby wedged the bipod legs of the Barrett under rocks and sighted through the scope.

The U.S. Army has adopted the M82A1, the Barrett fifty-caliber, as their special-purpose long-range sniper rifle. The official designation for the rifle is XM107 Long Range Sniper Rifle. It has a maximum effective range of 1500 meters or 1640 yards. Bobby could shoot pop cans with it from over a mile, so hitting a terrorist from their position, a couple hundred yards max, would not be a problem. Bobby's weapon had a ten-round box magazine and weighed thirty-two pounds. But as far as portability goes, it was way too heavy for most snipers.

Bo also had an M24 Sniper's Weapon System (SWS), the U.S. Army's bolt-action sniper rifle similar to the U.S. Marine Corps C M40A1 sniper rifle. The M24 uses the Remington 700 action, although the receiver is a long-action made for adaptation to take the .300 Winchester Magnum round. The stock was made of a composite of Kevlar, graphite, and fiberglass, and had an aluminum bedding block and adjustable butt plate.

It was set up to fire 7.62 × 51-millimeter NATO ammunition, adaptable to .308-caliber Winchester with a five-round built-in magazine. Bo was using a 10x42 Leupold Ultra M3A telescope sight with Mil-Dots. With this weapon she could fire with accuracy all the way out to 875 yards.

Many in the know consider the M24SWS the world's very best sniper weapon. It didn't have the power of Bobby's, but it certainly had the portability and weight that made it more feasible to carry.

Bobby and Bo had extra magazines for their Glock 17s,

and both carried M4 rifles as well, to grab and run to the vehicles with when the arrests went down or if they had to give chase. They both got Gatorades out, and they started eating their sandwiches. As soon as they finished eating, Bobby's sat phone rang. It was Ramsey. The terrorists had gone to the storage facility and gotten their other vehicles and were now on their way. He gave the license numbers and descriptions and told Bobby he would inform the others. He and the other FBI vehicle were leapfrogging, so they would not be noticed, and the bogies were getting close to the Glen Canyon Dam.

Bobby and Bo's plan was to let the terrorists make the parking lot and actually start the operation, so a good case could be built to nail them for terrorist activities. To that end, Bo also had a digital video camera set up on a sandbag on a rock to catch the whole scene. When the suspects' vehicles first appeared, Bo would simply turn it on. She just had to place it far enough away from the Barrett that the concussion from the muzzle blast would not knock it out of focus or off target.

Bobby and Bo took notice when the first black pickup pulled into the visitors center parking lot.

Both of them looked through the lens of the big sniper rifle and the standard one, and eased the safeties off. Two men jumped from one pickup and ran to the rear of the truck, pulling out two handmade ramps. They held a length of yellow nylon rope between the two ramps, spacing them, and set them up three feet from the cyclone fence bordering the parking lot.

Two more jumped out of the other truck and opened the sliding back door of the rental truck. They immediately pulled out sparklers and started placing them in the barrels. One was going to light them. Bobby aimed, not at them, but at an angle that would send the bullet into the driver's compartment of the truck. By preagreement, Bo aimed at them.

The officers, on a radio signal from Ramsey, converged, flying into the parking lot, sirens blaring, lights flashing.

The two Navajo tribal officers ran out from behind the visitors center, one on each side.

The one in the cruiser had his cruiser's loudspeaker on and said, "You are all under arrest. Lay facedown on the ground, hands spread—"

Rat-a-rat-a-rat-a-rat-a-rat-a!!!!!! Brackkkkkkkkkkkkkkk kkk! Boom! Boom! Boom!

Imaad Udeen emerged from one truck and started screaming directions in Arabic, and Bobby switched the sights to him, but immediately aimed back at the truck. He was dying to shoot the leader, but knew that he had to eliminate the threat of the truck going through that fence. He saw a puff of smoke as the driver put it into gear. Bobby fired one shot and the shot slammed through the truck, the driver's torso, the dashboard, the firewall, the upper manifold, radiator, and grille, and across Lake Powell, where the round buried itself in a cliff face. The truck, dead driver slumped over the wheel, started rolling forward, and Bobby again switched to the right front tire, shot it out, while Bo shot out the right rear and left rear, and finally Bobby slammed two quick rounds into the engine block from behind. The truck died before it hit the ramp.

Suddenly, Bobby realized there were muzzle flashes from automatic weapons pointed at him. Cracking sounds whizzed past his ears, and Bo's; then they both heard many whump, whump, whump sounds. Bobby's left leg stuck out to the left and something slammed into that sending him forward onto his face. Bo immediately jumped up and with bullets kicking up rock ricochets all around her, she fired, and a shooter with an Uzi submachine gun collapsed, his head a bloody mass. The one next to him, with a folding-stock AK-47, fell backward, blood and brain matter exploding through the back of his head. The others ran for cover, but the FBI and other cops chewed them up.

Bobby saw his bloody leg and ignored the pain. He looked for the leader again, who was running toward the man with the sparklers, who Bo had turned into a martyr. Bobby fired and blew the man's left leg off.

Bobby yelled, "Tourniquet him and keep him alive! We need intel!"

Bo said, "Bobby, bandage your leg, now!"

It was not a request, and Bobby complied. He pulled out his army pressure bandage and applied it right away.

Bo jumped up, saying, "Can you hang?"

Bobby yelled, "Go!"

Bo had grabbed her M4 and ran down to the site, while Bobby fought to stay alert. He now grabbed the video camera and focused on the scene, doing close-ups and pullouts as the officers converged. The white Navajo tribal police officer was on the ground unmoving, and Ramsey's partner had a crease along the bicep. Their vehicles were shot to doll rags. Distant sirens could be heard, and a helicopter was approaching.

Suddenly, a terrorist appeared, jumping out the back door of the truck, and ran toward the officers.

Bobby could even hear him yelling "Allah Akbar."

He looked through the Barrett and placed the dot center-mass and fired. The man's chest was torn out through his back and his body flung backward against the truck. He slumped forward onto the blacktop and his blood made a giant red O on the side of the truck. Bobby grabbed the video and focused and zoomed in on the big red O and then the body.

Bo turned and waved at Bobby, and all the others followed suit. The legs went out from under one of the cops, as he sat down in place cross-legged. Looking through the scope, Bobby saw that Bo had blood along her left hip. She had been shot.

Dead terrorists littered the parking lot of the Glen Canyon Dam's visitors center.

Bobby stood and limped down to the scene using Bo's weapon as a crutch. He carried an army pressure bandage in his hand. He immediately grabbed Bo and yanked out his Gerber knife and cut down through her jeans along her hip. Adrenaline winding down, she screamed in pain as Bobby placed the bandage on her hip. The bullet had torn along the hip and apparently chipped or severely bruised her hip bone.

Within minutes, there were cruisers flying into the lot. Bobby and Bo lay back against Ramsey's car side by side. Bobby pulled out his sat phone and called DC. He asked for General Perry. The white Navajo cop sat up suddenly and grabbed his chest. One of the FBI agents stripped his shirt off and they found three bullets in his Kevlar vest.

"Sir," Bobby said, "Bo and I are alive and the dam is safe. Yes, sir. Gotta do some mopping and scrubbing. Thank you, sir. I will pass it on. Wilco. Thank you, sir. Bye."

Bobby smiled at Bo and said, "He's a happy camper." Then he passed out.

Bo looked at Bobby and her eyes rolled up, and she fainted.

Ramsey took over and directed an ambulance and EMTs to the pair. Ramsey was called by Washington, and was told Bo and Bobby were to be taken to Bliss Army Health Center at Fort Huachuca, Arizona.

Bobby was being treated, and called Ramsey over.

"I would suggest that we keep it quiet that Captain Devore and I are involved," he said. "There are plenty of Americans who would get very concerned about soldiers shooting people on American soil."

Ramsey said, "We are sending you to Fort Huachuca. I have a Flight For Life on the way."

Bo was on the gurney next to Bobby's.

Ramsey looked at her saying, "Captain, before you two came. I guess I was a little arrogant and thought, two army cops, big deal. I'll tell you what. I would rather have you with me kicking in doors than any man I have ever worked with."

A tear forming in the corner of her eye, Bo shook hands

and smiled softly, saying, "Thanks, Agent. I enjoyed working with you, too."

Bobby had a flare-up of jealousy and tried to catch himself. What is wrong with me? he thought. He wanted a drink more than anything right now.

8

BLISS TO BLISS

Minutes later, they were airborne in a renovated Bell UH-1B Flight For Life helicopter, and both awakened mid-morning at Bliss Health Center, along with their legless enemy, who was barely clinging to life.

Each of them met with a major from Walter Reed in Washington, DC. He had flown in immediately on an air force jet, and was a surgeon who specialized in bullet wounds and had served several tours in Iraq and Afghanistan. He had brought his surgical team with him.

It was reported in all the press that a combined drug task force led by the FBI had a vicious shoot-out with illegal Mexican nationals who had trucks loaded with chemicals to set up a giant methamphetamine lab. The media reported that the Mexican drug dealers resisted arrest and fired at the law enforcement officers with automatic weapons, and were all killed.

MPs from Fort Huachuca were assigned to provide heavy guard around Imaad Udeen. A team of surgeons were working on him to save his life after the amputation of his leg by Bobby's shot.

Intelligence personnel from the DC-area agencies were already starting to arrive and hover like vultures waiting to catch his first words, hoping to get him to open up while he was on drugs, or to at least hear whatever he had to say before he died.

Bobby and Bo went into the operating room that afternoon, and both came out without complications.

Imaad Udeen also survived his surgery, and was stable when they moved him from post-op into the ICU. He was being treated like he was the President of the United States the way people hovered around him and checked on him left and right.

Bobby and Bo were sitting together in the hospital commandant's office reading e-mails, and Bobby looked over, saying, "I don't know about you, but I am in pain. But they transfused me to make up for all the blood I lost from the nicked artery. I don't have any broken bones, so I just have to put up with some pain."

Bo said, "I just had that chip out of my hip bone, but my wound is mainly soft flesh. Pain and soreness, too."

Bobby said, "So you ready to get back to work?"

Bo said, "Absolutely, partner. I have to check on the items I signed for from the 19th Group before we do anything."

Bobby said, "I already checked this morning. Ramsey secured everything, and it has already been returned to the 19th. He also got our video camera, and tapes have already been made from it and passed to each agency in the task force."

Bo said, "Ramsey turned out to be a good guy after all. He is kind of cute, too."

Bobby felt a little flame of jealousy again, and said, "He's not your type."

Bo said, "What do you mean, not my type?"

Bobby could not believe he'd blurted that out, and now he was stuck explaining himself.

"He just did not seem like he would be strong enough for you," Bobby replied.

Bo said, "Now, what in the world do you mean by that, Bobby?"

She thought to herself, "Is he jealous?"

Bobby said, "Look, we have terrorists to fight. Let's get the hell out of here."

Bo said, "Sounds good to me. How? The major is not going to release us."

Bobby called a nurse over and asked if the surgeon was around anywhere.

Five minutes later, he showed up.

"Are our wounds life-threatening now, Doc?" Bobby asked.

The surgeon replied, "Probably not, just painful, but you both are healing very well. Why?"

Bobby said, "Doc, we are involved in a top secret mission involving our national security, and it is much more important than us being comfortable. We have to leave and get back to work ASAP."

The major looked at his notes and then out the window.

He said, "Major, Captain, you both will be in pain, and the more you do, the more pain you will be in. You need to let your injuries heal, but I will clear you for discharge. Where are you headed now?"

Bobby said, "Fort Bliss."

The doctor said, "Is that in El Paso, Texas?"

Bo said, "Yes, it is."

The surgeon looked at his Blackberry and punched something in.

He said, "If you need anything, you go to Beaumont Medical Center at Fort Bliss. They have a pharmacy, too, so you can get your medication refilled there. Good luck. You can leave within the hour."

They all shook hands.

Bobby called Task Force headquarters and then ten minutes later, got a call from General Perry.

"What is this crap I hear about you and Captain Devore checking out of the hospital, Major?" the general said.

Bobby replied, "Sir, is this a secure line?"

"Roger, it is scrambled."

Bobby went on. "We have nukes to find, and we cannot find them sitting on our asses in hospital PJs, General."

"Good point, son," the general replied. "You are headed to Fort Bliss?"

"Roger, sir," Bobby came back. "Needed a military jumping off and resupply point."

The old man said, "When will you arrive?"

Bobby said, "Haven't left the hospital yet, sir, but we'll take the next flight we can get."

General Perry said, "Well, I'm in my car now with the SECDEF and FBI director. Several of the task force heads are coming, too. I already called the CG of Fort Bliss and the command conference room is being set up for us. We're flying into Lackland outside San Antonio and are being brought in by Blackhawk from there."

"We'll get there ASAP, sir," Bobby said.

General Perry said, "Well, we can take care of you there, too, Major. There is a 305th Rescue Squadron, an Air Force Reserve unit, and an HH-60G 'Pavehawk' search and rescue helicopter is on its way from Davis-Monthan Air Force Base in Tucson. They'll fly you back to Davis-Monthan, and a C130 Talon is waiting there to fly you to the El Paso International Airport. A Blackhawk from Biggs Army Air Base at Fort Bliss will pick you up and bring you right to the Charley Gulf's (CG, Commanding General) helipad. The Talon will wait for you and be secured at El Paso."

"General," Bobby said, "why can't I borrow some stars to wear sometime so I can get things done like this?"

"God help us!" the army chief of staff said. "I'll see you later today."

Bobby related all the information to Bo. They packed and found out where the helipad was, and went there to wait. In a half hour, they were on board an air force rescue helicopter heading toward the Davis-Monthan Air Force Base, home of the 355th Wing of the air force. As they approached, Bobby and Bo noticed a lot of flight activity by A-10 Warthogs.

He pointed the strange-looking jets out to Bo, and said, "Now there is a great close-in fighter jet. Those puppies saved my bacon more than once."

Bobby remembered one operation where his USAF-SOC Air Force Special Operations Controller painted a target for Bobby and his team with his laser designator. It was a sand-colored bunker filled with bad guys in the middle of the desert. Bobby and his men were getting ready to enter the bunker, which they thought was abandoned, when all of a sudden one of his team members took a burst from an SKS and the team ended up against the back of the building where there were no windows. They could not throw grenades in the shooting portals, and could go nowhere, because any movement would bring fire from one of the firing ports in the building. They figured the bogies inside had been asleep until they were ready to enter the building, then awakened and started firing.

The AFSOC leaned out carefully and painted the front firing port on the side of the building and learned he had a pair of A-10s on station. He asked them to wait for Bobby's team to boogey out and then bring in their ordnance.

As Bobby tossed smoke grenades all around the bunker, the controller told his Warthogs that the team was scampering away from the building. When Bobby saw the first A-10 coming in from overhead, he thought the pilot figured his team were the bad guys, but in actuality, when they were far enough out that the concussion of the five-hundred-pound bomb would not hurt them, the jet put the bomb right through the front firing port. Many bad guys went to see Allah that day.

At Davis-Monthan, they were picked up in a limo by a really friendly brigadier general in a flight suit, who Bobby knew just had to be a tough old fighter pilot. He took them directly to a waiting MC-130E "Combat Talon I" Hercules, the army's workhorse for so many years. The MC-130E "Combat Talon I" is a specially equipped "Herk." The E-model has more instruments designed for covert operations. It can fly infiltration/exfiltration missions or can airdrop or air-land personnel and equipment in hostile territory. They also aerial-refuel special operations helicopters, and usually fly missions at night-with aircrews using night-vision goggles. The "Combat Talon I" also has an electronic countermeasures suite and terrain-following radar that enables it to fly extremely low, counter enemy radar, and penetrate deep into hostile territory.

Bobby and Bo ran up the ramp in the back, chocks were removed, and they started taxiing immediately before the ramp was even shut. The C130 Combat Talon I is powered by four Rolls-Royce AE 2100D3 turboprop engines generating 4,700 horsepower, and additionally has two jet take-off assists on the side of the fuselage. Within minutes, they were airborne with those jets firing and the big plane rising quickly into the Southwestern U.S. skies.

After they leveled out, Bobby and Bo went forward to meet the flight crew, and he pointed out two A10s flying escort.

Bo said, "What are they accompanying us for?"

The copilot said, "We were told two VIPs would be on board, ma'am, so I guess that is you. You two related to a senator or something?"

Bobby grinned, saying, "Nope, we are the government contractors who supply all the liquor for air force officers clubs."

The pilot was wearing earphones, so the copilot relayed Bobby's words. The pilot started laughing.

The pilot removed his earphones and said, "Very funny, Major. I read about both of you and saw your pictures in *Newsweek* and in *The Army Times*. I am very honored to be carrying you both. I would like to get a picture with you both for my son when we land. I also want you with me if a terrorist ever wants to blow up my craft."

Bo said, "Thank you. We are deeply honored."

In less than an hour's time, they were on the Blackhawk helicopter headed toward Fort Bliss, taking off on that C-130 climbing to altitude, then almost gliding in—if you can call four-hundred-plus miles per hour gliding. Minutes later, they set down on the commanding general's helipad at Fort Bliss.

Two MPs met them and escorted them into the three-story Post Headquarters, down two hallways, and into a double-doored conference room with armed MPs posted at the ends of the hallways and outside the doors. They came to attention as the pair approached, and came to port arms saluting them as they entered the conference room.

As Bobby and Bo walked very gingerly through the doorway, General Perry was already standing, and walked right over smiling and stuck out his hand. Both snapped to attention and a jolt of pain shot through Bo's hip and up her spine. Her leg collapsed and she started to fall sideways, but a man in a blue suit jumped from the table and caught her. She looked up and smiled. It was FBI Agent Ramsey Keats. He smiled at her and looked into her eyes. Bobby felt the flames again.

Bo came back to attention, and General Perry said, "As you were. Relax, Captain, sit down."

Bo said, "I apologize, sir. No disrespect intended."

"Bullshit!" Perry laughed, "Damn women heroes showing up all of us men. She is probably carrying twenty pounds of shrapnel in her hip."

Bobby Samuels shook hands with the general, saying, "No, sir. Captain Devore is a drama queen wanting to get attention from Agent Keats."

"Doggone, Bobby," he thought, "why don't you just rent them a hotel room, idiot?"

Then he started wondering why he was worrying about who his partner dated. None of his business.

The secretary of defense got up and walked over and shook hands with Bo and Bobby, who both jumped to attention again. This time Bo was okay, but Bobby had every muscle tense ready to grab her first if she fell.

The general took over and explained they had to make plans for the next concept of the operation. First, he explained to Bobby and Bo that both could have flown into

Biggs Army Airfield, next to El Paso International Airport, and it could even accommodate a B-52 bomber, but he felt that of all military bases in the U.S., Fort Bliss was probably the most closely monitored by enemies lurking south of the border. He did not want to call too much attention to their arrival. Bobby and Bo would be leaving by the same C-130 Talon I, but it would pick them up and take off at night using night-vision equipment and absolutely no lights at Biggs.

The general asked the CG of Fort Bliss to summon an orthopedic surgeon, and wanted Bo and Bobby examined immediately. He explained they were going to make a night parachute jump into Mexico, but Bo falling over really bothered him. Bobby's adrenaline kicked in and he was excited, readying himself mentally for battle. To that end, he excused himself to go to the latrine. Whenever Bobby knew he was going to go into combat, make an important jump, rappel, or do anything dangerous, he would have to void his bowels and bladder right away.

One night at Fort Bragg at the 82nd Airborne Officers Club Annex, he shared drinks with a major who was an army psychiatrist, who spoke with him about it at length. He said it is normal and comes from the warrior instinct for Type-A personalities. He said that Bobby was psychologically readying himself for battle, lightening the load so to speak. Emotionally, the shrink explained, he was shedding himself of all excess poundage that would encumber him during battle, and added that this phenomena even manifests itself before giving a speech or chairing a business meeting.

Bo wondered why Ramsey was there, and that was explained soon enough when the secretary of defense said, "Ladies and gentlemen, we have assets on the ground in Mexico who are keeping us apprised about any attempts to smuggle those nukes into the U.S. When we do get a hot lead, FBI SAC (Special Agent in Charge) Ramsey Keats here will be infiltrating Mexico by parachute along with

Major Samuels and Captain Devore at night to meet with our assets on the ground. Agent Keats's mother was from Mexico, and he grew up with Spanish spoken all the time in his household, so he will also serve as their interpreter."

Bobby thought to himself, "I want a drink."

Bo gave Ramsey a flirtatious look. He smiled in kind.

Bobby got mad at himself again for his thoughts, and then he figured he was just being protective about his partner.

Then he thought, "Man, we are making a night combat jump, and I have to baby-sit a civilian."

Just then, the SECDEF said, "Agent Keats already knows how to parachute, as he was a Navy SEAL and served in Iraq."

Without realizing it, Bobby moaned out loud, and everybody looked at him. To cover up, he immediately grabbed his wounded leg and held it a second.

General Perry said to his aide, "I want Major Samuels checked thoroughly, too. These two fine soldiers were just wounded and should really be in hospital beds, but they are both too damned stubborn, and they realize the threat to our nation and the world."

The secretary of defense went on. "One of the most porous places in the United States for illegal border crossings is right here at El Paso, Texas, and Ciudad Juarez, Mexico. We have Fort Bliss, of course, White Sands, and I can go on and on. Besides our reports about the backpack nukes, we have to also stand watch for this base, the army's headquarters for air missile defense, and White Sands. Additionally, we have identified NORAD in Cheyenne Mountain, north of here in Colorado, as well as Northcom; and in addition, for the psychological effect, the U.S. Air Force Academy, also at Colorado Springs. We have reports of serious activity south of us, folks, and we are prepared to move ASAP, but we think it will be right here."

The meeting went on, and it was learned that housing and BOQ (bachelor officer quarters) were hard to come by at Fort Bliss. Many people were billeted at the Inn at Fort Bliss, but it was filled up, so Bo, Bobby, and Ramsey would be given rooms at an Econo-Lodge that was just one mile from Fort Bliss and one mile from the El Paso International Airport. Bo hoped it had a pool, and it did, outside.

For the next weeks, the three of them and others would spend time at the hotel, tanning around the pool, or hanging out at the main Fort Bliss O-Club.

9

NASTY PEOPLE

The Hotel Lucerno is a five-star hotel located in the center of the city of Ciudad Juarez, Mexico on Triunfa de la Republica. Ramiro Maureo and Paola Mirari were thoroughly enjoying the generous breakfast buffet in the highly touted hotel restaurant. What Ramiro liked most was that the restaurant opened up toward the large foyer area and his seat gave him a commanding view of who was coming and going. What he also liked was the fact that al Qaeda had been paying for his stays at hotels like this and meals at restaurants all over town. Tariq Ubaadah and Abdul Qudoos did not like Brazilian henchmen, but they knew that buying him and his whore hotel rooms and meals all over town made him feel powerful, so it was a profitable investment.

Tariq was the al Qaeda moneyman who flew in from Iran, and Abdul, a Saudi by birth, spoke fluent Spanish and had lived as a cell member for years in Ciudad Juarez. By agreement, Abdul was the spokesman for the two. They, as well as other AQ bodyguards around the room at the small red tables with gray chairs, were dressed as Mexican businessmen.

Ramiro was dressed the way he always was, as a gang-banger leader with loose gold jewelry hanging all over his body. His "woman" Paola was dressed simply like a cheap whore, but she did possess the physical beauty of an expensive call girl.

Although Brazilians speak Portuguese, Ramiro and Paola both could speak fluent Spanish, so that was how all conversations were handled. Besides Abdul, all the bodyguards in the room had taken Spanish classes and also learned the customs of the country. Each had also learned some English, too.

Tariq would whisper in Arabic to Abdul, who would translate.

He said, "Señor Ramiro, Tariq Ubaadah has brought with him a large amount of money today, which is a down payment for what we need."

Tariq handed an envelope to Ramiro, and he nodded and opened it up. It contained $100,000 in large bills. He smiled and handed it to Paola.

"What do you want from O Grupo Grande?" Ramiro asked.

"We want you to take us across the border," Abdul translated, "And we will have two very important packages. We must get those packages across the border at all costs. If the U.S. Border Patrol catches you, they must be killed, but you cannot get caught."

"I want to know what I am transporting, *amigo*," Ramiro answered, "Is it drugs?"

Abdul said, "No."

"How much will we get paid after we get them across the border?"

Abdul responded, "An additional two hundred thousand American dollars."

Ramiro said, "What will be in the packages?"

Tariq and Abdul whispered back and forth for a few seconds. Then Abdul again translated while Tariq spoke. "We are smuggling two Soviet backpack nuclear bombs."

"*Hijo de mil putas* (son of a thousand bitches)!" Paola Mirari said.

Everyone looked at her, and Ramiro shook his head chuckling.

Tariq angrily said something to Abdul, who translated. "Why do you not beat her? Do you allow your woman to speak out like that?"

Ramiro did not like this. He stood up, his seven feet of muscle towering over the al Qaeda terrorists. Then he relaxed and sat down.

"Our society is different," he said.

Tariq was angry and stood up, and Abdul followed suit, as did their AQ bodyguards. They started for the door.

Ramiro stood again and said, "What are you doing?"

Abdul translated Tariq's dismissive words. "We will pay our money to the Mara Salvatrucha-13 (the MS-13 gang)."

They walked out the door, and Tariq tossed a wad of hundred-dollar bills at the maitre d' hotel.

Ramiro said nothing, but headed toward the door as his gang members followed at his nod. It was obvious he was not only upset, but deep in thought.

A bus boy who had dark complexion indicating he might have *indio* ancestry came over to the round red table where the killers had talked. He started bussing dishes and knocked a spoon on the floor. Looking around carefully, he reached up under the table with his other hand and pulled a taped hidden microphone from under the table, finished clearing the table, and carried the dishes to the kitchen.

Five minutes later, Ramiro and his gang-member bodyguards caught up with the group who had walked down the street together. At the same time, an American tourist snapped shots on the street, while his wife simply stood by the rented car and applied makeup, balancing a mirror on her purse. As the groups walked down the street, she turned her mirror at different angles to apply her makeup, the hidden digital camera in the mirror frame catching all of their moves.

Ramiro said, "Señor Abdul, please tell Señor Tariq to give me one minute privately to speak in that alley."

Abdul spoke in a whisper and Tariq stared, then headed toward the alley with his group following. Paola was holding Ramiro's hand. Both groups walked deep into the alley and stopped. Here, Tariq spoke in a normal tone of voice.

Abdul translated, "What do you wish to say, Señor?"

Ramiro, still holding Paola's hand, said, "It is very simple. We want to do business with your organization. Let me prove it."

He pulled Paola around slowly and smiled at her. Letting go of her hand, he raised his left hand up and caressed her cheek, and she smiled at him. Then suddenly, his face twisted, and he grabbed her throat. She tried to scream, but his powerful grip was just too much. He lowered his elbow and incredibly lifted her feet up off the floor, reached into his pocket with his right hand, and pulled out a large switchblade knife, opened it while she struggled and kicked, and plunged it into her torso over and over, until she went totally limp. He dropped her on the ground, then bent over and slit her throat from ear to ear. Ramiro tore her blouse off and wiped his hands and knife blade off on the clean part of the back of the blouse.

He turned and smiled at Tariq and Abdul, saying, "Okay, *amigos,* let's go somewhere quiet and talk business. *Sí?*"

Tariq laughed and nodded, but looked over at Abdul saying, *"Hayyaa binaa! Li-natruk hunaa!"*

Abdul responded, looking down at Paola's very bloody body, saying, *"Laqad ghaadarat haadha i-makaan."*

Tariq started laughing and everyone started to leave the alley together, but now Ramiro was angry and stepped in front of them, saying in Spanish, "What is funny? What did you two say?"

Abdul said, "Oh, Tariq said to me, 'Let's go! Let's get out of here,' and I said to him, 'She has already left here.' He thought that was very funny, Señor. Do not worry. I think you have convinced him."

They went down the street to a bar and went in.

Speaking in Arabic, Tariq said to Abdul, "The beloved and venerable Muhammad does not allow us to drink alcohol, but we are in the land of the infidels and must blend in. I will a have a drink or two and you should, too."

Abdul was very glad Tariq said that, because he used the same lame excuse many times when he traveled. They allowed the bodyguards to drink, too, and soon the gang-bangers and the terrorists were all getting drunk together.

They agreed to meet the next day at Tariq's current hotel, Hotel Villa Manport at Hermanos Escobar and Calle Panama, and from there they would walk to one of the many fine restaurants nearby such as the El Herradero Steak House, Villa del Mar, or the Mariscos D'Mazatlan.

While Ramiro Maureo loved staying at luxury hotels and getting room service and nice restaurant meals, such as staying at the five-star Hotel Lucerno, Tariq and Abdul, on the other hand, had been well schooled by al Qaeda and preferred the nice but much more modest Hotel Villa Manport, where the two of them and their bodyguards would be less noticeable. Tariq always checked the whole group in with a phony Mexican business name, usually a large national business with a known name.

Ramiro hired two prostitutes to accompany him to his hotel, so he could get the death of the beautiful Paola out of his mind, but he really did not care. Her death was the cost of doing business.

They met the next day for late breakfast at Mariscos D'Mazatlan, very noted for its seafood, which is why Tariq asked to meet there. He wanted some.

They made plans for Ramiro personally, and his other gangsters who would act as *coyotes,* to meet outside Cuidad Juarez at a spot not too far from the Rio Grande. The terrorists would bring their backpack nukes, and Ramiro would have his plan worked out for how they would smuggle them into the United States. Most of the al Qaeda members taking part in the operation had gone to college at various universities in the USA already.

The rest of Tariq's men were on their way from Mexico City riding in a large ambulance, which had been gotten for a large bribe. They had two very large iceboxes labeled with cautionary labels in English and Spanish, reading: DO NOT OPEN—HUMAN ORGANS—KEEP ICED. Each box contained a Soviet RA-115 backpack nuclear bomb.

In 1999, terrorism expert and author Yossef Bodanksy, director of the Congressional Task Force on Terrorism and Unconventional Warfare, and the man who first warned the world about Osama bin Laden, quoted a senior Arab intelligence official as saying, "Osama bin Laden has acquired tactical nuclear weapons from the Islamic republics of Central Asia established after the collapse of the Soviet Union."

According to Bodansky, "Bin Laden's emissaries paid the Chechens $30 million in cash and gave them two tons of Afghan heroin with a $600 million street value in exchange for nuclear weapons." This was done well before September 11, 2001. In his 1999 book, *Bin Laden, the Man Who Declared War on America,* Bodanksy wrote: "Evidence of the number of nuclear weapons purchased by the Chechens for bin Laden varies between 'a few' (Russian intelligence) to 'more than twenty' (conservative Arab intelligence services)."

Even Tariq did not know how many al Qaeda possessed, but he did know he had two of them and that the job before him and his men could get them all into Paradise forever.

In fact, he knew he would make Paradise detonating the two devices on American soil, because it was even addressed by the clergy.

In 2003, Saudi cleric Nazer bin Hamd al-Fahd wrote a fatwa entitled: "The Legal Status of Using Weapons of Mass Destruction Against Infidels."

Nazer bin Hamd's fatwa says, "Weapons of mass destruction will kill the infidels on whom they fall, regardless of whether they are fighters, women, or children. They will destroy and burn the land. The arguments for permissibility are many."

This gave Tariq great comfort. Like Osama bin Laden, he was an outcast from his own very wealthy Saudi Arabian family, and most of the activities of his adult life were

"I'll-show-you" actions, starting with his Penn State business degree and his MBA from Harvard.

The plan al Qaeda had laid out for this operation was even more complex than that on 9/11. They not only had to smuggle the two nuclear devices into the United States undetected, they had to take them both cross-country, get one into New York City and the other into Miami, and detonate them. But it was a little more complex than that. The bombs dropped from the Enola Gay on Nagasaki and Hiroshima were fifteen-kiloton nuclear bombs; and in Nagasaki a brick building, although a very well-built brick building, a little over two hundred yards from ground zero, essentially survived the atomic blast without being demolished, and a streetcar, which was just over a mile away from ground zero, also survived the blast.

Tariq Ubaadah had to emplace both bombs in both cities so they would create the most damage and also cause the most terror, which was always Osama bin Laden's concern. That was why his goal always was to detonate both bombs during daylight hours, simultaneously. He wanted to make sure the U.S. news media would replay the blasts and damage over and over.

The Soviet RA-115 backpack nuclear bombs only weighed just over fifty-seven pounds each, and could fit not in a backpack, but in a large suitcase, so they could be carried and hidden almost anywhere. But Tariq's other challenge was to put them where they could rain fire and fear on the U.S. populace.

With a nuclear bomb, over fifty percent of the damage done and lives lost is from the initial blast, and then over thirty-five percent is from the radiation wave, and then the rest from fallout and residual affects. Tariq and the other al Qaeda leaders had had a great many discussions on what to target. The blast from a one-ton backpack is considerably less than the fifteen kilotons that hit the Japanese cities in World War II, but the falloff with nuclear bombs is not really that great as the size decreases. The ground zero blast from a one-megaton nuke, which would be like one thousand backpack nukes, has only a seventy-percent increase over a two-hundred-kiloton nuke. Which is like comparing a hole in the ground seven to eight miles across with one four to five miles across.

An airburst nuclear bomb could spread radiation over a very large area, but would do significantly less blast damage, as most explosions blow up and out. So, to get the most out of the backpacks, it was determined to execute a ground burst detonation, but Osama bin Laden always favored the destruction of national monuments or symbols of America for the symbolism of their destruction, though many in the leadership wanted the practical destruction of strategic targets.

The attack on the World Trade Center was supposed to be a symbolic gesture of attacking America's free-enterprise system of capitalism, and the attack on the Pentagon was obvious. Flight 93 was intended to strike the White House, which would have made bin Laden ecstatic. He and none of the al Qaeda leadership had any idea that the World Trade Center towers would collapse from the intense heat. They had hoped for the deaths of hundreds, but when the buildings collapsed, they thought Allah was indeed blessing them.

Now al Qaeda was counting on two RA-115 backpack nuclear bombs to create more damage than Hiroshima and Nagasaki with one-fifteenth the blast power of each. To that end, and to satisfy the wish of Osama bin Laden, it was decided that Tariq Ubaadah would have to emplace one of the devices about halfway up the Empire State Building. Osama was in favor of blowing up the Statue of Liberty, but they had already tested the defenses, and the ground zero blast zone would have little effect on New York City proper, which would only get some radioactive fallout, and maybe some initial thermal blast that would be far less than the winds of a tornado.

They reasoned by bombing halfway up the Empire State Building, they would achieve bin Laden's goal of attacking a major American landmark, but as a practical result, they would destroy most of the building, sending pieces of brick, concrete, metal, desks, chairs, computers, and other items flying and falling as deadly pieces of shrapnel spread in all directions. Additionally, the upper half of the building would be gone and all the people within would die, and the radioactive fallout from the blast being raised high above the ground would spread over a large area, especially if prevailing winds were not blowing out toward the ocean. Had they blown the building lower, much of the shrapnel falling would not be deadly, but from the higher elevation, they reasoned, a falling coffeemaker could become a deadly weapon.

The initial planning was to detonate at Disneyland, but even though Nazer bin Hamd al-Fahd's and others' fatwas allowed the killing of women and children, the AQ leadership concluded it could bring disfavor from moderate Muslim nations. They did not care about non-Muslim nations, as anybody who was not Muslim was an infidel, an unbeliever, and some were simply to be used toward the end of achieving eventual Islamic world domination.

The metropolitan area of Miami had a population of 5,500,000 people, many celebrities lived there, and most importantly, the Miami metro area had a very large Jewish population, so most of the al Qaeda leadership saw it as a no-brainer over destroying Disneyland. Picking a target would be more difficult because Miami had no Empire State Building. It was simply famous for sun and sand and Cuban refugees, as far as the terrorists were concerned. Tariq himself was assigned the research for strategic bomb emplacement there, too. What he found was also a no-brainer to him.

The Four Seasons Hotel and Tower on Brickell Avenue in Miami had a height of exactly 788 feet, 9 inches, making the tower the tallest U.S. building south of Atlanta and tallest U.S. residential building south of New York City. So it was much more than the tallest building in Florida. It also had office space for lease, and hotel rooms, which would more easily facilitate unencumbered bomb emplacement. The building itself, if a room or office could be used halfway up, could serve the same purpose as the Empire State Building. The construction of the sixty-four-floor high-rise was a reinforced concrete structure incorporating core shear walls, post-tensioned slabs, and perimeter columns with spans between the columns that reached forty feet. It would work.

Tariq learned that the tower was supported by caissons six feet in diameter that ran 140 feet deep, which was about 40 feet down into the bedrock, so a ground zero at ground level would not be good, but the airburst effect halfway up could be ideal for their goals.

To make the planning even better, Tariq found that floors forty through seventy of the building housed residential units, ranging in size from 1,697 square feet to 6,603 square feet, while floors thirty through forty housed either hotel rooms or suites, which ranged in size from 600 square feet to 2,000 square feet, He also learned that the building also contained 184 condominiums and 84 condo/hotel units, 200,000 square feet of office space, and even had a 45,000-square-foot fitness and spa facility. When discussing the shrapnel effect with his murderous cohorts, Tariq happily reported that the building contained over twenty various types of finishes, including imported Italian marble, imported stones, and floor-to-ceiling glazed glass. He was very elated picturing shards of thick fancy glass flying through the air as deadly projectiles, as well as pieces of marble falling on the heads of aging Jews on the streets below.

To mock both the Hebraic and Christian religions, the code word with al Qaeda for "New York City" became "Sodom" and "Miami" would always be referred to as "Gomorrah," after the two famous cities of crime, lust, and sin in the Old Testament that are spoken about in many Bible verses, most notably Genesis 13:13, 18:20, 19:24, 29; Hosea 11:8; Deuteronomy 29:23, 32:32; Isaiah 1:10; Ezekiel 16:49; Matthew 11:23; 2 Peter 2:6; and Jude 7. They were two cities that were actually named afterward, with Sodom being the Hebrew word for "Burnt" and Gomorrah Hebrew for "Burning Heap." The word Sodom, in fact, because of the city's deviant sexual practices in the eyes of many, begat the modern words of "sodomy" and "sodomite."

Because it seemed like the emplacement of the back-pack would be easier in Miami than in New York City, where security measures had become so much more stringent since the World Trade Center attacks, it was decided that Abdul Qudoos would be the leader of that operation and Tariq, the overall U.S. leader of the operation, would emplace the New York City bomb.

The two men also had to decide how they would detonate the bombs. Would they become martyrs, or would they detonate the bombs by remote controls or timers? Using the excuse that they would have had the experience of smuggling bombs into the U.S. already and, in case something went wrong, they would be experienced operators, they decided against becoming martyrs. In actuality, it was the experience of Bobby, Bo, and most U.S. counterterrorism personnel that the mullahs never became suicide/homicide bombers, the al Qaeda leaders never became suicide/homicide bombers; only the young disenfranchised, usually uneducated men, and sometimes women, became suicide/homicide bombers.

10

ZIP ALONG DOTTED LINE

The cell phone call came in from Tariq's men in the ambulance. They arrived in Zaragosa, south of Ciudad Juarez, and were waiting for Tariq and Abdul to meet them. Miles and miles above, the cell phone intercept was picked up by the National Security Administration. Translators at NSA deciphered the call and determined that it was the bad guys. A message was sent to the Department of Homeland Security, and from there to the National Security Council, the Federal Bureau of Investigation, Central Intelligence Agency, Defense Intelligence Agency, Secret Service, the Immigration and Naturalization Service, Border Patrol, and several other offices. The Task Force immediately forwarded the information to General Perry and the secretary of defense.

Within fifteen minutes of receipt of the message, Bobby, Bo, and Ramsey were loading on the MC-130E Combat Talon I and had their parachutes on already. With lights out, it taxied down the long runway at Biggs Army Airfield and was skyborne. It circled out, flew west, and then south below Potrico, New Mexico, buzzing in at almost ground level under the Mexican radar screen. It made another ninety-degree turn to the east of Anarpa and headed on a southeast heading. The cargo ramp was lowered as the four-engined bird climbed in elevation, still flying lights out. Its FLIR (forward looking infrared) scanned the terrain one thousand feet below and out ahead for miles. Jump commands were given and the trio prepared for their ramp exit. They were not HALOing but instead were jumping static, and were finally given the green light and went off the ramp and into the night sky at one thousand feet elevation.

The MC1-1C parachutes of all three deployed. They checked their risers, suspension lines, and canopies, then released the quick-release on their equipment bags, which fell and dangled below them on fifteen-foot nylon tethers.

The night was still and the desert air was hot and very dry. All three turned so their faces were into the little wind there was, held their knees together, legs slightly bent, and sighted the far-off horizon. The breeze in their faces was three knots per hour, so they each landed going forward at five knots per hour, because of the open gores on the back of the canopy and eight-kph forward thrust. Each hit doing good PLFs (parachute landing falls), with the balls of their feet twisted to the right, and rolled forward, on the calf, thigh, butt, back muscles, and shoulder muscle, and rolled over coming up into a standing position, where they each collapsed their chutes and started S-rolling them over their arms.

They immediately grabbed their weapons, and Bobby answered a satellite phone call. He turned to the south and saw two quick flashes from a laser rifle sight, then a pause, then two more flashes.

Bobby said, "I see you, Come ahead. Our guns are down."

Three vehicles came forward with just parking lights on, then turned them off when they got to the three jumpers.

A tall Mexican male got out of the lead car and shook hands with all three, while one got out of the second and two from the third, and those three grabbed the chutes and reserves and put them in their car trunks inside aviator kit bags the three jumpers had carried, folded up, under their quick release plates.

"*Buenos noches!* Welcome to Mexico, *amigos,*" he said, "My name is Angel Valenzuela. I know who you all are. We must move fast. You weel ride weeth me."

They put on their tactical vests and assembled their weapons and equipment how they wanted, and Angel gave orders in Spanish and the three grabbed their equipment bags and tossed them in the cars, too.

The three got in the lead car, with Bobby and Bo in the back and Ramsey in the front, and were soon on an actual road driving to the east very fast.

Meanwhile, a general from the U.S. Air Force called Mexican Air Defense Command and apologized, saying they had a C130 pilot carrying a load of MREs (Meals Ready to Eat) for a National Guard unit on an FTX (Field Training Exercise), and it got out of position and accidentally wandered across the border near Juarez, and he would be court-martialed, and "we apologize profusely." This seemed to satisfy the Mexican government.

As they rode along toward a potential shoot-out with Muslim terrorists with nuclear bombs, Bobby thought about the denial Americans were in and how many wanted to appease the jihadists thinking they might lighten up if we could just get them to like us. He reviewed in his mind the facts on Muslim terrorists attacks on us in recent years.

1. In April of 1983, a large vehicle packed with high explosives was driven into the U.S. Embassy compound in Beirut. When it exploded, it killed sixty-three people.

2. In October 1983, a large truck heavily laden down with over 2500 pounds of TNT smashed through the main gate of the U.S. Marine Corps headquarters in Beirut and 241 U.S. servicemen were killed.

3. In December 1983, another truck loaded with explosives was driven into the U.S. Embassy in Kuwait.

4. In September 1984, another van was driven into the gate of the U.S. Embassy in Beirut.

5. In April 1985, a bomb exploded in a restaurant frequented by U.S. soldiers in Madrid.

6. In August 1985, a Volkswagen loaded with explosives was driven into the main gate of the U.S. Air Force Base at Rhein-Main; twenty-two were killed.

7. In October 1985, the *Achille Lauro* was hijacked and we watched as an American in a wheelchair was singled out on the passenger list and executed.

8. TWA Flight 840 in April of 1986 was hijacked, which killed four.

9. Pan Am Flight 103 was blown up over Lockerbie, Scotland, in 1988, killing 259.

10. In January 1993, two CIA agents were shot and killed as they entered CIA headquarters in Langley, Virginia.

11. In February 1993, a group of terrorists were arrested after a rented van packed with explosives was driven into the underground parking garage of the World Trade Center in New York City. Six people were killed and over one thousand were injured.

12. In November 1995, a car bomb exploded at a U.S. military complex in Riyadh, Saudi Arabia, killing seven servicemen and women.

13. In June of 1996, another truck bomb exploded only thirty-five yards from the U.S. military compound in Dhahran, Saudi Arabia. It destroyed the Khobar Towers, a U.S. Air Force barracks, killing nineteen and injuring over five hundred.

14. U.S. embassies in Kenya and Tanzania were attacked in August 1998. These attacks were planned with precision. They killed 224.

15. The USS *Cole* was docked in the port of Aden, Yemen, for refueling on 12 October 2000, when a small craft pulled alongside the ship and exploded, killing seventeen U.S. Navy sailors.

In all those incidents a total of 813 people were killed. There were twelve vehicle bombs, one boat bomb attack, two airliners bombed, and one gun attack at CIA HQ. And then came September 11, 2001; and now Bobby Samuels and Bo Devore might have a chance to alter U.S. and world history and prevent a coordinated attack that would make the events of September 11, 2001 seem like a kindergarten picnic by comparison.

Thinking about this, Bobby was absolutely awestruck.

There also had been so much political arguing back and forth about closing the U.S.-Mexican border, building a 2,900-mile fence, or wall, opening the border, offering amnesty, or even annexing Mexico as additional states of the United States; it was dizzying listening to all the arguments about the issue. What was important to him, though, was the fact that the border had become such a political football.

Bobby was a former Green Beret, besides being an army officer and a cop. This was not something political to him. It was something strategic. To Bobby, no political party or belief should come ahead of the security of our nation, but it seemed to him that was not the case with many politicians in both major parties. He did not understand all the "political correctness" and why every group of people in America seemed to have gotten overly sensitive. His concern was the survival of U.S. civilization, and he was constantly shocked at the number of Americans who aided the enemy with such actions as looking at anything and everything a few of our soldiers might do wrong in the War on Terrorism so they could decry the effort and the country's leadership. Bobby had heard all the horror stories from his father, a highly decorated and celebrated Special Forces sergeant major, who'd also been a POW in North Vietnam and had escaped. His father was so ashamed of so many Americans for "betraying our troops" with their disdain and disrespect that he actually saw his dad privately shed tears over it.

Then, there were those who hated any and all parts of our government that were the least bit conservative, and did all they could to cause disruption. One of them attended school with Tariq at Penn State, and they became good friends.

Otis Franklin Rabbe, Ph.D., was a fine professor of American history, but he was so radical as a citizen that he would embarrass any member of the sixties group SDS (Students for a Democratic Society). In fact, he had once been a vocal member of that group, too.

Now, he was the executive director of the Patriotic Posse Comitatus, or as Bobby and some members of the Department of Homeland Security called it, the "Comatose Pussies." Professor Rabbe had at one point decided to become proactive, and now headed this militia group, which just knew that the government of the U.S. would fall someday because of corporate and political greed heaping itself atop its own waste piles. PPC also decided they would do everything in their collective power to make this happen.

As the years went by, Rabbe and his friends became emboldened by earlier clandestine successes, and became even more brazen in their attempts to sabotage anything that had to do with the federal government, especially the military. After seeing the shock of 9/11, they became even more determined to utilize terrorism as their tool to get their message out, as they saw the publicity 9/11 got and how it strongly influenced everyone's lives.

Professor Rabbe had straight A's all through grade, middle, and high school and was the guy who was beaten up by every bully in each class. He attended Penn State with Tariq Ubaadah, where he graduated magna cum laude with a degree in American history. He then got his graduate degree and his doctorate from UC-Berkley, and was now a tenured professor at a large Western university. Dr. Rabbe was on a museum board, an art center board, and a local history board, as well as occasionally traveling to lecture on American history at other universities.

He was totally passionate and outspoken in all his years against the U.S. government, and was equally outspoken about eating meat of any kind. Because of all the vegetables he ate, his students would frequently joke that his ears looked like green stuff was growing out of them, but in actuality they were seeing unclipped hairs. His other eccentricity was that he had always, since the 1960s, had a beard and Beatles-type haircut, although now it was all gray and there was a big bald spot right in the back. He also always wore Nehru jackets, even having them custom-made when they could no longer be found.

He also had a photographic memory, and expected all students to have one, too. His classes were comprised of stating historical fact after fact with dates, and for exams and quizzes, he wanted to see the same dates and events listed back for him. Students were to memorize, not think. The smartest students would raise their hands when he mentioned any event that even half-looked like the feds had encroached on the rights of an individual or entity. The rest of the class would then be a raging diatribe against the U.S. government, and the students would have fewer facts to memorize. Otis knew, but did not care. These young minds were putty, and he was the artist, carefully forming them into his way of thinking, he thought.

As learned and as tenured as Otis Franklin Rabbe, Ph.D., was, he did not realize that he simply was just another punk, but one with more education than most, and an inflated sense of self-importance from the world of academia. A gang-banger with a sheepskin, he had the same insecurities and need to be recognized for something, anything. He hated Ronald Reagan so much that he had plotted often to try to assassinate the President, but to do so, he would have had to act alone and that was not his style. He had to have his other "bros" from his "hood" backing him. He had no woman. He was asexual. He had no relatives that had anything to do with him. He was "too weird." He needed his fellow conspirators to show off for. Group courage. It worked for all of them.

He had the ties to radicals with money, so he was tolerated as the leader, with most members privately saying about his leadership, "Hey, he'll listen, man. Money talks and bullshit walks."

These were the people who hated commercialism and materialism in America.

Tariq Ubaadah didn't care at all about his old college "buddy." He actually had no respect for Otis or any of his cohorts with the PPC, because to him, they were more puppets, stupid infidel puppets, to be used to devastate his hated enemies, the United Sates of America and Israel. Not its military, but every man, woman, and child. He hated them all. Including Dr. Otis Rabbe, born sucker.

Tariq and Abdul met with their cohorts in the ambulance, while Bobby, Bo, and Ramsey were heading east toward the rendezvous point.

On a typical day, more than one million passengers in 350,000 private vehicles, along with 30,000 commercial trucks, rumble past more than 150 established U.S. border sites with Canada and Mexico, according to U.S. Customs data.

The three nations have been dropping travel and commercial barriers over the years to create the biggest free-trade zone on the planet. Cross-border business between the United States and its largest trading partner, Canada, has expanded to over $1.4 billion a day.

So, Canada had started looking more attractive to al Qaeda. But officials in several border cities such as Ciudad Juarez, realizing this, decided that they had to do some helping if they wanted the American tourist dollars to continue coming into their communities at an uninterrupted flow.

This is where Professor Rabbe would be used by his treacherous classmate. Otis had flown to Ciudad Juarez and met with several officials while carrying money from a large wealthy donor who hated the Bush family, the Republican Party, the free enterprise system—although he had made billions using it, even middle-of-the-road liberals, and pretty much hated most of what was considered good about America. He had funded PPC activities before and was happy to do it now.

Rabbe explained that he wanted to bring a large class of students from Penn State for a history tour of the town and area. While in Ciudad Juarez, he explained just how much money would be spent by the wealthy American college students. In exchange, he said that he had a small number of Mexicans who wanted to come to the United States to work and then bring their wages home to their families. He further explained that they had some equipment to carry, and maybe even some weapons for protection from gangs in America.

Otis then said he was so grateful for this meeting, and so hopeful for cooperation in this endeavor, that he wanted to just thank each man in the room with a small gift. He then handed each official an envelope with five thousand dollars cash, with a promise for more gifts if they would guarantee his passage across the border.

The Associated Press reported that: "The United States has sharply intensified inspections and antiterrorist surveillance along its Canadian and Mexican borders, reshaping the face of two of the most open international frontiers maybe for years to come.

"More inspectors on more overtime are asking more questions at the overland border stations. They are opening more trunks and peering at cars more often with imaging equipment. More agents are taking to the air also, patrolling the vast stretches of forest, desert, and waterway along more than six thousand miles of border shared by the United States with its two neighbors.

"Waits up to fifteen hours have been reported at border crossings. Most travelers are accepting heavier security with patience and patriotism, but some border towns feel pangs from their pocketbooks. Some Americans favor even more inspectors and stricter screening to snag terrorists before they strike."

The problem Otis now faced was figuring out how to smuggle everyone across the border without arousing suspicion or getting inspected by the Americans.

It was simple in his mind. He arranged for a historical visit with U.S. Border Patrol in that area on their way into Mexico. He arranged for a senior agent to explain to the college students the history of the Border Patrol, give them a tour, and they were even given U.S. Border Patrol baseball hats. The man who was picked to do the public relations was considered the biggest screwup bureaucrat wannabe in the El Paso area. That was just what Rabbe needed.

In his initial planning with Tariq, the Islamic terrorist simply said, "Bribe them."

Rabbe laughed and talked with Tariq about the patriotism of just about all of the U.S. Border Patrol agents, even jingoism, and their anger since 9/11, and said he would be hard-pressed to find someone they could bribe. This actually made sense to Tariq, with Otis adding he might have been able to find someone to bribe before 9/11, but not since.

It was actually Otis's idea to use the heart transplant con to move the two nukes across the border. He also used university computers, creating phony, official-looking documents, written in both Spanish and English, regarding the transport of the so-called organs. They would use the ambulance to transport them across the border, with just two men in the front seat of the ambulance and two in the rear. The rest of Tariq's terrorists would ride the buses along with the college kids, but then both ideas were scrapped in favor of using O Grupo Grande, as they had much experience smuggling drugs and weapons across the border.

So now, Otis Rabbe was waiting in an old adobe ranch-house near the Franklin Mountains area north of El Paso, outside the two-thousand-person town of Tularosa in what was referred to actually as the Tularosa Basin. He had put a down payment on the property, and Tariq, using AQ funds, gave Otis the money to pay it off. This would be the safe house for the bad guys. Otis could not show off for the students, or do all the amazing things he had planned.

Tularosa, New Mexico, in Otero County is about thirteen miles north of Alamogordo at the junction of U.S. 54 and U.S. 70, with White Sands Missile Range to its left and Fort Bliss to its right and below it, and the Mescalero Apache Indian Reservation above it. The community was founded in 1862 by Mexican settlers who chose the marshy land where Tularosa Creek fans out with many tributaries among reeds and marsh grass approximately one mile from the mouth of Tularosa Canyon.

In 1863, during the Indian Wars, several sheepherders were killed on Tularosa Peak, which is six miles southwest of Tularosa and overlooking the Tularosa Valley. Because of that, this peak was called Dead Man's Hill for a little while. Then In 1868, a U.S. Army soldier, Sergeant Glass, defeated a band of Mescalero, Apaches on what was then called Round Mountain, but now Tularosa Peak gets credit for most old legends in the area.

Nobody but a satellite tens of thousands feet above could actually see it, but there was a very slight movement near a ridge near Tularosa Peak. On the ground, it was two FBI agents, and they were taking turns watching the ranch with Oberwerk 25/40×100 Military Observation Super-Giant Binoculars on a large wooden tripod. The manufacturer says; "Oberwerk 25/40×100 mm Military Observation Super-Giant Binoculars are two feet in length and weigh over twenty-six lbs! For decades, this Carl Zeiss-designed binocular was available only to the East German and Chinese militaries. Now the same factories are producing these for Oberwerk Corporation for the civilian market. Oberwerk 25/40×100 mm Military Observation Super-Giant Binoculars are the ultimate optical instrument for terrestrial observation as well as astronomical viewing."

From three or four miles away, the two agents were able to watch what was going on at the ranch, through windows, even between curtains. They watched in shifts and regularly reported to the Task Force headquarters set up at Bliss headquarters.

Unfortunately for bad guys, they often do not think that a man will be watched closely who has made statements about assassinating a previous President and often is way beyond far left in his comments to students.

One of the FBI agents, before getting his CPA and then becoming an agent, was in the Marine Corps and was a sniper. He had a good idea about the fortifications at the ranch, and was very concerned about the tactics of attacking the place.

Back at Fort Bliss, General Perry and the secretary of defense were being given a private briefing and shown a video by a pair of high-ranking British SAS officers. The had flown to Fort Bragg, North Carolina, to meet with the commanding general of the USA John F. Kennedy Special Warfare Center to brief the commander of the Green Berets, and he was so impressed, he flew with them to MacDill Air Force Base in Tampa, Florida, to brief the commanding general of the U.S. Special Operations Command, in charge of all Specops, not just USA Special Forces. General Perry was contacted, and he immediately thought of their mission and knew that Bo and Bobby had done a lot of sport parachuting or sky-diving, in addition to Bobby's extensive experience with HALO. The two SAS officers were immediately flown from MacDill to Bliss to brief the SECDEF and COS (chief of staff) of the Army Jonathan Perry. All others were excluded from the briefing room as they watched and listened.

According to the briefing, British Special Forces troops would be dropped behind enemy lines on covert missions by trading their traditional parachutes in favor of strap-on stealth wings.

The lightweight carbon fiber mono-wings would allow them to jump from high altitudes and then glide 120 miles or more before landing—making them almost impossible to spot, as their aircraft could avoid flying anywhere near the target.

The technology was first demonstrated in 2003 when Austrian daredevil Felix Baumgartner—a pioneer of free-fall gliding—"glided" across the English Channel, leaping out of an aircraft thirty thousand feet above Dover, England, and landing safely near Calais, France, twelve minutes later.

Wearing an aerodynamic suit, and with a six-foot-wide wing strapped to his back, Felix soared across the sea at 220 mph, moving six feet forward through the air for every one foot he fell vertically—and opened his parachute one thousand feet above the ground before landing safely.

Now, military scientists have seen the massive potential for secret military missions. Currently Special Forces and Specops, such as the SAS, which this was initially proposed to, rely on a variety of parachute techniques to land behind enemy lines.

Existing steerable square parachutes, or parafoils, are used normally, but when opened at high altitudes above twenty thousand feet, jumpers have to struggle to control them for long periods, often fighting very high winds and extreme cold, while breathing from an oxygen bottle.

They can also free-fall from high altitude, open their parachutes at the last minute, but that severely limits the distance they can "glide" forward from the drop point to just a few miles.

But the German company ESG developed the strap-on rigid wing specifically for Special Forces and Specops use.

Looking like a six-foot-wide pair of F-15 Eagle wings, the device should allow a parachutist to glide up to 120 miles, while carrying up to two hundred pounds of equipment.

Not only that, the stealth wings are fitted with oxygen supply and navigation aides. Ultimately, Bobby and Bo could wear the wings, jump from a high altitude breathing oxygen, while their transport aircraft can stay far, far away from enemy territory, or in this case, could avoid detection or suspicion by staying close to commercial airliner flight paths.

The manufacturers claimed the ESG wing is "100-percent silent" and "extremely difficult" to track using radar.

When they would approach their landing zone, Bobby and Bo could pull their rip cord to open their parafoil canopy and then land like they normally would.

The briefer pointed out that even their weapons, ammunition, food, and water could all be stowed inside the wing, although caching the six-foot-wide wings after landing would be much more difficult than caching or burying a traditional parachute.

The SAS officers also said that in the future, ESG claims the next stage of development would be fitting "small turbojet drives" to the wings to extend range even further.

The secretary of defense looked at Jonathan Perry and said, "If you want some, just tell me."

Perry winked, looked at the two SAS officers, saying, "Did you bring any of these wings with you?"

Colonel Heath Weatherill said, "Yes, sir, we most certainly did. We brought two sets. Would you like to see them?"

Perry laughed and said, "Did they come with a manual?"

The SECDEF chuckled.

The other officer, a major, said, "Aye, General. Actually they do."

Jonathan said, "Can we keep the two sets and try them out a little and let you know if we want to order some? I am very impressed."

The secretary of defense said, "I concur, gentlemen."

The colonel said, "General, please keep both sets with the compliments of the British army."

General Perry and the secretary of defense stood and shook hands with both British commando leaders, and then invited them as their guests for supper at the O-Club. The men of course accepted.

Jonathan Perry had no clue if these were something Bobby and Bo could use, but they certainly would be handy to have around in case they could. He and the SECDEF, in fact, had a lengthy discussion in regard to the use of the new stealth wings for special operations forces needing to enter enemy territory undetected.

Bobby's force continued to speed toward the general direction of the terrorists' rendezvous, but the bad guys were now already meeting. In fact, they were now caravaning, including the ambulance, and following Ramiro Maureo as he wound his way northwestward through the city. Traffic was heavy. Hitting Laredo, he traveled northward, getting closer and closer to the Rio Grande. Then turned west on Ignacio Mejia.

Zorion Duarte knew they were heading to a large warehouse, and was wondering how he could signal the Americans. He had sworn an oath to O Grupo Grande. He feared Ramiro more than anything, but his brother was in prison in Sao Paulo facing a death sentence, and the Americans who met with him told him that they would insure his brother's release, transport him to the U.S., and Zorion, too, if he would help them, agreeing to never join a gang again. Plus they would give him $400,000 cash, tax-free. He had to try to take advantage of it, so he had been feeding information by his cell phone to the two Americans, who both spoke Spanish and looked and acted Mexican. They'd approached him in a restaurant.

In actuality, one was named Carlos Lopez and grew up in Decatur, Georgia, and was bilingual. The other, Dan Jones, had spent twenty years in Special Forces, and had learned Spanish starting in high school at Bakersfield, California, then attended Spanish language school, several of them in fact, and was a heavy weapons sergeant on A-Detachments all over South America and Central America with the 7th Special Forces Group, for almost his entire career. Carlos was a naval intelligence officer. The two of them, after retiring from the military, both avoided training at "The Farm." They were field operations officers who were recruited to work for the CIA, but had they not had their military job experience and been so fluent in Spanish, they would have had to have been under thirty-five, have a degree with a high GPA, and to become Field Operations Officers, would spend time at "the Farm," the CIA's training ground at Camp Peary near Williamsburg, Virginia. The course, which is referred to by many as "Outward Bound with guns," requires a few days' training and living in a swamp escaping human predators. Besides the outdoor skills sets they learn, candidates also learn how to gather information at cocktail parties, set up clandestine meetings, see if they are being tailed, learn how to slip tails, learn how to effectively use shortwave radios—as well as other clandestine communications gear, and report-preparation. There is also a phase, simply called a "jail sequence," in which officer recruits are put in a cell, deprived of food, water, and sleep, and then interrogated for nearly two days.

Both agents had been assigned to Ciudad Juarez and had a good net of agents working the area, as well as working their own little projects like Zorion Duarte, who was now paying off for them in spades.

The problem now was that he knew the gang would soon be in the United States, and he had to tell the men. If the gang was successful, the American spies or policemen, or whatever they were, would not do the things they promised or pay him any more money.

Finally, riding next to Ramiro, he punched the cell phone number for Dan Jones, who he knew as Enrique Acosta. He looked down at the pad until he saw that it read "connected."

Then Zorion said, in Portuguese, "Ramiro, are we going to the empty warehouse near Laredo with the tunnel entrance in it?"

Ramiro was not the leader of such a notorious gang because he was stupid. Zorion's leading question was unusual and out of place, and Ramiro immediately whipped out a monstrous Desert Eagle .44 Magnum automag and said, "Do not move."

He literally shoved the barrel into Zorion's left ear.

Then Ramiro said, "Raise your right hand slowly and do not push any buttons on your phone."

Zorion raised the cell phone cautiously as tears started to stream down his face.

Ramiro pulled over right in the middle of traffic and got out, telling Zorion to get out, too. The caravan stopped, as did many other cars.

The gang leader smiled broadly and said in English, "Hey, Yankee, here is your little rabbit and what we do to traitors."

Dan heard Zorion scream and then a loud bang. The head shot blew the back of his skull all over a car. Ramiro kicked the still-twitching body, spit on him, and got back in the vehicle, driving off.

Bobby, Bo, and Ramsey found themselves in the southern outskirts of Ciudad Juarez, where Zorion had called from. They got a call from Task Force headquarters, with the translation of Zorion's last words. They immediately headed north.

Was this task force going to work?

Bobby wondered to himself, and thought about how al-Zarqawi was nailed. It was not some hit-or-miss event, but the culmination of a long concentrated effort. Immediate news reports would credit every unit from the 101st Airborne Division to the Iraqi Police, but he knew that the killer got nailed by a concentrated long-term tireless pursuit by Task Force 145.

Abu Musab al-Zarqawi, the late commander of al Qaeda in Iraq, was a powerful symbol of the al Qaeda mindset, a ruthless commander willing to exercise the most extreme brutality on the battlefield. Zarqawi was a living gruesome role model and legend in the jihadi community, and was every bit as popular as Osama bin Laden. He became a video and Internet star. His image and videotapes were widely distributed.

Task Force 145 was the driving force behind the killing of Zarqawi, Sheik Abd-Al-Rahman, his spiritual adviser, and other lieutenants during a high-level meeting. For many months, TF-145 tracked his whereabouts around Iraq, conducting numerous raids, and killing or capturing many of his leaders. After many raids searching for him turned up AQ leaders all over Iraq, al-Zarqawi was finally identified and targeted in a farmhouse just outside Baquba, a city with a heavy al Qaeda involvement.

Task Force 145's operations were based on intelligence on al Qaeda's organization, and their intelligence sources tried to identify his locations close to Baghdad, because Zarqawi focused his activities in that area trying to influence the news media and incite a civil war, which would destabilize the newly formed Iraqi government.

The numerous raids they made around the area started netting plenty of cell leaders, helpers, backers, and terrorist commanders, which provided intelligence for follow-up strikes, which ultimately led to the attack of Zarqawi's safe house, which they actually targeted.

The death of Zarqawi certainly did not end the insurgency in Iraq, but Bobby remembered how much it helped make a dent and upset al Qaeda. Now he hoped this task force would do just the same.

The first task at hand, however, was to find Ramiro and al Qaeda before they could cross the border with the nuclear bombs. The outlaws were now speeding toward their faux-warehouse/real tunnel entrance, which had been years in the digging and construction.

Bobby had read the translation of the document found at al-Zarqawi's safe house after he was nailed, and was shocked at the detailed planning and thinking about apparently all al Qaeda undertook. It amazed him how much they manipulated what was happening. The document, that al-Zarqawi apparently had written, read:

"The situation and conditions of the resistance in Iraq

have reached a point that requires a review of the events
and of the work being done inside Iraq. Such a study is
needed in order to show the best means to accomplish the
required goals, especially that the forces of the National
Guard have succeeded in forming an enormous shield protecting the American forces and have reduced substantially
the losses that were solely suffered by the American
forces. This is in addition to the role played by the Shi'a
(the leadership and masses) by supporting the occupation,
working to defeat the resistance, and by informing on its
elements.

"As an overall picture, time has been an element in af-
fecting negatively the forces of the occupying countries,
due to the losses they sustain economically in human lives,
which are increasing with time. However, here in Iraq, time
is now beginning to be of service to the American forces
and harmful to the resistance for the following reasons:

"1. By allowing the American forces to form the forces of
the National Guard, to reinforce them and enable them
to undertake military operations against the resistance.

"2. By undertaking massive arrest operations, invading
regions that have an impact on the resistance, and
hence causing the resistance to lose many of its elements.

"3. By undertaking a media campaign against the resistance resulting in weakening its influence inside the
country and presenting its work as harmful to the population rather than being beneficial to the population.

"4. By tightening the resistance's financial outlets, re-
stricting its moral options, and by confiscating its ammunition and weapons.

"5. By creating a big division among the ranks of the resistance and jeopardizing its attack operations, it has weak-
ened its influence and internal support of its elements,
thus resulting in a decline of the resistance's assaults.

"6. By allowing an increase in the number of countries and elements supporting the occupation or at least allowing them to become neutral in their stand toward us in contrast to their previous stand or refusal of the occupation.

"7. By taking advantage of the resistance's mistakes and magnifying them in order to misinform.

"Based on the above points, it became necessary that these matters should be treated one by one:

"1. To improve the image of the resistance in society, increase the number of supporters who are refusing occupation, and show the clash of interest between society and the occupation and its collaborators. To use the media for spreading an effective and creative image of the resistance.

"2. To assist some of the people of the resistance to infiltrate the ranks of the National Guard in order to spy on them for the purpose of weakening the ranks of the National Guard when necessary, and to be able to use their modern weapons.

"3. To reorganize for recruiting new elements for the resistance.

"4. To establish centers and factories to produce and manufacture and improve on weapons and to produce new ones.

"5. To unify the ranks of the resistance, to prevent controversies and prejudice and to adhere to piety and follow the leadership.

"6. To create division and strife between America and other countries and among the elements disagreeing with it.

"7. To avoid mistakes that will blemish the image of the resistance and show it as the enemy of the nation.

"In general and despite the current bleak situation, we think that the best suggestions in order to get out of this crisis is to entangle the American forces into another war against another country or with another of our enemy force, that is, to try and inflame the situation between America and Iraq or between America and the Shi'a in general.

"Specifically the Sistani Shi'a, since most of the support that the Americans are getting is from the Sistani Shi'a, then, there is a possibility to instill differences between them and to weaken the support line between them; in addition to the losses we can inflict on both parties. Consequently, to embroil America in another war against another enemy is the answer that we find to be the most appropriate, and to have a war through a delegate has the following benefits:

"1. To occupy the Americans by another front will allow the resistance freedom of movement and alleviate the pressure imposed on it.

"2. To dissolve the cohesion between the Americans and the Shi'a will weaken and close this front.

"3. To have a loss of trust between the Americans and the Shi'a will cause the Americans to lose many of their spies.

"4. To involve both parties, the Americans and the Shi'a, in a war that will result in both parties being losers.

"5. Thus, the Americans will be forced to ask the Sunni for help.

"6. To take advantage of some of the Shia elements that will allow the resistance to move among them.

"7. To weaken the media's side, which is presenting a tarnished image of the resistance, mainly conveyed by the Shi'a.

"8. To enlarge the geographical area of the resistance movement.

"9. To provide popular support and cooperation by the people.

"The resistance fighters have learned from the result and the great benefits they reaped, when a struggle ensued between the Americans and the army of Al-Mahdi. However, we have to notice that this trouble or this delegated war that must be ignited can be accomplished through:

"1. A war between the Shi'a and the Americans.

"2. A war between the Shi'a and the secular population (such as Ayad 'Alawi and al-Jalabi.)

"3. A war between the Shi'a and the Kurds.

"4. A war between Ahmad al-Halabi and his people and Ayad 'Alawi and his people.

"5. A war between the group of al-Hakim and the group of al-Sadr.

"6. A war between the Shi'a of Iraq and the Sunni of the Arab countries in the gulf.

"7. A war between the Americans and Iraq. We have noticed that the best of these wars to be ignited is the one between the Americans and Iran, because it will have many benefits in favor of the Sunni and the resistance, such as:

"1. Freeing the Sunni people in Iraq, who are (thirty percent) of the population and under the Shi'a rule.

"2. Drowning the Americans in another war that will engage many of their forces.

"3. The possibility of acquiring new weapons from the Iranian side, either after the fall of Iran or during the battles.

"4. To entice Iran toward helping the resistance because of its need for its help.

"5. Weakening the Shi'a supply line.

"The question remains, how to draw the Americans into fighting a war against Iran? It is not known whether America is serious in its animosity toward Iraq, because of the big support Iran is offering to America in its war in Afghanistan and in Iraq. Hence, it is necessary first to exaggerate the Iranian danger and to convince America and the West in general of the real danger coming from Iran, and this would be done by the following:

"1. By disseminating threatening messages against American interests and the American people and attribute them to a Shi'a Iranian side.

"2. By executing operations of kidnapping hostages and implicating the Shi'a Iranian side.

"3. By advertising that Iran has chemical and nuclear weapons and is threatening the west with these weapons.

"4. By executing exploding operations in the west and accusing Iran by planting Iranian Shi'a fingerprints and evidence.

"5. By declaring the existence of a relationship between Iran and terrorist groups (as termed by the Americans).

"6. By disseminating bogus messages about confessions showing that Iran is in possession of weapons of mass destruction or that there are attempts by the Iranian intelligence to undertake terrorist operations in America and the West and against Western interests.

"Let us hope for success and for God's help."

* * *

Bobby knew that O Grupo Grande was dangerous, but was simply another tool to be used and manipulated by al Qaeda, which by 2006 was being characterized by much of the American media as split up with no major chain of command. This was ridiculous, but for right now, the man of the hour was Ramiro, along with what Bobby considered his gang-banger punks. Ramiro was a mover and shaker himself, from a criminal point-of-view.

A major drug smuggler and *coyote* had a construction company and had purchased the warehouse and adjacent lots years before, while his brother had moved to El Paso legally, also years prior. He was the U.S. connection, and the two brothers both had warehouses, one on each side of the Rio Grande. Both had worked heavy construction for years, and both had specialized in road construction, particularly working mountain regions in Western mountain states.

Using heavy construction equipment such as backhoes and bulldozers, even a road grader, they purchased the property next to each warehouse, so they could control the neighborhood, so to speak. They started projects in the lots next to each building as if they were digging foundations, and they then started a large tunnel, which traveled literally under the Rio Grande River. Working toward each other, they met in a few years' time, and the tunnel became one of the biggest conduits for drug importation into the United States of America. The brothers not only stepped up their drug trade, but also got a percentage of every batch of drugs being taken through the tunnel. They were the highest-priced, but most effective *coyotes* in the El Paso area, and the word was they were the people you dealt with if you felt like your name was on a list with the Border Patrol.

Ramiro Maureo, when he learned all about the virtual gold mine of a tunnel, affected its purchase easily. He set up a meeting with the two brothers in a nice restaurant in Ciudad Jaurez. In the meeting, he produced a legal document prepared for each to sign. Jessan lived south of the border and Javier lived north, and each had the deed to each property in their chosen location. A third brother, Jorges, worked for them as their head of security. He, too, attended the meeting. Ramiro had his nasty gang-bangers all over the restaurant, and after enjoying a nice meal of *pollo asado, tamales,* and a dessert of *flan,* he produced the bills of sale and other legal documents and announced that each was selling their real estate to him, as well as all their heavy equipment.

Jessan started laughing and looked at his bodyguards, and they began laughing. Then he looked at Javier, and he started laughing, followed by Jorges laughing, too. Then Ramiro pulled out his ever-present Desert Eagle .44 Magnum automag and shot Jorges right in the forehead, with the back of his skull and a lot of brains landing on the plate of a young woman eating tamales and fried tomatoes. She began screaming until Ramiro gave her a shushing gesture. As soon as each bodyguard started to move, Ramiro's men, wielding either guns or switchblades, killed them. Then Ramiro pointed his .44 at Javier and then Jessan, as they both stared at the carnage around them.

Ramiro, in Spanish, said, "I was going to pay you, but now the price is your lives. Sign and you leave and can leave town. Don't sign and you both die. If one signs and one does not, both die. You will then pack and must leave this part of Mexico."

Both anxiously signed the contracts and fell all over themselves running out the door.

Ramiro put the papers in a folder and slowly walked out the door, stopping to pull some Cuban cigars from the pocket of one of the dead bodyguards. Paola, still alive then, hung on his arm strutting like a peahen at an NBC network convention.

After that the O Grupo Grande gangster boss simply took over the major drug smuggling trade into the U.S. as well as ferrying illegal Mexican border-crossers back and forth between the U.S. and Mexico. He had large homes, estates actually, in both countries, as well as another home in Bel Air, California. He increased the take for the gang by literally tens of millions of dollars per year, and was a hero to all his wealthy gang members.

The tunnel itself was crude but large, big enough for a road grader to be able to go back and forth between the two sides. Very far underground, it was not detected by Border Patrol seismographs, and was deep enough and carved through bedrock so that it did not leak water where the river basin ran above it. It had lights and ventilation and was like a toll road for the O Grupo Grande with diamonds and gold as the toll.

In each warehouse there was a large room with a garage door and a door for people, with cans of paint outside and a large air-pressure tank. There were numerous signs, in Spanish in Juarez, of course, which read: PAINT BOOTH DO NOT OPEN DOORS. Of course, inside was the tunnel entrance and no paint or painting material at all.

Ramsey said, "Look, up ahead. Way up, about four vehicles up there are smoking it in and out of traffic. I bet that's them."

Bo glanced at him, saying, "Good eye," in kind of a flirtatious way, and Bobby felt himself getting jealous again.

He did not have time right then, though, for anything other than total concentration.

Ramiro turned right again, off Ignacio Meija, heading north, with his vehicles following somewhat behind, but still keeping up by weaving in and out of cars. The ambulance had stayed in the lead the whole time with flashers and sirens going, and the rest of the cars followed closely behind. So far, Bobby and the others had seen the several speeding cars in the distance, but were always just out of sight so they could not see the ambulance.

To make matters worse, Bobby and Bo now had another matter to concern them. In the distance, several Mexican police cruisers were now giving chase because of the shooting of Zorion Duarte in the middle of the busy road. Neither of the military cops, nor the FBI agent, were carrying any identification allowing them to be involved in a high- speed chase on Ciudad Juarez streets in pursuit of anybody. Bobby pictured the international incident as they drove, the interrogations, the delays, the bad guys making it across the border and into the U.S. and detonating nukes in two U.S. cities. Bobby remembered the horrors of September 11, 2001, and all the mental images. He pictured in his mind's eye what the death toll would be like with two nuclear devices being detonated in two major U.S. cities. He saw the carnage in his imagination, and it made his back shiver unwillingly. He glanced out of the corner of his eye, embarrassed, to see if anyone noticed the movement. He simply could not allow them to be caught by the Mexican police, and he could not afford to be held up at the border.

Bo and Ramsey were also processing pretty much the same thoughts as Bobby. The three were cops, too, and had a singleness of purpose, and that was to catch up to the outlaws before them.

The pursuing cars slid around the corner off Ignacio Meija just in time to catch a glimpse of the last al Qaeda vehicle turning into the lot behind the warehouse. The gangsters roared into the big warehouse garage doors, and Ramiro pushed the remote to lower the doors again. They pulled up to the tunnel entrance inside the faux-paint booth, and the gang leader jumped out to eliminate the menace they had seen in their rearviews.

Ramiro ran back and got several of his men to jump out and take cover positions for an ambush. One was armed with an Uzi, another with an SKS converted to automatic, and still another with a scoped .308 sniper rifle, who started for the ladder to climb up into the high trusses honeycombing the upper part of the entire warehouse building.

Ramiro ordered one man into the driver's seat of the ambulance, and told him to pull down into the tunnel and wait for him. He then instructed the drivers following to pull into the booth and enter the tunnel behind the ambulance.

The gangster leader waited by the pedestrian door of the paint booth pulling apart the M-72 LAW (Light Anti-Tank Weapon) cached by the door. He opened the hinged end, and pulled the disposable rocket launcher apart with the plastic sight popping up by its spring-loaded mechanism. Made popular during the Vietnam War, the LAW could only be fired once, and the small rocket would hit a tank, bunker, or whatever with an explosive charge that generates immense heat that can literally instantly bore through the armor of a tank and use the tank's steel to also turn into molten projectiles to ricochet around the insides of the armored vehicle.

He pulled the safety clip out, rested the small metal tube on his right shoulder, wrapped the fingers of his right hand over the trigger with his thumb under the tube, and sighted through the clear plastic pop-up site.

Outside, Bobby, Bo, and Ramsey and a couple others were in the lead vehicle. They slid to a halt at the large warehouse door and all jumped out, but the unsettled dust was too obvious and the tracks in the dirt went right through the large now-closed door. This indeed was the place.

Bobby told Angel Valenzuela to hop in the back, and he jumped behind the wheel, yelling to the others, "Hop in!"

Doing it himself, he hollered, "Buckle up!"

In the excitement, all Bo thought of was having her M4 at the ready, and she did not replace her own seat belt. In the confusion, nobody noticed.

Bobby spun the car around in the dirt lot in a large circle, yelling, "Hang on!" and he steered into the skid and, straightening the car out on a head-on course with the large door, he floored it.

He slammed into the door with the large Hummer, and the door flew into the warehouse, crashing out and falling down in before them with a loud bang.

Ramiro, the patient and experienced killer, waited and squeezed the trigger as they passed over the door, aiming at the license plate, automatically knowing the car's speed would put the vehicle forward slightly before the rocket hit.

As Ramiro calculated, it hit right through the grille with a crash on an angle from just inside the right headlight, through the engine block, and exited out the driver's side below the rearview mirror and missing the driver's leg by inches. There was a loud explosion as hot molten steel from the block being hit pierced the gas tank, and the car engine compartment was about destroyed by red-hot fragments flying all around.

The Hummer went up and spun to its left, and the passenger door flew open, as Bo came flying out, her M4 boomeranging through the air at the same time. The auburn-haired beauty was tough and a survivor, and her immediate thoughts were to survive this. She was preparing for a shoulder roll, and saw she was fortunately going to miss the concrete floor, but unfortunately about to hit on wooden shipping crates. She hit with a crash, doing a shoulder roll, and felt several splinters dig into the flesh in her back and shoulders, also having the wind knocked out of her and banging the back of her head.

Bo rolled up right to the feet of Ramiro Maureo, who grinned at her while evilly pointing his Desert Eagle at her face. Bo Devore thought for certain she was dead. They were pursuing this man, and were not only in the middle of a high-speed chase of a murder suspect, but a shoot-out as well. He was a cold-blooded, cold-hearted killer. This man had plunged a knife over and over into the abdomen of his lover, simply to get brownie points with two al-Qaida men. Bo immediately thought of all this, and felt he would dispatch her with a head shot and keep running, so she did the only thing she could think of doing. Bo gave Ramiro the finger and spit on him.

He laughed, and she saw the arc of the Desert Eagle streaking down at her left temple. Then everything went black.

Bobby and Ramsey both crawled out of the twisted wreckage at the same time, blood seeping from several wounds.

They were groggy and both shook their heads to clear them. With horror, they saw the limp body of Bo Devore slung over the wide shoulders of the giant Ramiro as he disappeared into the large paint booth.

Bobby crawled into the twisted burning car, and crawled back out dragging a Mexican undercover agent who was knocked out cold. He also had two plastic bottles of water from the ice chest in the vehicle. Bobby unscrewed the cap while moaning in pain and poured the icy water all over his head. He tossed a bottle to Ramsey, who did the same.

It now hit Bobby full force what had happened. Bo was a hostage. He never would have carried her during a shoot-out if she was dead, so she had to be unconscious. He grabbed his own M4 and ran toward the paint booth. Bobby kicked the door in and swung his rifle from side to side, his eyes frantically searching for Bo and somebody to shoot. He reached over and pushed the electronic door opener and ran into the massive tunnel, oblivious to anything but rescuing Bo, even if he had to run to America to do it.

Ramsey was shocked seeing Bobby run through the door on foot, but he jumped up and ran out the big door to get the other vehicles to continue the pursuit. He took over the lead SUV and sent the men that were in it back to the other cars. He and Bobby would ride in the front in case of any more LAWs, but he did not want to ask Mexican nationals on the U.S. payroll to ride "point" after the rocket attack. It was not that he was being noble, just practical. His reasoning was simple. He asked himself how many Mexicans or any other foreign nationals, even if very dedicated, would actually lay their lives on the line to nail criminals fighting against American authorities.

Ramsey peeled in the dirt and floored it into the warehouse, and was shocked to see the tunnel entrance inside the paint room. He called it in and flew into the large tunnel. Ramsey wondered what had happened to Bobby, but he could not slow down. He had to catch up and try to rescue Bo Devore before she could be murdered, or even tortured and then executed.

Bo awakened inside the ambulance to find herself handcuffed and gagged. She was strapped on the floor next to Ramiro and could not see sideways out the windows, only up. It was clear to her that she was in a massive tunnel speeding along. Her first reaction was to slam on the brakes, but then she looked down when her legs would not move, and realized her ankles were tied off to the frames of both front seats using some type of nylon ribbon apparently from the medical supplies.

He saw that she was awake, and he grinned down at her menacingly.

Bo struggled as he slid his right hand down inside her blouse and bra and started fondling her left breast.

Ramiro, in broken English, said, "You weel be very wile in bed later."

Bo tried to curse him, but had tape over her mouth. He got the idea, however. Enjoying any kind of altercation, even verbal, he yanked the tape off her mouth.

He said, "Now you speak, *sí*? I doan wan a cover that pretty mouth. Eet weel be very busy soon."

Bo said, "Try it. Just try it! I swear to God, I will bite it off, even if you blow my brains out."

He started laughing loudly while he sped along.

"You weel geeve eet up to me and all my guys, baby. I weel make you scream and want to die."

Bo said, "You all may rape me, but you will be raping a dead body, you cowardly son of a bitch, because you will have to kill me first."

He laughed loudly again and said, "*Sí*, that might be fun. Maybe I keel you first."

He really enjoyed his own joke and kept laughing while he drove. Grabbing the wheel with his left hand, he grabbed Bo's blouse and bra and ripped them from her body with one quick swipe. Her breasts were now totally exposed, and she could do nothing about it, hands cuffed behind her back.

"*Meu Deus!* (Oh, my God!)" he exclaimed, looking down at her naked beauty.

Ramiro firmly grabbed her breast again, hurting it. Bo bit her lip and stared straight ahead. He pinched her nipple, and she fought back tears, but would not make a sound.

Ramsey tore down the tunnel and saw something moving ahead of him. He slowed as he got closer, seeing it was Bobby Samuels running as fast as he could, and he had already run three quarters of a mile down the tunnel.

The FBI agent skidded to a halt.

Blood seeping from several leg wounds, Bobby jumped in and yelled, "Go! Go!"

They tore out of there flooring the car.

Bobby was very much out of breath, but managed, "Can you imagine how many billions of dollars of drugs has come through this thing?"

Ramsey replied, "I know. I wonder how long it is."

Bobby said, "We'll find out soon enough. Bo is alive."

"Are you sure?"

"Absolutely," Bobby said, "We were chasing the guy. He would not stop to pick up a body and carry it."

"I don't know," Ramsey said, "The guy is obviously a sicko, and Bo is very, very beautiful. You never know how these guys think."

Bobby's jealousy boiled to the surface and his anger flamed over. "Look, She's alive! Period! And we have to find her fast!"

Ramsey said, "Hey, sorry. I know she's your partner. We'll find her."

Bobby crawled over the back of his seat and looked around for water. He found an ice chest in the back with a bottle of water and Gatorade. He started drinking, poured more water over his head, and opened a bottle, handing it to Ramsey.

"Thanks."

Bobby was really worried about Bo. She was his partner and they had been through an awful lot together. He thought about how good it would be to just go to a bar and have a couple drinks. The army cop really wanted the comfort of that right now, but he also knew that was the very last thing he needed.

Ramsey drove as fast as he could, and they were soon coming to the end of the tunnel. Ramiro had considered stopping to shoot the driver of the last car, and blocking the tunnel with it, but there was no way he could do that without his men seeing him, and he could lose his power base.

In the meantime, back in the warehouse in Juarez, the last car of Bobby's people had gotten out of their vehicle and opened fired on the three ambushers Ramiro had left there. One of Bobby's people actually made his way into the paint booth and found another LAW, then used it on the sniper up in the ceiling. They shot all three and rushed into the tunnel with their own vehicle.

Ramsey came out in another warehouse in a downtown section of El Paso, and Bobby, now able to use communications again, called in the location of both warehouses. There was a satellite, a Border Patrol helicopter, and a Highway Patrol helicopter up in the sky looking for the gangsters.

Suspecting this, Ramiro drove out of the warehouse slowly, but first changed into the coat and hat of an ambulance driver. He had four of his bodyguards riding in the back of the ambulance, plus his al Qaeda partners, and warned them all to stay out of sight.

As they pulled out of the American warehouse, he tousled Bo's beautiful auburn locks and laughed again, saying, "My boys back dere. Dey all bang you real good weeth me. We weel use every hole you got."

Ramiro laughed again at his crude obscene comment.

Bo stuck her chin forward and ignored his taunting.

At the first traffic light, Bo looked up at him, and this

shocked him. The calm demeanor made him shiver sub-consciously, as she spoke in a very matter-of-fact manner, saying, "Before this is all over, I'm going to kill you."

Bobby gritted his teeth, saying, "I'm gonna kill Ramiro Maureo."

Ramsey said, "I know she's your partner, but is she more than that?"

Bobby thought briefly and responded, "Yeah, Bo is my friend."

Bobby could not help himself. As they drove, he was alert, but kept thinking back to Arianna. Bobby used to tell her that her hair looked like it had been dipped in fresh honey and the sun slowly melted it off the ends of each strand. She was a ravishing woman with very intelligent eyes, and Bobby knew that Bo was the most like Arianna of any other woman he'd known. He also realized that, if she was not his partner, he would be able to fall in love with her. She was also his best friend. In fact, a much better friend than any male pal he'd ever had.

He'd loved Arianna so deeply and been so excited about the son she was carrying, he just could not ever allow himself to love that way again. Love hurt too much. He knew it really didn't. Bobby was very macho, but was also very much a romantic. He used to tell Arianna that the only reason he ever dared to accomplish anything of significance was simply because he wanted to show off for her. Now, he knew, he also wanted to show off for Bo, but that was because she was his friend and partner.

Bobby knew what the giant Ramiro was capable of, and all he could do was picture al-Zarqawi sawing off the heads of hostages with his long knife. He quickly fought to push those pictures out of his mind.

Ramiro looked down at Bo as he drove carefully through El Paso traffic.

He said, "Maybe we gangbang you, then cut off thet preety head."

Bo said sarcastically, "Gee, with my hands cuffed. What a big stud you are!"

He looked at the traffic. At his direction, his other cars were now speeding through traffic northeast toward the distant safe house, but they were taking a different route.

The Muslims could not understand why he kept talking to the woman. She should be used, her throat slit, and then tossed aside, they both thought.

Bobby hung up the cell phone, having just gotten a fix on the caravan, but the ambulance was now driving through traffic at normal speed and was unnoticed from the sky above.

Now the El Paso police were also involved, and were starting to set up roadblocks at various intersections. The cars were now heading down one of the most historically storied streets in Texas history, called simply El Paso Street. In fact, had it not been for the famous shoot-out at the O.K. Corral in Tombstone, the shoot-out in El Paso known simply as the "Four Dead in Five Seconds Gunfight" would have been the West's most famous cowboy gun shoot-out.

There were five men involved in this gunfight: the El Paso Town Marshal Dallas Stoudenmire; J. A. Ochoa, a college-educated Mexican, who was an innocent bystander; former El Paso Town Marshal George Campbell; El Paso County Constable Gus Krempkau; and a local rancher who was also into cattle rustling named John Hale. On April 14, 1881, at about six P.M., the Four Dead in Five Seconds Gunfight became a page in Western folklore that started as quickly as it ended.

A wealthy Mexican rancher hired an armed posse of about seventy-five Mexicans to cross the Rio Grande and locate two missing young Mexican vaqueros of his, Sanchez and Juarez, who never returned home. The land and cattle baron was also missing over thirty head of cattle. A local El Paso rancher named John Hale was considered the likely suspect. But a Mexican posse was not something that would go over well with the local populace.

The leader of the posse asked El Paso County Constable Gus Krempkau to join in the search for the missing vaqueros and cattle by helping them check the ranch of John Hale, which was about a dozen or so miles above El Paso in what was known as the Upper Valley, in the general area where the professor was now waiting to rendezvous with Ramiro Maureo and the two al Qaeda and Maureo's men.

On Thursday, April 14, 1881, the posse, along with Krempkau, did indeed find the bodies of the two vaqueros and the missing cattle at John Hale's ranch. The posse went to El Paso, and a large mob gathered with John Hale and his buddy, former El Paso Town Marshal George Campbell, in the crowd.

An inquest was quickly set up, and the Mexicans were allowed to retrieve the two bodies of the dead vaqueros and the few head of stolen cattle and leave town peacefully. Although there was a lot of anti-Mexican sentiment, not a shot was fired or a voice heard as they left town.

Then Marshal Stoudenmire crossed the street for dinner at the Globe Restaurant, while Krempkau went to a saloon next door to the restaurant to retrieve his rifle and pistol, which he'd left there during the inquest. However, a confrontation erupted when George Campbell accused Krempkau of taking the side of the Mexicans.

Campbell yelled, "Anybody that is a friend of the Mexicans ought to be hanged!"

Furious, Krempkau said, "George, I hope you don't mean me!"

"If the shoe fits, wear it!" Campbell yelled back, and walked away.

Then a very drunken John Hale, standing next to Campbell, yelled at Krempkau, "George, I've got you covered!"

Then Hale reached over and pulled out one of Campbell's two pistols and fired a shot at Krempkau, hitting him in the chest, and he suffered a sucking chest wound.

Krempkau drew his own pistol, just as Marshal Stoudenmire ran out the door of the restaurant and onto El Paso Street, drawing his twin .44 Smith and Wesson pistols. All the businesses immediately closed and locked their doors and according to witnesses, Mr. Ochoa was running right behind John Hale, who took off running, when Stoudenmire initially fired and killed the innocent Mexican by mistake. Hale jumped behind a pillar, but Stoudenmire's second bullet hit him right between the running lights, killing him instantly.

Then Campbell, seeing Hale die, drew his other pistol, and Krempkau, dying, fired twice, hitting him in the gun hand, breaking his right wrist, and then shot him in the foot. Campbell, screaming in pain, picked the gun up with his other hand, and Stroudenmire whirled, shooting him in the stomach, and he now slumped to the ground dying, holding his stomach.

Stroudenmire walked forward still holding his gun on Campbell, who rolled over onto his back and yelled, "You big son of a bitch! You murdered me!"

He then died and the gunfight was over. It actually all took place in less than five seconds according to numerous witnesses, and four men died from that quick storm of gun smoke. Stroudenmire was not hurt.

Although the town aldermen praised and recognized Stroudenmire, others later hired an assassin to kill him, as they were all afraid of him now, The assassin got drunk and slipped when he was getting ready to shoot Stroudenmire with a double-barreled shotgun loaded with 00-buckshot. Stroudenmire drew, aimed, and fired, and accidentally shot him in the testicles, and the would-be-assassin bled to death.

Wyatt Earp, Billy the Kid, Pat Garrett, President William Taft, and Pancho Villa had all made foot tracks in the dust of famous El Paso Street, and now another legend in the making, Major Bobby Samuels, was making skidmarks on the same street with burning squealing tires.

The police were closing in from all sides and in less than a mile, the lead SUV came to a halt and four members of O Grupo Grande jumped out brandishing various weapons. There were El Paso police positioned behind cruisers in front and on both sides of them. One drew up his Uzi and started to fire, when five officers fired at once, and he slumped into a bloody pile right where he had been standing.

The other three looked at what used to be their bro, and their hands could not have gone skyward any faster. While several officers covered, others came forward warning the three to drop to their knees and lock their fingers together behind their heads. They were soon cuffed, searched, Mirandized, and placed in the back of cruisers. The other three SUVs still had men inside trying to figure out what to do. An El Paso police sergeant using a cruiser's PA system warned them to toss weapons out of their cars and stick their hands out the windows.

Bobby arrived on scene and took a position behind a cruiser, gun in hand. He told the sergeant in charge to remind everyone that Bo was a hostage. He did not know that Bo was miles away cruising along at the speed limit in an ambulance.

Humberto Inigo grew up outside Brasilia, and was the highest-ranking punk of the remaining gangsters. He was in the second car and all were waiting to see what he would do. Humberto called Ramiro on his cell phone, but he did not know he was facing a terrorism task force, and he was not aware, just like insurgents in Iraq, that Bobby's people were just waiting for a phone call from a cell phone, as they had the technology to trace, eavesdrop, and pinpoint the location of both cell phones.

Unknown to the notorious O Grupo Grande was the unmanned aerial rotor vehicle UARV, or similar helicopters hovering over the El Paso area and being controlled by men and women sitting at large computer screens and digital video screens in Langley, Virginia. The one almost over Humberto, operating on silent mode, had special monitoring equipment on board the five-foot-long helicopter. Humberto dialed Ramiro, who answered immediately, and the device successfully attacked on the A5/1 algorithm of the cell phone transmission and bounced its signal to a satellite miles overhead, and right into the headset and onto the digital audio monitor of the helicopter controller in Langley at the same time it was also displayed for an intelligence analyst a few offices away. The entire conversation was not only recorded, but the bird over Humberto shot a directional azimuth on the cell phone, as well as one on the cell phone being used by Ramiro.

At the same time, an old Mohawk propeller-driven aircraft miles out, equipped with some of the most expensive radio equipment available, was also shooting an azimuth on both cell phones. More intelligence analysts in Langley and in Washington, DC, in the basement of the Pentagon, were seeing the bisection of the azimuths, giving an exact location on Ramiro's cell phone, even while he moved, as the UARV and Mohawk kept shooting azimuths so they could also get his direction of travel and speed.

Bobby got a call from General Perry.

"Son, one of the guys you have surrounded is on a cell phone with Ramiro Maureo," Jonathan Perry said, "We have satellite imagery, and Bo is inside an ambulance that Ramiro Maureo is either driving or riding in. They are several miles from you heading northwest. We can track them as long as the ambulance is in sight from our satellite or as long as he is on his cell phone. Why don't you let us use the UARV that is over you now and sprinkle the guy's vehicle with Smart Dust and let him go somehow. If there is an alternate rendezvous point, he might lead us to it."

Smart Dust was something most terrorists did not know about, but had been in development by our government over ten years. The al Qaeda members who did know of it referred to it as "magic dust," but were not sure how we operate it. "Smart Dust" is basically very miniaturized electronic devices. Very similar to stuff like RFID, or smart cards, or EZ Pass, and even those rice-grain-size tracking devices you can have injected into your pets. But Smart Dust is even more amazing than any of these. Smart Dust takes tracking devices to a whole new level, and Bobby was excited because he knew that Smart Dust was used to help track al-Zarqawi when he was taken out. Smart Dust takes electronic tracking to a whole new level by being small enough to be disguised as dirt, the kind you can pick up in your shoes or clothing. As small as these little bits are, each bit of Smart Dust can be given a unique serial number that, when hit with an "interrogation signal" from troops on the ground, or an aircraft overhead, is broadcast back giving a radio signal to our interceptors hidden overhead, such as the small unmanned helicopters.

If they brought the UARV down in a silent hover over the outlaws' vehicle, they could hit it with a cloud of Smart Dust, and barring a major thunderstorm, they could follow the vehicle wherever it went.

The Defense Advanced Research Projects Agency began funding aspects of this work at the University of California, Berkeley, in 1998.

Smart Dust devices are tiny wireless microelectromechanical sensors (MEMS) that can detect everything from various types of light to vibrations. Thanks to recent breakthroughs in silicon and fabrication techniques, these "motes" are the size of a grain of sand. Each MEMS will eventually contain sensors, computing circuits, bidirectional wireless communications technology, and a power supply. Motes will eventually gather and store data, run computations, but currently can communicate information using two-way-band radio between the MEMS sensor and the receiver aboard UARV choppers approaching one thousand feet in elevation. In silent mode, the UARV could fly a thousand feet above Ramiro or Humberto without probable detection. In the dry desert air, it was also found that the so-called dust particles could effectively transmit to the airborne receivers well above one thousand feet in elevation.

Bobby told the general to stand by and he would call back. He worked his way over to the sergeant in charge and flipped his badge.

"Sergeant, we need you to communicate with the guy who is the leader of this group," Bobby said, "We have a tiny unmanned helicopter overhead, and we are going to mark his car with it, and then somehow we have to let him go so we can track him."

The sergeant looked at Bobby like he was crazy.

"Bullshit!" he said, and looked back at the sight of his rifle aiming at the closest car.

Bobby grabbed the stock of the rifle and pulled it off the car with a jerk.

He said, "Sergeant, if I can produce a tiny unmanned helicopter that is hovering up there right now, but you cannot even hear it, if it comes down out of the sky like I said, and you see it with your own eyes, are you going to say 'Bullshit' and end up looking like a dufus, or are you going to cooperate fully for the sake of national security?"

The sergeant said, "You show me an unmanned helicopter, and I damned shore will cooperate, but right now I am about ready to call the boys in white coats for you, son."

Bobby grinned saying, "Thanks, Dad."

He lifted his cell phone, speed-dialed, and said, "General, I need the UARV to come down and attach our devices to all four vehicles. ASAP, please, sir? Thank you, wilco, out."

The sergeant grinned, saying, "Talkin' to yore spaceship, are ya? Beam me up, Scotty."

Seconds later, Bobby tapped the sergeant's arm and pointed. Barely discernible was a small unmanned helicopter, but much larger than a remote-control helicopter. The sergeant's mouth dropped open as he watched it maneuver over each vehicle and release what looked like a puff of dirt blasted down onto the vehicles by the rotor-wash. The noise from the chopper was barely audible, and it rose again into the darkness.

The police leader looked at Bobby like he was a creature from outer space.

He said, "Damn Sam! You boys are way out of my league, but you sure are the real McCoy. I am not gonna end up on *World's Wildest Police Videos* looking like an idiot. Whatever you need, Officer, you got our help."

Bobby said, "For the sake of the War on Terrorism, you might want to keep quiet about what you saw and ask your men to hold it back, too. Can you ask who is in charge and tell them you want to talk?"

The sergeant said, "Shore," and he reached for the microphone and turned on his PA. "You in the cars, I just want to speak to your leader. We won't shoot. Just want to talk with you. Will your leader just roll down your window and give us a wave?"

Bobby said, "Great. Look," as they saw Humberto's arm waving from car number two, a Ford Expedition.

Bobby said, "Why don't we back up your cruiser and that other one to let them out, then see if they don't just take off? We can pretend to be Keystone Cops and not get after them."

"Good idea," the sergeant said sarcastically. "Let's make my department look like idiots."

"You said you would cooperate fully. I know what I am doing," Bobby replied.

"Okay," the sergeant responded hesitatingly.

He grabbed the mike again, saying over the PA, "You, the leader. Bring your car up here slowly, and we will let you through here so you can get out and talk. We'll move these two cruisers. The rest of you remain in your vehicles."

He pulled one cruiser back, telling his men that this car was probably going to run, but they did not want it stopped.

The two cars were backed up and the second car, the Expedition, slowly drove through. As Humberto drove through, he noticed that the two police cars were facing each other, and not on an angle toward his car but the other way. They could not just spin and chase him if he took off. The others were on other streets, so they would have to travel around a block or more to get to his car. They also would have to worry about the other cars getting away if they gave chase, so he made a decision.

Humberto waited and told his compadres in Portuguese to tighten their seat belts. When the two cruisers pulled back together, he floored his accelerator and in his rearview, saw two cops starting to get out of the cars, but now getting back in. They tried to move the two cruisers, but almost rammed into each other.

He laughed heartily.

Humberto actually did not grow up in Brasilia. His father was one of the Candangos, construction workers who came from all over Brazil to build the country's planned capital city. Núcleo Bandeirante was a city built near Brasilia to house the workers who built it. The city was then later called Cidade Livre, which meant "Free Town." This is where Humberto grew up, but every night after dinner, all he did was listen to his father talk about the many projects he had worked on.

Brasilia was constructed between 1956 and 1960, during the government of President Juscelino Kubitschek, and was inaugurated as Brazil's new capital on April 21, 1960. Its master plan, or *Plano Piloto,* was conceived by Lucio Costa, and most of Brasilia's major buildings were designed by Oscar Niemeyer.

It was originally planned to house 500,000 inhabitants, but Brasilia had seen its population grow much more than expected. Several satellite towns were created over the years to house all the extra inhabitants, which now includes over 2,000,000 if the outlying communities and suburbs are included.

Humberto was never asked anything by his father. He only heard what a great builder his father was and how the man helped create the Cathedral, Dom Bosco Sanctuary, Igreja Nossa Senhora de Fátima ("Our Lady of Fatima Church"), which is usually called "Igrejinha," and many other buildings.

By the time he was a teenager, he ran away from home, and eventually made his way to Rio de Janeiro, where he met Ramiro Maureo. He wanted to make his own name in life, and so he had by being murderous and daring in O Grupo Grande, but Humberto was certainly not a doctoral candidate.

He headed down the street as if the end of his Expedition was on fire, and Officer Ev Franklin had seen too many episodes of cop shows where the hero disobeys his superior, goes after and dispatches the bad guy, and all is forgiven when he makes his department look good.

Everett Franklin was a young black El Paso police officer with political ambitions. He did not want to be a cop to help people or make a difference. He wanted to save a life or two, make a major bust, or anything of that nature, while TV cameras were around, so he could achieve fame, which could be parlayed into votes. He saw himself as El Paso mayor someday. Maybe then governor of Texas.

On the next street over, he jumped in his cruiser and tore off trying to overtake Humberto. There was some construction along the way, and a natural ramp where workers had put thick planks down over dirt piles so they could push wheelbarrows filled with concrete up to fill in a wall of bricks laid on the corner as a fancy planter. Everett figured he could shorten his drive and add to his splash by soaring up the ramp, and he calculated his flight would take him right over the roof of Car Number 519 parked there. He would land on the street in a shower of sparks and tear off after the bad guy. He would initially make the sergeant mad, but when he overtook and had a shoot-out with the bad guys, he would be a hero to one and all.

Unfortunately, about two hours earlier, the foreman of the construction crew working on the planter had told the men not to use the ramp because the main plank on the right was cracked.

Everett Franklin learned this the hard way. As visions of sugar-plum assignments danced in his head, he headed toward the ramp and into it, not onto it. The board broke when the front tires hit the expedient ramp, and the car pitched on its right side, smashed through the top of the dirt mound, completely turning the left front fender and hood into a nonmusical accordion, and smashed into the front of the driver's door of Car 519, totaling both cars, and knocking Everett's four front upper teeth out, which would hardly make for a good appearance during political speeches.

"Dumb ass," was all that the sergeant muttered as he watched and shook his head. "Somebody call for an ambulance and two tow trucks. Holmes, I want you to get your ass to the hospital and write him a ticket for reckless endangerment, careless driving, and whatever else you can come up with. I wish he would have gone through the damned windshield, so we could write him up for leaving the scene of an accident."

Northwest El Paso, much better known as West El Paso, or to locals simply as the West Side, is an area of El Paso, Texas, that is located north of the downtown area and on the west side of the Franklin Mountains. It is also a home to some of the more affluent neighborhoods within the city of El Paso, Texas. Many really magnificent mansions are perched high on the mountains, as well as some spectacular homes in the Upper Valley. The West Side is most likely the fastest-growing area of the city, and it was where Ramiro was now driving.

There was much construction going on in the area, and he felt it was time to ditch the ambulance and switch to another vehicle. He also kept looking down out of the corner of his eye at Bo's magnificent body, especially her breasts every time the car went over a bump. Ramiro thought of her fiery spirit, and this excited him sexually beyond imagination. If he could possess this woman and make her afraid and scream in terror, that would be one of his best conquests ever. Then he would turn her over to the others to use before they slit her throat.

He saw a dirt driveway that was to be paved, and it led to a high mansion under construction up the side of a ridge covered with creosote bush, mesquite, and some gnarled cedars. A locked chain stood guard across the end of the driveway, and several construction company vehicles sat atop the hill. There was no activity, and his sense was that the site was deserted for the day. The house was going to obviously be stucco, and was shaped to follow the contours of the ridge. Ramiro simply crashed through the chain with the ambulance and went up the driveway, parking the ambulance in the large garage with no walls yet on two sides. They all got out, and Ramiro had his men unload the two backpack nuclear bombs and move them over by the construction vehicles.

They put them in a big red Chevy Suburban that was loaded with extras.

Tariq Ubaadah and Abdul Qudoos had been very silent for some time, as Ramiro was paid to get them and the nukes safely across the border, but they knew he had just about outlived his usefulness.

Tariq, in Spanish, asked, "Why are we here?"

Ramiro said, "To switch vehicles, *amigo*. They will be searching, investigating, and many of my men will talk to save themselves, I think."

This seemed to satisfy Tariq, and Ramiro went on. "Besides, we need a short break to see if they are looking for the ambulance. The woman can give us some recreation."

Tariq decided to be patient and said, "So then what? What are your plans?"

Bo knew she was in deep trouble. She was still in great pain from the crash, and looked to her right at her shoulder and saw a nail, apparently from one of the wooden pallets she'd crashed on. It was sticking through her shoulder with the point protruding through the front of her supraspinatus, the muscle at the top of the shoulder that runs from the neck to the deltoid. It was right at the top of the muscle, and gritting her teeth, Bo now raised her shoulder and reached back with her neck twisted as far as it would go, and grabbed the head of the nail with her teeth and pulled it out of the wound. She was in sheer pain, but her adrenaline would not allow her to even think of it, and when she saw the nail she could only think of Bobby Samuels sticking a screw up his rectum to use to pick his shackles when he escaped from al Qaeda in Iraq. He had described exactly how he manipulated the lock like a burglar using a rake and pick. She had to leverage the tumblers by twisting something in the cuff while she used the thin nail to push each tumbler aside.

Bo knew she must escape or she would be brutally raped, probably beaten and tortured, then killed. She guessed correctly that it would happen here at this house. She worked feverishly to push the lock hole against a screw head on the bucket seat, while she held the bloody nail in her teeth and tried to pick the lock. Bobby had told her that some locks such as some cuff locks would actually come loose if you kept moving both rapidly and continuously, so she did this desperately. Tears started flowing down her face, as she did not want to die like so many women who were victims. Bo Devore would never be a victim again. She kept picturing her uncle over her sweating, panting. She cried more, making it hard to see.

Finally, the cuff suddenly sprang free, and she raised her head, saying, "Thank you, dear Jesus."

She quickly untied her ankles. Now, she peeked out the window and saw the men were headed toward the ambulance again, and she panicked.

"Oh, my God! Help me, God please!" she whispered desperately.

Bo suddenly knew what she would do, and set her jaw firmly.

She reached back and grabbed the mattress pad off the gurney and pulled it over her head and body. Anything would be better than the fate she knew awaited her.

Bo reached up with her right hand and started the ignition, slammed the ambulance into reverse, turned the sirens and flashers on, and shoved her foot down hard on the accelerator. The tires spun, and she flew backward out of the garage, as bullets tore through the side, and the vehicle flew over the lip of the steep hillside. She turned the ignition off, and then Bo lay flat, flinging the mattress over her, and she held the base of both seats and gritted her teeth. The siren died as the vehicle hit and somersaulted backward down the hillside.

Tariq yelled in Spanish, "Forget her! We must go now!"

Ramiro growled, but translated in Portuguese, and they all hopped in the Suburban and flew down the driveway.

Bo held on for dear life as the ambulance rolled and tumbled down the hillside hundreds of feet, and finally came to rest on its roof.

Rudolpho Jorge Santana was one of the key players of the Republican Party in El Paso county. He owned a chain of martial arts schools teaching song moo kwan tae kwon do, freestyle karate, kodokan judo, and jujitsu. He was a former world karate champion with NASKA, the biggest and main tournament circuit, and won Grand Championships at the Battle of Atlanta, U.S. Open in Orlando, Diamond Nationals at Minneapolis/St. Paul, the late Ken Eubank's Bluegrass Nationals, the Compete Nationals in LA, and John Chung's Sidekick National Championship in DC.

He was one of the most outspoken proponents of a secure Mexican border, and he spoke about how proud his parents were, after years of study and testing and waiting, that they legally became United States citizens. He felt a fence should be built and all illegal Mexican nationals should be jailed and prosecuted.

His next-door neighbor, Francis Murray, was a member of the Fund for Animals, Operation Greenpeace, the Democratic National Committee, and many other liberal organizations. He felt that all Mexicans coming to America, illegally or not, were entitled to government benefits, should be welcomed with open arms and amnesty. At a neighborhood picnic the two got into a friendly quarrel a year earlier, which escalated into a shouting match, with Francis actually doing the shouting. Rudolpho was too busy laughing after the pacifistic Francis swore he was going to kick Rudolpho's "ass all over the street."

The two had not spoken since, nor had their wives. Bo was dazed but unhurt in the totaled ambulance, and the two men arrived at the same time. They smiled and nodded at each other as they looked inside and saw Bo naked from the waist up with various cuts and bruises. Both men immediately removed their shirts and laughed at each other that they both thought 'of helping her immediately. Rudolpho had the better build and darker shirt, so they both recognized this and Francis replaced his shirt.

He stood and halted other neighbors running up. In the confusion, the red Suburban speeding down and out of the driveway was hardly noticed.

Someone yelled, "I called 911."

Rudolpho carefully put his shirt on Bo, and she smiled through a veil of tears, saying softly, "Thank you, sir."

His wife ran up carrying a first-aid kit, and Francis's wife ran up, too.

Francis's wife took the kit and softly said, "Why don't you let me do that, Connie? I'm a nurse after all."

Connie smiled and said, "Sure, Peggy. Let me know what I can do."

Bo tried to get up, but her left wrist was still handcuffed to the driver's seat. This shocked the men and women.

Bo quickly said, "I am a law enforcement officer. I was

kidnapped. Somebody please get me a cell phone, and can you get this handcuff off of me?"

Francis said, "I have bolt-cutters," and ran to his home nearby.

Bo called 911 and said into the phone while the neighbors, amazed, listened in shock and awe, "This is a police emergency. I am Captain Bo Devore, U.S. Army Criminal Investigation Detachment at Department of the Army Headquarters, the Pentagon. Call headquarters at Fort Bliss and ask for anybody in the Task Force headquarters. Tell them where I am and that I escaped. I will put a person on with you in a second to give an address. Tell them the terrorists escaped in a large red SUV. Did anybody get a license number?"

One neighbor said, "That belongs to a construction company on the West Side. I know the owner. I'll call him and get the particulars."

"Good," Bo said, "Call 911 with the license number!"

Back to the 911 operator, Bo said, "Are you getting all this?"

The 911 operator said, "I have patched you through to El Paso Police headquarters. They are listening, ma'am."

"Good thinking," Bo said. "There is an American C.I.D. agent, my boss, Major Bobby Samuels. He was in Ciudad Juarez, but is probably in El Paso by now. Let him know I am okay and tell him I lost my Glock and M4 and need weapons and have to be picked up right away."

Francis showed up with the bolt-cutters, and snapped the cuffs, freeing Bo from her trap, and a familiar voice came on the phone saying, "Bo, it's Bobby. I'm in a police chopper on our way. We had a twenty on the ambulance and don't need an address. Are you okay?"

Bo said, "I'll live. We have to get them, Major, They have the packages that were reported with them, both packages."

Rudolpho took the cell phone out of her hand and said, "Sir, this is a neighbor on the scene. This young lady is very brave, but she should be taken to the hospital. She looks like she was in a gang fight with no weapon."

Bobby laughed, saying, "Sir, I'll look at her when I get there, but believe me, she would win the gang fight."

Bo said, "Major, someone has to get the names and addresses of these people for me. They have been wonderful."

Bobby said, "I just got a thumbs-up from the police. They'll take care of it."

Bo smiled at everyone around her. Francis's wife was still cleaning and dabbing her wounds, and used an Ace bandage to hold an ice pack on her bleeding shoulder. She had Connie behind her with another woman holding her dark green shirt up carefully, while Connie pulled splinters from her back with tweezers and applied first-aid cream to each wound.

Bo said, "You all have been so nice. Thank you."

Rudolpho said, "We are all Americans, Captain. Thank you for your courage."

All the neighbors started clapping and were soon cheering, and that is what Bobby saw when he topped over the trees in the police helicopter. The neighbors first heard sirens in the distance, and then heard the unmistakable whop, whop, whop of the UH-1D rotor blades. The chopper descended just yards from the wrecked vehicle, and the officer set it down in the middle of the street. Bobby jumped out, amazed at all the people clapping. He ran to Bo, and they hugged, neither caring how it looked. The neighbors just kept applauding.

A well-endowed young woman ran up and asked to speak to Bo alone. She took her behind some trees and handed her a bra and yellow blouse that looked like it would fit her. Bo hugged her and thanked her. She removed her shirt from Rudolpho and handed it to the young lady. Then she put on the bra, which fit, and then the blouse, which looked good on her.

Bo said, "Let me pay you for this."

The girl said, "I would be insulted. Please, I want you to have them. In fact, I am going to go down and enlist in the army."

Bo pulled out a business card from her back pocket and handed it to her.

She said, "You e-mail me and let me know when you go in and how you are doing."

"Okay," she said, "I promise."

They went out, and Bobby handed Bo her Glock 17 and another belt holster he probably got from an El Paso officer, she figured. She checked her magazine and the gun functioning, and holstered it.

They ran for the helicopter and waved at the crowd.

Bo said, "Wait."

She ran back and handed Rudolpho his shirt and gave him and Francis kisses on their cheeks, then hugged their wives. Waving, she half-limped, half-ran to the chopper, and it lifted off with the whole neighborhood clapping and cheering again. Francis reached out a hand to Rudolpho and the two shook hands, then hugged. So did their relieved wives.

11

RACE AGAINST TIME

The police chopper set down where the standoff was still going on, and Ramsey ran over and gave Bo a long hug. Too long, Bobby felt. He felt his ears burning again, and really wished he could just get away from there and have a few beers.

The sergeant greeted them and introduced himself to Bo. She thanked him for the support and asked him if he could suggest some special award from the PD for the neighborhood that had helped her. He felt it would be a great idea. He then introduced them to the lieutenant who had taken over, and to the SWAT lieutenant, who was waiting for the armored SWAT vehicle.

Bo was re-outfitted with weapons and ammo, even a tactical vest with help from the El Paso police. Ramsey said he would stay and take care of his group while they pursued Ramiro. The police helicopter took them to Biggs Army Airfield at Fort Bliss, where General Perry and a few others waited on the tarmac with the Specops U.S. Army CH-47E Chinook Special Operations Helicopter, this chopper and flight crew formerly of the 160th Special Operations

Aviation Regiment (Airborne), commonly known as "The Nightstalkers." As soon as the police bird touched down, they thanked the cop, and ran up the ramp of the Chinook while giant twin rotors slowly turned.

They were greeted by General Perry and others, who checked to see if Bo was okay physically, and then sat down and started planning. The big helicopter revved up, and was soon airborne.

General Perry said, "We have the red Suburban under surveillance by satellite, and the other car, with, we believe, one of Ramiro's gang leaders, Humberto Inigo, and three others, is heading north, with both cars, we believe, heading toward what we expect will be a rendezvous with Dr. Otis Frankin Rabbe at the safe house he has in the Tularosa Valley. Two FBI agents are keeping his place under watch and report that it is like Fort Knox."

Tariq Ubaadah saw a large shopping mall and asked Ramiro to pull in there. He had him drive around the mall, and then saw an entrance to an underground parking garage, which seemed to be very busy. Ramiro was puzzled, but complied. One ramp before the exit, Tariq had him stop, and he and Abdul got out, opened the trunk, and removed the two bombs, setting them down on the ramp.

Ramiro, in Spanish, asked what was going on.

Tariq said, "You got us across the border. That is all we wanted. You can go to the meeting with Dr. Rabbe and he has even more money for you. Just kill him and take it, but here is what we promised you."

He tossed Ramiro an envelope, and the gang leader looked inside and saw many bills.

Ramiro said, "But I thought we were going to . . ."

Tariq said, "We are where we want to be. Thank you. Good-bye."

Ramiro started to speak again, but Tariq smiled and said again, "Good-bye," and Ramiro felt that would be a permanent thing if he did not leave right then.

He pulled out with his followers.

Abdul said, "Why did you do that?"

Tariq responded, "Because all of those fools will be arrested or killed by the infidels. That Yankee whore crashed that ambulance, so the Americans could find her and see where we were."

Abdul said, "How?"

Tariq said, "Satellites. They have them everywhere in the sky and are always watching us."

"Really?"

Tariq said, "The infidels even have magic dust, which they can sprinkle on people or things, and it makes a satellite look at them."

"How?"

A car approached, and Tariq waved and smiled as one housewife drove by, then another.

"I think that their satellites have a special camera and the magic dust shows up very bright green," Tariq said, trying to sound like he had all the answers.

A mother-of-pearl Cadillac Escalade came around the corner, although they actually call the color White Diamond Pearl. It had wire wheels, all-wheel drive, large tan heated leather seats. It was what Tariq was watching for.

With a big smile on his face, he held up his hand, and the silver-haired man driving the SUV slowed to a stop. He smiled and rolled down his window and started to speak, but he couldn't as a Colt Python .357 Magnum barrel was shoved into his mouth. Tears started to run down his cheeks, and he shook all over.

Tariq said in broken English, "Open zee trunk."

The man reached over carefully and pushed the button, and the back gate unlatched. Abdul hoisted the backpack nukes into the back and closed it, while Tariq forced the man into the backseat. He looked all around.

The man said, "Please! I am a grandfather. I have seven grandchildren and my wife and I are celebrating our fiftieth anniversary next month. Please don't kill me? Please?"

Tariq raised the pistol up and slammed it down on the

man's left temple. He slumped unconscious on the floor of the backseat.

The al Qaeda leader hopped behind the wheel and drove out of the garage.

By this time, Ramiro Maureo was eight blocks away driving north. Tariq headed east just wanting to distance himself from Ramiro and not show he was headed the same direction. He would head due east on U.S. Highway 62, and eventually make it to Interstate 20 and follow the blue lines back east. In the Midwest, he and Abdul would each take a bomb and head to their respective cities and their destination with world history.

General Perry got a scrambled call on the sat phone, and told Bobby and Bo about the parking garage diversion. They all discussed the possibility that the group was thinking of changing cars. General Perry called back and asked if they'd digitally taped the satellite views. They had, so he told them to review all vehicles that exited the parking garage within fifteen minutes of them entering. This in case of what did happen.

Tariq decided they would stop in one major city and rent one car, and then dump the Cadillac in another town, then rent a second car in the next large city, so the FBI would not check for car rentals in the same city where the Escalade was dumped.

He found an old adobe house that was crumbling a bit off the road about a dozen miles or so due east of El Paso. Tariq quickly pulled in to the old dirt driveway and behind the shambles of a building.

In Arabic, he told Abdul to watch for cars and warn him if any were coming. He opened the back door and pulled the distinguished-looking man from the backseat. The man had a large blue goose egg over his temple and his left eye was blackening and was totally bloodshot. Tariq dragged him back up behind the old house and pointed the .357 at his head, cocking it. The man started to cry again and begged, throwing his hands up protectively.

Tariq laughed and yelled, "Allah Akbar!" and fired into the palm of the man's right hand. The round then traveled through his left hand, and dead center into the forehead, finally mushrooming.

He called Abdul, and they hopped in the car with Tariq explaining that by the time someone found the man's body, they would be long gone and the authorities would probably be busy killing or arresting the O Grupo Grande gang members. Another thought was not wasted on the grandfather who was going to celebrate his fiftieth anniversary. In fact, that made the killing sweeter for Tariq.

Sheriff's deputies, Border Patrol, FBI, and many types of cops were on their way toward Rabbe's outpost. The helicopter set down miles beyond the far side of the hill from where the FBI agents had been maintaining vigilance. Rabbe and several others had been spotted over the course of the past couple of days doing activities you would normally associate with such a place.

One hour later, the SUV with Humberto arrived, followed just ten minutes later by the red Suburban. When they went down the long gravel driveway to the ranch house, two men wearing rifles at sling arms ran out and moved an old school bus that had been placed across the driveway to block the entrance. The rest of the ranch yard was bordered by an adobe-covered brick wall.

Minutes later, a command post was established several miles down the road leading to the southern end of the compound. The general had the Chinook fly over there. Inside the compound, for want of a better word, Otis Rabbe and his five volunteers kept going from window to window to try to figure out what was going on.

Back in the city of El Paso, every single one of the hard-core rough, tough gang members of O Grupo Grande surrendered without a shot being fired. Ramsey Keats bummed a ride on the same police helicopter, which was going out to the Rabbe site command post.

Ramsey and Bo got off in the corner by themselves, and spoke at some length while Bobby joined the general, the senior FBI agents who had come, an arrogant Homeland Security boss, a Border Patrol lieutenant, several sheriff's supervisors, and several more boss-cops. His eyes kept inadvertently straying toward Bo and Ramsey, who really seemed to enjoy each other's company. Bobby felt the flames of jealousy worse than ever.

Why did she seem to like Ramsey so much? he wondered. He was an FBI agent and seemed to be good. He was very good-looking and well built. Bobby wondered why she seemed more interested in Ramsey than himself, and then he once again got mad at himself for even thinking that.

The meeting ended, and the FBI supervisor spoke. "We must, before we do anything else, give the suspects an opportunity to surrender. They have not answered any phone calls, so we will send two volunteers with a loudspeaker in a cruiser to the front gate where the bus is parked and tell them to lay down their weapons and surrender."

Ramsey saw this as an opportunity to further his career, plus he was simply gung ho.

He immediately said, "Sir, I would like to volunteer," and a sheriff's deputy said, "I'll drive him."

Bobby and Bo did not even have a chance to volunteer. General Perry had already decided he would not let them volunteer, as they were members of the army, and he wanted to really keep them as low-profile as possible because military and civilian law enforcement do not mix well. People can and should worry about martial law and government intrusion. Plus, both of them were still walking wounded. If national security were not at stake, both would be in the hospital by his orders, especially Bo after what she had just gone through.

Ramsey came over and shook hands with Bobby, but Bo leaned forward and kissed him on the cheek. He smiled at her, and she at him, and Bobby Samuels could hardly contain his jealousy. He wanted to get out of the rental house they were using and hop in a cruiser and drive to a bar somewhere and have a few drinks. Thoughts like that were interfering with his investigation, and he was developing a newfound respect for AA. He really wished now he could go to a meeting and learn more about this disease he now understood he suffered from.

Ramsey and the deputy went out and hopped in the cruiser, pulling out the driveway with two other cruisers going as backup. The rest watched with a video camera being used by the two FBI agents who had been maintaining surveillance, and another in the highway patrol helicopter now airborne and slowly circling over the ranch area.

Bobby and Bo walked outside, knowing how the general would react, then quickly hopped in a cruiser and hijacked it, tearing down the road, and caught up, following the others toward the ranch. General Perry looked out the window, shaking his head and chuckled to himself.

The FBI supervisor said, "You want them back here, General?"

Perry laughed. "They partnered up with your man. You want to try to stop them from backing him up now?"

Bo and Bobby and the cruisers stopped at the end of the driveway, while the deputy and Ramsey went forward down the long gravel driveway.

They pulled up in front of the school bus barricade.

Ramsey lifted the mike up and said over the PA, "Dr. Rabbe, Ramiro Maureo, and all residents inside the house. This is the Federal Bureau of Investigation. . . ."

The staccato bursts of automatic-weapons fire from inside the darkness of the windows stabbed flame out of the blackness of the building's interior, and shot horror into the hearts of those witnessing the carnage. It was eerie to Bobby, Bo, and the others to see the flame of bullets and the shattering of windshield and rear window, and from there, a mile away, the blood was visible.

Bobby yelled at Bo, "Get out!"

He ran to the back of the cruiser and opened the trunk, pulling out a tow chain.

He quickly affixed it to a brace under the rear bumper, hopped in, and tore down the driveway, yelling out the window, "Cover me!"

The other officers were in shock at the outpouring of gunfire, but Bobby's actions awakened them.

Bo jumped in the lead cruiser and snapped, "Get down the driveway, Deputy. We can't cover him from a mile away."

He was fearful and said, "We are outgunned. We need to wait for backup."

Bo looked at him, saying, "Tough shit! Drive!"

He snapped out of it and tore down the driveway, stopping a hundred yards out. They took cover behind the cruiser. The other one followed him and parked to his right.

Bobby's vehicle took some overhead fire as he approached, but right behind the other cruiser, he slammed the brakes on and whipped the wheel to the left, and let off the brakes and stomped on the accelerator. The cruiser did a complete 180-degree spin, and Bobby jammed it into reverse and backed up to the back of the other cruiser.

In the meantime, Bo called General Perry saying, "Sir, we need the big bird for medevac. ASAP. That will be fastest."

Perry said, "Wilco, out!"

Bo thought, "A four star general, chief of staff of the army, and the man still understands combat."

Perry had already had the chopper warming on the expedient pad, for just such an occurrence. He ran in, dragging a paramedic Border Patrol officer with him, carrying a first-aid kit without explaining. They were ready to touch down at the end of the driveway within minutes, but waited and went into a hover instead.

Bobby jumped out of his cruiser under another burst of 7.62-millimeter automatic weapons fire, and ran back to the back of Ramsey's cruiser, where he quickly affixed the tow chain. They fired at him, ineffectively.

He called in from behind the cruiser, "They have at least two AK-47s on full automatic with armor-piercing ammo! Cover me! Out!"

Bobby jumped up and opening up with his M4 in one hand, he fired round after round in thee-shot bursts from his thirty-round magazine, and with his Glock 17 in his other hand, he fired round after round at the windows. He wanted fire superiority, pure and simple. Bobby did not care if he hit anybody. He just wanted them to duck because of the heavy volume. While shooting, he dashed forward to the driver's door, reached in, and slammed the car into neutral. It was still idling.

He glanced at Ramsey and the deputy, but they were covered with blood.

Bobby ran back to the rear of the cruiser, but they were waiting for him in the house. Every time he tried to move, despite the covering fire from Bo and the others, he was pinned down.

Then, suddenly, "God bless Jonathan Perry," Bobby thought as he heard the distant giant Chinook approach, and he looked back at it. It was leaning forward and made it to the ranch house in seconds, where it went into a hover, descending slowly, its gargantuan rotor blades producing a dust cloud that enveloped the house and provided the cover for Bobby's escape.

He hopped into the cruiser, slammed it into low, and floored it, towing the other cruiser backward down the driveway. He flew past the other two cruisers, who withdrew, and just kept going, shifting up into drive. Three fourths of the way to the road, he slammed on his brakes, and the other cruiser struck the back of Bobby's cruiser and stopped.

The Chinook was already almost overhead, ready to land, and Bo and the other cruisers pulled up, backing down the driveway at high speed. Bo jumped out and Bobby ran up slamming Ramsey's driver's door. Signaling Bo to get in her cruiser, he ran back to his own cruiser and hopped in.

The giant Chinook came overhead and went into a hover, sand-blasting the cruisers with dust and sand as it set down. The ramp opened, and the general, carrying a CAR-15, led the paramedic out and over to the cruiser, where Bobby and Bo met them. When Bobby opened the door, they saw the real damage. The paramedic reached in to feel for pulses only as a formality, already shaking his head, "No." Both officers had had their heads literally shredded by bullets.

Bo shrieked and started crying. Bobby held her protectively. She bawled, and Bobby made a face at the general, who shook his head.

Bobby explained over the rotor sound, "They had become very close already."

The general walked over and grabbed Bo's shoulders and in a fatherly way, escorted her into the Chinook.

Bobby looked at the paramedic, saying, "Their bodies are safe here for now. It is not worth risking more lives. Get the Chinook out of here now."

Bobby signaled the other cops to leave with him, as he detached the chain and spun around. The ramp went up on the Chinook, and it lifted off.

Bobby figured the general had already called the command post, as he heard many sirens approaching, and then saw the vehicles. They reestablished their command post at the end of the driveway. The Chinook set down on the other side of the CP. A trailer was brought in from the Texas Rangers to be used as a mobile command post.

General Perry's aide walked over to him, saying, "General, it is the commander in chief."

Perry whispered, "Personally?"

The aide mouthed the words "Yes, sir."

The general took the sat phone, saying, "Hello, Mr. President, Jon Perry here, sir."

The President said, "If I end up with another Waco, I will personally kick your ass into the Gulf of Mexico, General. And if I ever hear of the chief of staff of the U.S. Army grabbing an M-16 and combat-assaulting in to help out a major with automatic-weapons fire going on, I will shove my foot straight up your ass. Are you crazy, Jon, or just can't help always being a hero?"

"Yes, sir," the general replied, "I will certainly relay your well wishes to the people."

The President said, "Jon, you are something else. Please do not let our country down. Make this work out."

"Not a problem, Mr. President," he said gravely. "I will pass on your feelings verbatim."

General Perry hung up and called everyone around him.

He said, "Ladies and gentlemen. That was the President of the United States. He said those terrorists in there may have two nuclear bombs and we have to be so careful and professional how we handle this, but the whole nation is behind us, and he is behind us and knows we will all handle this menace."

People seemed impressed.

Bobby took Bo off to the side.

She said, "I know we have to get through this mission. I am sorry I got emotional."

"Nonsense," Bobby said, "I saw you and Ramsey had some chemistry going, and . . ."

She interrupted, "Bobby, he and I became friends, that's all."

Bobby said, "Yeah, but I could tell you both were attracted to each other."

She stopped him again, saying, "Bobby Samuels. We did not. Ramsey was gay. He had a major crush on you, but would never tell you."

"What?"

Bo said, "Look, we became friends, and he told me that

in the strictest confidence. He said he was a professional FBI agent and would never jeopardize his career or insult you by mentioning anything at all, but he joked with me about fantasizing about you."

"Holy cow," Bobby replied in an uncharacteristically soft response.

He sat down as if his legs gave out from under him. Bobby wanted to cry, he was so embarrassed and furious with himself for all the jealous rages over Bo.

Bobby Samuels gave Bo a reassuring hug and walked away. They had to get back to work, and he could not afford to be shook up now. Bo could not either.

Bo yelled, "What are you doing?"

He said, "My job! We cannot afford to let down right now, girl."

She gave him the thumbs-up and said, "Rog-O!"

Bobby went to General Perry and said, "Sir, can you give me a quick brief on the Batman or Jimmy Jet getup, whatever it is?"

The chief of staff said, "Stealth wings. Yeah, who is going with you, son?"

Bobby said, "I can do better alone on this, sir."

General Perry said, "I had the same thoughts about sneaking in from on high, but you will not go alone."

"Yes, sir," Samuels said, "but nobody can go in with me. You are the only guy here besides me who is HALO-qualified."

"Captain Bo Devore," the general said, "is an expert sports parachutist, and you know it. You're trying to protect her, aren't you, Bobby?"

"Sir, with all due respect to Major Samuels," Bo said, walking up from behind Bobby, "I do not need protecting. I'm a big girl, sir. Major Samuels already put himself in the line of fire today without me. If he wants to do it again, I need to concern myself with my O.E.R. (Officer Efficiency Report) or worry about sexual discrimination."

"Now hold on, Captain, " Bobby said, turning, and saw a big grin on her face.

He laughed and pretended like he was going to punch her, and she scrunched her shoulders and laughed.

"Okay, you two clowns," the old man said. "If you are going to get yourselves killed, at least I have to train you so you can do it. Come on into the Chinook."

An hour later, Bobby and Bo emerged from the big chopper, briefed, fitted with weapons, night-vision devices, high-altitude suits, oxygen bottles and masks, parafoils, and their new experimental flight wings. The Chinook started to rev up, so the engines could warm up. It would do this for close to a half an hour before the two took off.

When the big helicopter took off, Ramiro followed its flight with high-powered binoculars until its flashing lights disappeared from sight. It clearly was heading toward Biggs Airfield.

Bobby and Bo were at twenty-three grand and twenty-three miles away when they exited the chopper wearing O2 and night-eyes. They tracked back toward the command post traveling in excess of two hundred miles per hour. Bobby and Bo were both amazed at these experimental wings. Their target was the flat roof of the attached adobe barn. There was a wall around the top that they could use for cover, plus it was away from the CP, so it would not be watched the same way the driveway was watched.

General Perry called the President back. His secretary put the chief executive on immediately.

"Sir," Jonathan said, "I apologize for calling you personally and for breaching the chain of command, but this is—"

The President interrupted. "Jon, you are doing the right thing. What do you need?"

Perry said, "Sir, I know how bad it is to use troops in

civilian operations, but I have had the First Special Forces Operational Detachment Delta on standby, and would like to bring them in as backup to our current operation, or even complement it."

"Jon, our nation is faced with a nuclear threat on our soil," the President of the United States said gravely. "I trust your judgment and will back whatever play you make. Just eliminate the threat. Our citizens do not know about this, but they are counting on you nonetheless. Bring Delta Force in as you wish and let them kick ass and take names, and call me day or night, just use secure phone."

"Of course, sir, thank you," Perry said.

The President replied, "We're praying for you. Good luck."

The general made a quick call on his sat phone.

He said, "This is General Perry. This is a secure line. Crank up the jet and send Delta Force. Make sure they have parafoils, night vision, and O2. I want them jumping in tonight. I'll brief the CO while they are en route, and I want them locked and loaded."

"Roger," the other person said, "out."

The Delta Force, no longer housed in the old Fort Bragg Stockade, but now in a new state-of-the-art facility, was already on the jet on the tarmac and the turbines of the jet had been spinning for some time.

In less than ten minutes, Bobby and Bo were "on target" and opened their chutes, jettisoning the gliders out over the dry prairie below. The night was clear, still, and dry. If they were spotted, they would fight and the task force would come in like the cavalry. If not discovered, they would use stealth to work their way into position to place cameras and microphones through the roof and walls.

Both had taken off their oxygen long before, and they kept their eyes glued to the windows facing the barn. They also wore earpieces and had constant reports from the two FBI agents out on the hill.

They came in, popped their risers, and set down like an athletic duck on a small goldfish pond. Immediately, they collapsed their chutes and lay side by side on the roof of the barn for a full ten minutes before moving at all.

Now, they were up on their knees, weapons in hand. When they were getting ready for the mission, General Perry had opened his briefcase and produced a semiautomatic pistol with a very long barrel, almost seven inches long, in fact. The very end of the barrel was threaded, and the general also handed Bobby a long metal tube.

"Ever use one of these, son?" Perry asked.

"Yes, sir, thank you. This will be very helpful, General," Bobby replied.

General Perry said, "Probably do not want the press to get a picture of it. Been a great SF weapon for years, the whole time I've been in SF, in fact."

Bobby cleared the weapon, then screwed the silencer onto the end of it. He admired it and checked the ten-round magazine. It was a High Standard HDM, a modified target *pistol* equipped with an integral sound suppressor, but the general had added an even more effective silencer to the end of it, so when fired it made about the same sound as an air rifle, if that much. Originally adopted by the *Office of Strategic Services* (OSS) during World War II, the pistol is still found in U.S. inventories, including those of the *CIA*, U.S. Army Special Forces, and other Special Ops commands. It is ideal for assassinations and is loaded with full-metal-jacketed .22 LR rounds. In fact, instead of the standard issue, the general had loaded his with CCI .22 long-rifle copper-jacketed hollow-point mini-mags.

According to the military, the technical description is: "The High Standard HDM is a conventional blowback-operated semiautomatic pistol fitted with an integral suppressor decreasing its report in excess of twenty dB. This pistol design was originally delivered 20 January 1944, and original contract models were blued with a *Parkerized* (phosphate) finish on the suppressor. Follow-on models were completely Parkerized. Post-World War II models produced for the CIA were also blued. The ten-round box magazine was interchangeable with that of the Colt Woodsman. The weapon has a frame-mounted safety lever on the left in a similar position to the *M1911A1* and *Browning HiPower*. The front sight is a fixed blade with a square notch rear sight adjustable for elevation and windage zero."

Jonathan Perry, however, had made a few changes. Because it would often be used at night, he added a Meprolight M21 reflex sight, which used laser optics for daylight shooting and tritium at night, so no batteries were required but the shooter could essentially point, stick the dot on the target, and shoot. He was going to add a laser sight, but felt it could more easily give away the shooter's position if spotted.

Bobby would be able to pop any of the bad guys with very little noise if they got spotted.

Bobby reached into his black nylon backpack and pulled out two pairs of large black boot socks and a roll of army OD tape. He handed Bo one pair and put his own on over his black tactical boots, then held the tops of the socks in place by wrapping several wraps of army OD tape (olive-drab duct tape) around the tops of the socks. Bo smiled and followed suit. When they stood and started to walk, there was virtually no noise from their feet. Bo smiled at him and pointed at his head, indicating he was really smart.

In actuality, Bobby had learned that trick from a Vietnam veteran, a former Green Beret officer who had served with his father in Vietnam. The guy, named Don Bendell, lived in Colorado and had become an author. He had bowhunted since early childhood, and been a licensed big-game guide and outfitter in the mid-eighties in Colorado. Bobby was amazed at how good and young the man looked for his age, and hoped he could like that good when he got older.

They stopped at one spot on the roof, and could see the light from two windows on the interior yard, with the movement of shadows in each frame of light.

Bobby knelt down, while Bo maintained watch, and he took a small cordless, silent tactical drill from his pack. He carefully seated a very long industrial-diamond drill bit into the drill and tightened it. He drilled quickly down through the roof, and slowly through the layers of insulation and then the ceiling. This last part took many minutes of stop-and-go patience. With a hole through the ceiling of the room within, Bobby inserted a miniature tactical video camera and microphone, which immediately transmitted audio and video to the mobile command post. Bobby used the flexible metal tubing to move the camera around the room and see all who were within. In the corner, seated and looking very peaceful, was Dr. Frankiln Otis Rabbe, with his throat slit and his tongue pulled out through the slash. The blood was all dried, so he had been dead for hours. With perverted humor, Ramiro had crossed the man's legs and put a drink in his hand, which was now rigid with rigor mortis, fingers wrapped tightly around the piece of crystal.

Bobby then placed a small box over the tube. This contained a miniature motor, which would move the camera and mike around when activated by a toggle switch in the mobile command post. For the next two hours, Bobby repeated this operation in various spots of the ranch house roof. Now, the officers in the mobile command post could see all the terrorists and keep them under surveillance. Perry had them do a scrambled satellite uplink to the Defense Intelligence Agency, where Portuguese and Arabic translators sat waiting to translate anything mentioned in native tongues by the Brazilian and Arabic terrorists. Spanish translators were not needed since there were so many in the command post from several different agencies.

Bobby and Bo decided to take turns sleeping, waiting a few hours until the breach. Bo stayed awake first and allowed Bobby to set his head on her lap, while she sat with her back against the lip on the back of the house.

* * *

Because there was moonlight, General Perry had Delta Force jump out past the command post, and they walked a mile carrying their chutes in aviator kit bags. A breaching plan was made to insert Delta Operators as well as a couple of very experienced Texas Rangers who were SWAT specialists.

After one hour, Bobby and Bo switched positions. Within minutes, she was asleep with her head on his lap. He looked down at his partner and smiled, seeing the beginnings of bruises high on her neck, and a few scratches and marks. The woman was incredibly beautiful, he thought, but was still the original American badass, and he would want nobody else in a situation like this. She was the best partner he could imagine having. Bobby wondered if she had been raped during her ordeal with Ramiro. He flamed up again thinking about the possibility, and thinking how angry he would be if that were the case. They had not even had time to discuss it.

Finally, after she had been asleep about forty-five minutes, Bobby awakened her. He had been briefed. He turned his head, while she squatted on the roof and relieved her bladder. Then she turned hers as he, chuckling to himself, stood at the roof and peed on the roof of Ramiro's stolen car.

The operation had been very carefully planned because they thought that there were two backpack nuclear bombs inside. Bobby and Bo watched with their night-vision devices while the members of Delta and the Texas Rangers came across the prairie from the direction of the hilltop where the agents were. At the end of the driveway, they saw men getting into cruisers, but all lights were off.

The army had supplied everyone there with night-vision capability. Out on the road, a car with no light moved slowly down the road.

Bobby and Bo put on black nylon rappelling harness seats from his backpack. They affixed nylon ropes to the air vent coming from the roof, and tossed them over the side. The Delta Breach team came silently over the adobe walls in back and took their places at doors and windows around the house.

The on-site commander was the Delta Team commander, and all heard him speak into his mike. "Do not forget. We cannot afford a nuke going off. Double taps in the forehead, everybody."

Bobby and Bo had quietly rappelled down the front of the house, and each stood against the wall, leaning back, bodies parallel to the ground.

The leader said, "On my count, three-two . . ."

Bo and Bobby pushed hard with their feet, went out, and crashed feet-first through their respective windows as flash-bang grenades went off all through the house. They hit the floor and dropped their ropes and raised their weapons. Bobby had switched to his Glock 17. Bo wielded one, too.

A large body entered the room, and Bo recognized it as the giant form of Ramiro Maureo. She pictured him putting his hands all over her breast, as she quickly squeezed off two quick shots, both hitting him dead center in the forehead.

The entire house was a cacophony of gunfire and loud yells of "Room clear!" and as quickly as it started, the gunfire ended.

Just prior to the breach, the electricity had been turned off to the house, but now, at the bearded Delta team leader's command, it was turned on, and he told all the members to remove their night-vision devices.

Now, each body was checked and the entire ranch house was searched, while numerous police cars approached from the outside. The Chinook returned and was overhead, as well as two law enforcement helicopters. When the team leader gave the all-clear, General Perry in the Chinook and the other officers in cruisers came into the compound, the first moving the bus out of the way.

Bo looked down at the massive body of Ramiro Maureo, and Bobby walked up.

He said, "We didn't even have a chance to talk. Did he rape you while he held you?"

Bo said, "He tore my blouse off and fondled me, but no man will ever rape me, not ever!"

Bobby smiled at her, and said, "Good for you, partner. Keep that attitude."

The general came up and shook hands with both of them, and Bo said, "No nukes and only gang-bangers here, sir, and a few supporters of Rabbe, not Arabs."

The general said, "I already heard. We are scrambling to gather up what we have from sat of every vehicle that left the parking garage. They must have had one parked there, kidnapped somebody, or carjacked one."

Just then he got a call from the command post.

He spoke and said, "Thanks. Get a plate number and full description, and alert every cop between New York City, Miami, and here on every possible route to get there."

Bobby said, "Sir, what's up?"

"A man who parks in that garage was reported missing by his wife, and his body was just found east of here, executed, no robbery, just his car missing."

Bo said, "General, they would have ditched the car and either carjacked two more, so they can split up and take the nukes to Miami and New York City, or more likely rented two cars, so they would not attract attention."

General Perry took them to the command post and called the other leaders over to brief them. The FBI immediately alerted agents all over the country to check car rentals for either of the fake Mexican names the two al Qaeda terrorists were using.

He said to Bobby and Bo, "Hop on the Chinook."

They took off for Briggs on the Chinook with the Delta Force team and Bobby and Bo on board. They took their parachutes with them, and started folding and repacking them on the short trip.

The President and secretary of homeland security were both called. The entire nation's homeland security force was abuzz with activity, but all behind closed doors. Two transports for Bo and Bobby had already been called for, and the Delta Force team was taking the same C-18 cargo jet they came with.

General Perry already had two loaded B2 Spirits, the famous stealth bombers, sitting on the tarmac. They had flown in from their base in Missouri at Whiteman Air Force Base.

They set down near the jets and the crews were summoned. One would take Bo to Miami, and the other would take Bobby to New York City. Every available source around those two cities was on alert. Spotters were on alert at the Empire State Building, Statue of Liberty, and every major landmark they could think of. In Miami, law enforcement personnel were dispatched the same way. Rough photos were finally discovered of both men, in native Arab dress and as Mexican businessmen, and these were in the possession of spotters.

As the two stealth bombers taxied for takeoff, the word came in and was passed on to Bobby and Bo that the FBI had uncovered the rental of two different Cadillac Escalades, one silver, and one black, under the Mexican name of each man.

The U.S. Air Force says this about the B2 Spirit: "Northrop Grumman is the prime contractor for the U.S. Air Force B-2 Spirit stealth bomber. The B-2 is a low-observable, strategic, long-range, heavy bomber capable of penetrating sophisticated and dense air-defense shields. It is capable of all-altitude attack missions up to fifty thousand feet, with a range of more than six thousand nautical miles unrefueled and more than ten thousand nautical miles with one refueling, giving it the ability to fly to any point in the world within hours. Its distinctive profile comes from the unique 'flying wing' construction. The leading edges of the wings are angled at thirty-three degrees and the trailing edge has a double-W shape. It is manufactured at the Northrop Grumman facilities in Pico Rivera and Palmdale in California.

"Twenty-one B-2s have been delivered to Whiteman Air Force Base in Missouri, the first in December 1993. In the first three years of service, the operational B-2s achieved a sortie reliability rate of ninety percent. An assessment published by the USAF showed that two B-2s armed with precision weaponry can do the job of seventy-five conventional aircraft."

The War on Terrorism was a showcase for the speed and efficiency of the Spirit, and now two of them were carrying out their most important mission: to prevent a nuclear attack on two of the largest American cities.

Bobby and Bo were halfway across the country when both got a conference call from General Perry. "Major Samuels, Captain Devore, a Department of Homeland Security investigator found the definitive plans of these terrorists in their apartment. They intend to go into the Empire State Building in New York City, carry a bomb halfway up, leave the bomb in a suitcase in a hallway, closet, or restroom, set the timer, and leave. Even if the police find it, they will send the bomb squad, and it will take more than the hour on the timer, so the bomb will still go off. They plan the same thing in Miami at the Four Seasons Hotel and Tower on Brickell Avenue. Except there, they will rent a hotel room and ask for the highest floor. They will be housed better than halfway up. Again, the coward will then leave and an hour later, the bomb explodes. They are supposed to coordinate and set the timers to detonate at the same time. If anything goes wrong, they both agreed to blow themselves up."

Bobby said, "Sir, any knowledge of where they might be?"

"They rented one car in Memphis and the other in Nashville," the general responded. "The other car was ditched a little beyond Memphis. It is believed they must have split up at Nashville and should be arriving around the time you two arrive. Hopefully, a little after you get there. The President said you are to have anything you want or need to stop these bastards."

"Thank you, sir," Bo said. "We will."

"Roger that, General," Bobby said from his jet.

"Good luck and God bless," Jonathan Perry said.

12

DEATH OR DISHONOR

The jihadist looked up at the tall building rising up so many feet above him. He had called Tariq, and Tariq was then outside the New York City building with a perfect entrance planned. They would not even be able to detect him. Now Abdul would go down in history. He sat in the parking lot for a half an hour and watched the building and saw nobody. No cops, no army. He would rent his room, set the timer, and quickly leave and drive north out of Miami, and tens of thousands would die, probably millions. As simple as that. At the same time, Tariq had been carefully watching the Empire State Building, and was simply waiting for some attorneys to return he had seen earlier. He was going to enter with them, and knew he would blend in perfectly. He had even heard them say earlier to someone they would return soon.

In New York City, Tariq was well pleased. He knew they had outwitted the stupid infidels. There was no way that the Americans could unravel their trail and get there quickly enough to stop him or Abdul. Osama bin Laden's longtime goal was about to be realized, the American Hiroshima.

Two nuclear bombs were about to be exploded on American soil in two of its biggest cities at the same time in the middle of the afternoon. The terror would be extreme. The infidels would break. Someday soon the United States of America would be ruled by mullahs and freedom would be no more.

Abdul Qudoos had really worked on his Mexican accent, and was ready to employ it now for the most important mission of his life.

The desk clerk at the Four Seasons Hotel and Tower looked at the Mexican businessman with the large black suitcase and said, "Double or a single, sir?"

"Seengle, please, Señorita," Abdul said.

He heard clapping, and whirled around to see Captain Bo Devore with a Glock 17 in her right hand. Nonetheless, she was applauding.

Bo now leveled the gun at him with a double-palm grip, saying, "Congratulations Abdul, that sounded exactly like an Arab trying to speak English with a Mexican accent. You are under arrest. If you even move one inch toward the suitcase, I will kill you."

His hands went up, and the color drained from Abdul's face. The clerk screamed.

Bo said, without looking at her, "Be quiet, now!"

The young lady stopped crying and started whimpering softly.

Bo said, "I am Captain Bo Devore, of the U.S. Army Criminal Investigation Detachment, Specops section, Department of the Army."

Abdul licked his lips, and Bo knew he was going to try for it. Two Miami Police officers ran in the door, guns drawn, and saw Bo. They aimed at Abdul.

One said, "That him, ma'am?"

Bo said, "Meet Abdul Qudoos, major al Qaeda operative and soon-to-be martyr if he moves one inch toward that suitcase."

The other cop said, "What is in the suitcase, Captain?"

Bo said calmly, "A nuclear bomb."

The other cop said, "Holy shit!"

The clerk started to faint, but caught herself before she hit the floor.

Bo said, "Young lady, grab one of those complimentary bottles of water you have on your counter and pour it over your head. Quickly."

The woman complied, and suddenly knew what was going on. Her entire body was shaking.

Bo said, "Officer closest to me."

"Yes, ma'am."

"Without blocking my shooting lane," Bo said, "move up along the side, my right side, and retrieve the bomb."

Bo said to Abdul, "You have the right to remain silent."

He thought about moving toward the suitcase, and just the thought made him move toward it ever so slightly, and Bo's gun boomed twice. The first bullet hit him dead center between the eyes, and the second caught him above the left eyebrow. Blood and brain matter splattered all over the wall beyond the clerk, who started screaming bloody murder. She wet herself.

Abdul's body fell face-first on the floor. Bo walked forward, pointing her Glock at the twitching body. She stepped on one wrist and reached down with one hand and felt for a pulse in the neck. The girl, now fascinated, stopped screaming.

Bo said, "Clear," and she and the two officers holstered their weapons.

Bo looked back at the dead terrorist, saying sarcastically, "I see you want to exercise that right."

One cop laughed, and the other was rubbery-legged.

Bo said to the clerk, "What is your name, honey?"

The clerk said very timidly, "Katherine Marie Jace."

Bo said, "You are doing really well. I know this is all very scary, but it is about over. Now, I need you to do something for me. Set off the building's fire alarm."

Katherine Marie complied and started calming down, although seeing the gore of Abdul's shattered skull made her somewhat sick to her stomach. Soon, the building started clearing out and fire engines could be heard.

Bo said, "Officer, call in immediately and tell them we need your chief, assistant chief, everybody down here right away. We have to evacuate a large area."

"You got it, ma'am," he replied, "By the way, nice shooting."

Bo looked at the other officer, saying, "Can you take Katherine Marie away from here? Take her home if she lives several miles way. That will be safe."

Katherine Marie said, "Thank you, Captain."

Bo walked over and wrapped her arms around her, and she started bawling.

Bo pulled out her sat phone, but first said, "Katherine Marie, you did good and all we are doing is taking precautions. Now, if the news interviews you, you're going to say there was a bomb threat and this crazy man tried to shoot this officer, and some lady cop shot him. If you mention the word nuclear bomb or anything else, we will have to discredit you and make you look goofy. You understand, don't you?"

"Yes, ma'am," Katherine Marie said. "You don't want fifty old men in Miami having heart attacks."

Bo said, "Perfect. I just have to evacuate for everybody's safety until the army gets here to remove the bomb. They have been watching and listening the whole time, so the EOD, the Explosive Ordnance Demolition, people are already on the way."

Katherine Marie said, "Ma'am, one little question."

Bo said, "Yes?"

"Ma'am. I heard you say that guy was al Qaeda," she said, "but he didn't have a weapon. Can't you get arrested for murder yourself?"

Bo said, "No, absolutely not. I warned him not to move an inch. If he dove toward the bomb and I missed, we would not be here talking. This building would not be here, or that building over there, or that building. He had a much bigger weapon than mine."

Then Bo winked at Katherine Marie and said, "Remember, Katherine Marie, size doesn't matter when it comes to weapons. It is how well you use what you have."

The clerk started laughing and laughing, and the tears started rolling again as the chuckling officer escorted her away.

A fire chief ran in the door, passing hordes of building residents running out. The officers pointed at Bo, and she put her hand up as Bobby answered his sat phone.

Bobby said, "I heard you smoked him. Are you okay, partner?"

Bo said, "I am fine. I am taking the stealth up there. Get there as quickly as I can."

Bobby said, "I hope this will all be over before you get here."

Tariq Ubaadah had waited over an hour, and now the attorneys were on their way back, carrying all the evidence for their case in large briefcases, a suitcase, even file boxes. Even security looking for him would never notice him. He would slip right on an elevator with the attorneys and would blend in. The group entered the building and joining them, Tariq came in the front door of the Empire State Building, pulling the big suitcase on built-in wheels like several in the group of attorneys. One was even using a handcart to carry file boxes from the court case.

Tariq made one big mistake. No matter how many degrees he had or how much money, he was still simply one of those black silhouette figures you would see taken from F16, F15, A10, or maybe B2 Spirit jets right before our smart bombs wiped them out. Those black figures who thought infidels were stupid, and they were superior. Who thought they had the answers because they had some money from oil. Who thought women were possessions and anybody who did not believe as they did would have to be eliminated from the world. They always forget Ameri-

can resolve, ingenuity, and the call to service in the fight
for freedom.

Bobby had just hung up when he saw him. Tariq pushed
the cart rapidly forward, and Bobby noticed an FBI agent
and a New York City police detective both followed him in
the building. Bobby remembered their faces and sport
coats from his briefing earlier. Both were palming their
weapons under their sport coats, but obviously were waiting on his move. He was thankful for that.

Right in front of the elevator, Bobby brought his gun up
in a standard double-palm grip and yelled, "Tariq
Ubaadah, you are under arrest. Freeze! Don't move!"

Eyes opening wide, Tariq reached for the suitcase latch,
and Bobby's gun boomed twice, while the detective's .45
and FBI agent's Glock both boomed, and the man's head exploded in several directions and his body dropped onto the
floor with the suitcase falling on his bloody body. All three
officers approached, guns still drawn, and the FBI agent
kicked the terrorist's lifeless hand away from the suitcase.
Bobby moved the suitcase ten feet away from the body.

He said into the microphone on his lapel, "Tariq is dead,
bomb secured."

In the Oval Office, Department of Homeland Security,
U.S. Border Patrol, FBI headquarters, CIA, DIA, NYPD
headquarters, the city's Mayor's Office, and Task Force
headquarters, it was as if everyone let their breath out at
once, and everyone started cheering and dancing.

Bo's phone rang and a secretary said, "Captain Devore."

Bo said, "Yes?"

The woman said, "Please hold for the President."

She put Bo on hold.

There was a click and the President said, "Major
Samuels, Captain Devore, are you both there?"

They both said, "Yes, Mr. President."

He said, "The citizens of this country will never know
what you did, but God knows, and we know, and we can
never thank you enough for your extreme courage and

your professionalism. I heard you both have been walking wounded, so after you have taken some medical leave to heal up, the First Lady and I would love to have your for dinner at the White House."

Bobby said, "I would be deeply honored, sir."

Bo said impishly, "I'm not sure, Mr. President. Will you be serving any Mexican food. I am staying away from that for a while."

The President chuckled, saying, "Captain, I will let you dictate the menu to the chef."

Bo said, "Sir, I, too, would be deeply honored."

EPILOGUE

After the medical checkups and care, and debriefing with General Perry and celebration with other bigwigs, Bo and Bobby hugged each other after being given thirty days' convalescent leave that would not count against their annual leave time.

Bobby said, "Where are you going?"

Bo said, "I'm going to get some sun. What about you?"

"Me, too," Bobby said. "I'm going to get plenty of sun."

Two days later, Bo chuckled at a joke, and took another bite of barbecue, and asked for a can of beer. The neighbors in that nice neighborhood in the Franklin Mountains in northwest El Paso sure knew how to throw a block party, she thought.

Bobby looked at the front of the building and remembered the first day he went to kindergarten. He was so scared and apprehensive. The building was so white and clean, the grass green, and there were palm trees everywhere. He looked at the sign with the address, 39000 Bob Hope Drive, Rancho Mirage, California.

He walked through the arched doorway and up to a reception desk. A pleasant-looking woman smiled at him.

Tears filled Bobby's eyes, and he was embarrassed, saying, "My name is Bobby Samuels. I have reservations."

She smiled broadly, saying, "Major Samuels, we have been expecting you. Welcome to the Betty Ford Center. This will be your new home for the next month."

Bobby tried to smile, but was really fighting to hold back the tears right now. He could not wait to climb into a bed and get some sleep, lots of it.

ABOUT THE AUTHOR

Don Bendell is the author of twenty-two books and a motion picture with more than 1.5 million copies of his books in print worldwide. As an enlisted man, he served as an MP at Fort Dix, New Jersey, and as an officer, he was a Green Beret captain and served on a twelve-man A-team in Vietnam in 1968–1969, as well as the top secret Phoenix Program and three other Specal Forces groups. A seventh-degree black belt master instructor in four different martial arts, Don also owns karate schools in southern Colorado and was inducted into the International Karate Hall of Fame in 1995. Don's political editorials have been published far and wide, and he has been interviewed on *Fox News Live* and many other national radio shows. A real cowboy with a real horse, Don, and his black belt master wife, Shirley, live on a large mountain ranch overlooking Cañon City, Colorado. He has four grown sons (one a Green Beret), two grown daughters, and five grandchildren.

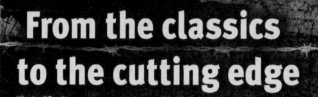

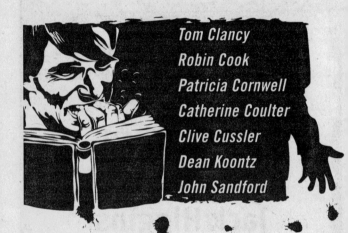